My Conversations with THE KING

D.M. FREEDMAN

Ordering Information:

Prime Seven Media
518 Landmann St.
Tomah City, WI 54660

Printed in the United States of America

DEDICATION

Elvis Presley's death was a milestone event in my young adulthood. I was a fan, but his music did not dominate my playlist. However, for many it was a life-altering phenomenon. As with many icons, it was difficult to comprehend how a man with such talent could pass from this Earth at such a young age. For those who did not easily believe it, there was a hope that perhaps it was not true. Most of us have experienced the loss of a loved one or close friend. Sometimes, we "see" them on the street and our heart jumps for a second. We realize that we are seeing someone else, but a part of us cries out to the mirage in our mind and we yearn for the opportunity to say one last thing to our close one.

Over the years, I've read of the many Elvis sightings and of course laughed them off. I started this project with a preposterous idea and tried to create a story of possibilities. Imagining being in Elvis Presley's head was one of the most difficult things I have done as a writer. It was also one of the most painful, for I had to empathize with a person I had never met and to whom I had paid scant attention to growing up. Elvis was a sad and complicated person. I wanted to give that sadness a place to be heard. It became my sadness, a sadness for me to work out.

I will never know what his ultimate life plans would have been or what would have happened had he lived. This story examines one possibility and how that fictional life might have developed. I tried to show Elvis' sweetness, his love, and in the end his determination. It is a determination he may have never known in real life. I hope I did him justice.

I dedicate this book to my wife Chaya and my children Chaviva and Menachem. I also dedicate it to those who were murdered by the Nazis and Ukrainians in the town that my family originally came from. The story of Skalat portrayed in this book is based upon true events. The names of the victims were changed to protect their privacy. Other names with the exception of Mendel Tackett are the actual names. Their crimes should live in infamy. The Skalat story reflects what was a systematic plan to kill the Jews throughout Galicia in Europe. I owe a great debt to Mr. Abraham Weissbrod, who lived through the slaughter and recorded a written history of the events which led to the decimation of the Jewish community there. His story formed the basis of the Skalat story in my book and although by now, he is long passed on, his account helped me to understand more of my own legacy. Thank you, Abraham, and may you rest in peace.

I also want to give a special thanks to my editor and friend Carolyn Bahm. You did an amazing job helping me convert my storytelling into a coherent literary work.

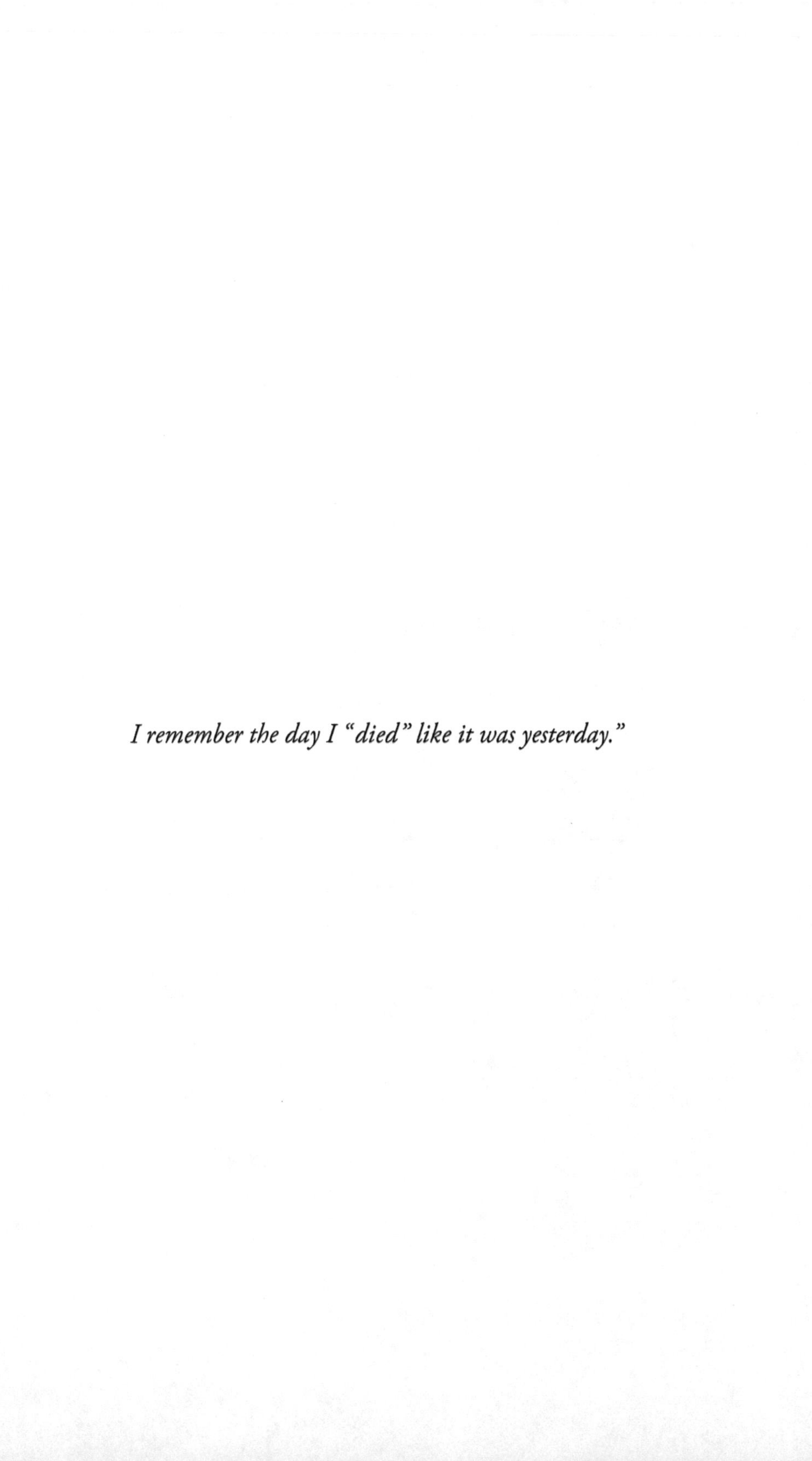

I remember the day I "died" like it was yesterday."

PROLOGUE

It was an unusually chilly day in late October. The McDonald's in Dearborn, Michigan was very busy, as it was noon and people were arriving to grab a quick lunch. The restaurant was filled with teenagers from the local high school, so it was bustling and noisy.

The lines moved slowly but steadily up to the counter where people ordered, picked up their trays or their bags with food, and moved on. On the line furthest to the right, a tall man with a long beard, a black jacket and a stocking cap waited patiently. He rubbed his hands together to warm them until it was his turn to order. He looked down at the pretty teenager working the register and ordered his meal.

"I'll have two Big Macs and an order of fries, please," he said in a southern drawl. "And a large Coke and an apple pie."

She acknowledged his order and took his money. As she gave him his change, she narrowed her gaze and tilted her head at him. She asked, "is this to stay or to go?"

"To stay."

She went back to the service area and put his order on a tray. She came back to the counter and placed the tray in front of him. He lifted it off the counter, looked at her briefly and went to find a seat. He settled into a booth facing the counter. The teenaged girl kept glancing over, but he stayed unaware, and just opened his food and began eating. He was unsuspecting that he had become the subject of someone's repeated curiosity.

During a lull, she called a coworker. Pointing with her pinky at the man, she whispered into her friend's ear. Her friend studied the customer and laughed.

"Silly girl, no way! It can't be him. He's been dead since last summer."

"I know that! Maybe it's some relative. The resemblance is eerie. I'm going to tell my Mom about this. She was a huge fan."

CHAPTER ONE

His head was pounding and really hurt, and Abraham believed it would be awhile before he got some relief, so he put water in the teapot and placed it on the stove to boil. Soon he heard the low whistle and shut off the fire. He prepared a coffee for himself and shuffled into the dining room.

"Good to see you again, Abraham," a voice boomed.

Abraham was so shaken he nearly dropped the coffee. He recovered quickly and glanced toward the voice. He saw a man sitting at the table, halfway facing him. He wore a long black coat and had penetrating eyes, and a white beard that reached mid-chest.

"Do you remember me, Abraham?"

"Of course, I do, Isaac."

"I scared you?"

"Well, I wasn't quite expecting to see you at my table. Frankly, I was not expecting anyone." He tapped his chest, "But I'm alright."

He put the cup on the table and froze. The headache was gone. Isaac smiled. "You have to admit it worked," he said with a wink. "I guess it did."

"Why are you here?"

"I need your help."

"You…need my help?"

"Yes."

Abraham sat down and faced him. "And how exactly can I help you?"

Isaac looked carefully at him. He looked deeply into his eyes and sat back in the chair. Taking a deep breath, the visitor leaned forward and reached across the table to clasp Abraham's hands in his own.

"There is a man. A famous man. Very, very famous! He is in trouble. Terrible trouble. You should know that he is also a very sad man. And soon, he will be coming to you to ask for help."

Abraham eyebrows shot up, "Why me? And how will he know to contact me?"

"Don't worry about how. But you will recognize it when you are contacted. You are wondering why he will contact you, are you not?"

Abraham nodded.

"Because in your unique way, you will be able to help him."

Isaac looked over and sighed deeply.

Abraham stood up and leaned over the table. "What can I possibly do to help this man, a man I don't even know? This stranger/ You expect that I can do this?" he said glaring. "I am just an old man!"

"Oh, you are more than that, and you know it. You can live by your wits, even though you would never let on about it to anyone. And you will be able to help him. You know why? Because of what you learned escaping from Buchenwald."

"What are you talking about?" Abraham chuffed out a breath and sat back down. He was quiet for a few moments. "Besides, that was a very long time ago." He stared into his coffee and fell silent. Isaac waited, not moving.

Abraham muttered, "I learned a lot of things in Buchenwald." He sipped from his cup. Lowering slowly onto the table, he asked, "Exactly what could I use to help this man?"

"The ruse you used when you escaped."

"Don't ask that of me! Not now! Are you telling me I am to help someone escape from somewhere?" Is that what you want me to do? Agh! Isaac, what I did to escape from Buchenwald… I don't talk about it ever! I try not to even think about it. It haunts my dreams and that wakes me up." He paused to collect his racing thoughts. Finally, he said to Isaac, "Why do you want *me*? I am an old man. I'm not meant for this!"

Isaac threw his head back, made a two-handed pleading gesture upward, and retorted, "Yes you are! You are exactly the right man for this! Why do you think I am here? He softened his voice. "Help this man to escape from a life of destruction so he can build a life of happiness and good."

Abraham shook his head. "And how am I supposed to do this? By myself?"

"You will not be alone. You will be the guide for others to get this man to the place G-d meant for him. There will be a time to get him out and there will be a time when you will need to listen to the man himself. You will be the messenger and the guide for this man for the rest of your life and even after you are gone, he will remember, and you will be his guide. So, listen to what he needs and work out a plan to bring him close to you here in Brooklyn. Your old student Rabbi Fried will contact you."

"And how is he involved in all this?"

Getting no response, Abraham got up to rinse out his cup. When he looked again, Isaac was gone!

CHAPTER TWO

L et me tell you a story about my next-door neighbor. On the surface, he might seem to be a rather unremarkable fellow, but in reality, his story is the one every reporter wants to tell. And boy, oh boy, am I going to tell it to you. I am going to tell you this story, to keep my word to this marvelous man. And, most important, because he allowed me to tell it when the time was right.

So, who am I that I get to tell this extraordinary story? I am Stan Eisenberg, a somewhat hotshot sportswriter, at least in my own mind, as well as to some of the others of importance at the New York Daily News. It seems that I am always in the right place when a great sports story breaks in New York. If there is someone in the sports world with a story, I get it. I personally know all the owners, the managers, the coaches, and the players. Before there were "Sports Doctors", there was yours truly. I am the expert on New York sports. For years, my column has run under the banner, "The Authority". In this town I am the man when it comes to talking about sports. Pretty big deal. Right? Ha! I have also written books about sports, as well as ghostwritten sports autobiographies with many famous players.

But I have my share of demons. Unfortunately for me, I have an incredible capacity for looking someone right in the eye and telling them to go, you know… themselves. In this profession, this ordinarily shouldn't cause too many problems. But for some inexplicable reason, I tell off the people most responsible for my success. I can't wrap my head around why I always seem to do that. Eventually, people get tired of dealing with "the man" despite the fact I am that brilliant reporter and an unusually dazzling teller of the story.

I do sound full of myself, don't I? Well, it belies the deep disappointment I sometimes feel about myself.

Hey, and I had a wife as well. Trudy and I met on a blind date at a City College party, and we were married for twenty-four years. We had a lovely apartment in Manhattan, raised two beautiful daughters, married them off, and were left to live with each other alone for the first time in many years. Not so suddenly, we both realized that we really didn't like each other. She quit first and asked me to move out four months after our youngest was married. I obliged her, because, well, the truth was, I didn't really care anymore, and thought it would be more fun to be single. It wasn't! It was just the same old sad stuff. I moved into a tiny bachelor pad on the Lower East Side and married my bar stool until my ulcer cried uncle.

I got very sick. The ulcer was the size of a pancake. Well, that's an exaggeration, but when they were done cutting me up, I returned to my stinking apartment, where it would be months before I was able to return to what I was doing before. My edge was gone, and I found that I had started hating my life. I'd look out of my window onto Avenue A and get sick to my stomach. I had nothing! At least nothing that I had before. Just a sore belly, a dingy place to live, and none of the drive to get out there and be the man I once was.

Enough with this pity party!

So, let me tell you this story about my neighbor. How I got to be this man's neighbor is another story, probably best left to another time. But, I'll tell you anyway.

Soon after I went back to work, I had to cover a story about this young Orthodox Jewish man who was playing for the Brooklyn Cyclones. The Cyclones are a minor league team in Brooklyn. They play in a small ballpark in Coney Island. The Cyclone is the name of Coney Island's biggest attraction. It's an old wooden roller coaster built early in the twentieth century. People come from far and wide just to brag that they've ridden on the Cyclone. Hence the name of the team.

This kid played every day but Friday nights and Saturdays. He was tearing the cover off the ball and had become somewhat of a local celebrity. I went to interview him at his home in Flatbush, a quiet section of Brooklyn.

I finished interviewing him in his house and walked down to Ocean Parkway, one of the major roads in Brooklyn. It was a warm late- spring night and before going to the subway, I decided to sit on one of these benches along the roadway. The benches are on these pedestrian islands that separate the main traffic lanes from the residences bordering the road. When I was a kid growing up in this neighborhood, there was a bridle path there for horses you could rent from a stable in Prospect Park. I remembered that as a kid, I used to take my dog and walk on this bridle path. But now, it has been paved over for people to walk on and to ride their bicycles upon. The benches have been built for resting and people watching. While sitting on one of those benches, if you weren't careful, you could easily fall asleep gazing at the passing traffic. It was that hypnotic.

As a teenager, I would go out there every night with my gang of friends over the summer, to watch the pretty girls sauntering by, and maybe if I got lucky, one of them might take the time to flirt with me. Now things are different. The neighborhood is mostly Orthodox Jews, but as I watched, it was obvious that behaviors don't change, just the outfits of the boys and girls. It was a lovely evening, and I enjoyed the warm breeze. All around me were young couples and their children. Young girls dressed in long skirts sat on the benches. Young men were seen in their black skullcaps, white shirts, and black pants with their four fringes hanging out. It was an idyllic scene. People everywhere seemed happy and connected. I ached for that, deep, deep in my heart I longed for that. It had been a long time since I had experienced it.

I had bought a takeout sandwich in a local deli and sat down to eat it on one of these benches. As I ate, I felt a little bit like a kid again. It felt good.

I decided to stroll around a few blocks and take a look around. I had grown up nearby in an apartment building on East Third and Avenue P, so I knew the neighborhood pretty well. It had changed a lot since I was a kid, but it was still familiar, very much as I remembered it. I headed down Avenue P to East Seventh Street and then turned on a whim up the street. As I moved on toward Avenue O, I saw a house for sale on my left: 1650 East Seventh Street. It was the right-side unit of this semi-attached house. I copied the real estate agent's number and decided I would call her when I got to the office in the morning. The next morning, I set up an appointment to see the house on the following Thursday.

So, that Thursday I went back to Brooklyn and saw the house. Liked it right away and decided to put in an offer. My offer was accepted, and three months later, on a blazing August morning, my moving van pulled up in front, and the moving men started placing my things into my new home.

As I stood on the stoop directing the moving men, I saw some movement behind a curtain in the next-door neighbor's window. As I watched, a woman intermittently peeped through her curtains. She kept doing this all morning, while the truck was being emptied. She never came out to say hello, she just watched.

The moving men finished, and now I was in my new house in my old neighborhood. The thing is, I didn't know anybody living there, but I couldn't care less. The block is quiet. Trees overhang the street. I have a pocket-sized patch of grass in front of the house and a shady porch to sit on where I can get relief from this damn heat. It's all right. The world is good for me again. I don't have to see the Manhattan filth. And I can walk to the subway to go to work. Not so bad!

The following morning, I got up, went to work, came home and started living a whole new life in my old stomping grounds. Except I am not stomping anymore. It's home.

Next came the weekend, and I saw that the entire neighborhood shuts down for the Sabbath. Families from all over were going back and forth to synagogue or to visit each other. On Saturday afternoon, I stepped onto my porch, and saw my neighbor sitting quietly on his porch, staring at nothing in particular. I walked down the steps on my way to the Avenue, and as I passed him, I waved. He didn't wave back, rather he got up and came down the stoop. We shook hands. He looked me in the eye closely, which kind of unnerved me. But I looked right back at him.

"Ah, my new neighbor! Hi, my name is Elijah Pressler, you can call me Elie." He spoke in a slow Southern drawl and grinned.

"Stan Eisenberg. I moved in a few days ago."

"I noticed. Stan or Stanley? Which do you prefer?"

"Either or. Most people call me Stan. But whatever works for you, works for me."

He nodded.

"Elie, it's a pleasure to meet you. Is it E-l-i-e or E-l-i?"

"It's E-l-i-e, short for Elijah."

"Like the Elijah in the Bible?"

Elie smiled, "That's the one!"

"Elie, how long have you been living on this block?"

"My wife and I bought this house about twenty-five years ago. It is a nice block. Mostly Jews like me, you know Orthodox. But some not! There are few Italian families living on the block, but it's mostly just us Orthodox Jews."

Stan laughed. "Well, you see I'm not one of the gang." He said pointing to his lack of a skullcap.

Elie laughed as well. "It doesn't matter; I wasn't always Orthodox. In fact, I barely knew I was Jewish. I came to this life about thirty-five years ago, and it's done well for me. So, I have a taste of both worlds. And I appreciate both."

"Elie, what do you do for a living?"

"I'm retired."

"Been retired for a while?"

"About ten years."

"You don't sound like you grew up here. I hear a touch of the South in your voice."

"Memphis. I grew up in Memphis."

"I hear there is a big Jewish community there."

"Not so big, but active!"

"And what did you do before you retired?"

"I was in the entertainment field," he said, laughing, "I was a Cantor."

"Really. For some reason I don't associate being a Cantor with being in entertainment, but I guess it is."

Elie's dimples deepened, "Yes, I consider it to be so. I've been doing it for years. I just sing occasionally now, but that's what I did for a long time."

"Did it pay well? I've heard that Rabbis and Cantors don't get paid so much."

"We got by. I also did funerals and weddings and Bar-Mitzvahs, so, there was some money coming in. I taught Bar-Mitzvah lessons as well." He shook his head and gave a quick laugh.

Elie turned to Stan, "And you?"

"I write for the New York Daily News. I'm a sports columnist. You may have heard of me. They call me the "Authority" when it comes to New York sports."

"Oh, you're that Stan Eisenberg! I read you all the time." Visibly impressed, Elie said, "Wow, Stan Eisenberg. Nice to meet you."

"The one and only! At least, the only sports columnist with that name."

Elie reached to shake his hand again. "Well, it is a real pleasure. I love your articles; read them every time I see them in the paper. I am a huge fan."

"Well, I'm glad you enjoy them."

"You were sick, weren't you? I didn't see your column for a while." Stan smiled and said "Ulcers! Took me out for quite a while. But I'm back making trouble all over New York."

"Glad to hear it. I missed your column."

"Thanks, that's nice of you to say."

I turned to go. "Listen, I don't want to disturb your Sabbath, and I have to cover a game. But it was a pleasure to meet you, and we'll talk. Good Shabbos."

"You too! It was a pleasure!"

And so that was how I got to meet Elie. We were to become close friends over the next year.

CHAPTER THREE

It was a brutal winter, unusually cold, and it snowed like crazy. The subways were a mess, and often Stan didn't get home until very late. He was busy covering the Giants and the Jets, then the Knicks and the Rangers.

Winter ebbed into spring, and then in late April, Passover was celebrated throughout the neighborhood. He didn't see Elie much all winter, but one morning as Stan was leaving for work, he ran into him in front of the house and they both went down Avenue P to the Subway.

Elie asked, "Do you have a place for the Seders (the Passover festive meal)?"

"I am going to my daughter's house." Stan told him even though he knew it wasn't true. Elie seemed satisfied with my answer.

"Well, if something changes and you find that you need company, join my family, next door. There is always room for you, my friend." Stan thanked him, but he could not imagine spending the Seder with the Pressler family. They were so "Jewish". Stan mused that he probably would be happier with a ham and cheese on a matza then going to a Seder. It seemed an odd thought. As a child, he loved the Seder. But he had drifted away into indifference to all things religious, and Stan realized it kind of scared him to entertain the notion of going to his neighbor's home. They split ways when they reached the subway.

The weeks passed, and Stan was settling in well. The house was comfortable and a nice place to escape from the pressures of work. He walked out one night and wrinkled his nose at the untended patch of ground in his front yard. It was shaggy, used up and ugly. That Saturday, he drove to Staten Island and bought trays of marigolds and petunias and a bag of grass seed. He needed some small hand tools and gloves, so he bought them in a hardware store. He brought them home and stored them temporarily in the garage. Opening a beer, Stan flipped on the TV and watched the Rangers lose another playoff game. Their season looked about done.

The next morning, he gathered the plants, seeds, and tools and set them in front of his stoop. Stan surveyed the lawn and saw that the soil in his front was pebbly and hard. He needed to rake it. Only he didn't have a rake and it would be a waste to throw seed down without softening the ground up and making it reasonably level. Stan stood there with his hands on his hips, frowning at the ground, when he heard Elie's voice behind him.

"Stan. You look perplexed." Stan slowly turned around and spotted Elie on his porch, where he was comfortably planted with a big religious book open on his lap.

"Hey, Elie. I bought all this stuff to grow a garden, but I forgot to buy a rake."

"What do you have to buy a rake for? I have three different kinds in the shed." He got up and motioned Stan to follow him along Elie's driveway to the backyard. He fiddled with the combination lock on an old metal shed and it opened.

"Ta-da! Magic." He slid the door of the shed open pulled out an old tire, some boxes, and a hose. He kept rummaging, muttering to himself.

"Elie, please don't go to any trouble."

"No bother, they are here somewhere. I just have to look. I haven't used them in years but unless my wife threw them out, they are here." Elie poked around some more. "Aha, found them!"

There were some scraping metal sounds, and then sure enough, he pulled out three distinct types of rakes. One for leaves and two for grooming soil. He gave them to Stan.

"There you go. This should fix you up." Stan said his thanks and took them while Elie locked up the shed. They returned to the front of the house. Elie went back to his book, and Stan started to break up the soil. It took a couple of hours for him to get the soil smoothed out and ready to seed. It was getting hot, and he was not a young man, so he stopped and sat on a step, mopping his brow with a handkerchief. Elie got up and went into the house. He returned to his book and Stan sat recovering his strength and letting the breeze cool him down. Elie's wife Shoshana opened the screen door and asked Stan if he would like something cold to drink. He nodded yes and she returned shortly after with a glass of iced tea. It tasted so good and was perfect, Stan thought. He thanked her, and she went inside. He had only met Shoshana in passing a few times. She was a tall, painfully thin woman with large square glasses. She was what one would call a plain woman. She was the mother of eight and grandmother of nine. She normally covered her head with a kerchief or a snood, although on the Sabbath or holiday, she wore a wig. Sneaking out from the front of her kerchief were wispy strands of red hair. Stan didn't get the wig thing. But all the women in the community seem to do it, although sometimes young women wore a baseball hat. Shoshana always came off as reserved and Stan didn't think he had ever seen her really smile, only a quick upturn of the creases of her mouth.

Refreshed, Stan decided to go back to work. Elie had gone inside for lunch, so he had no one to talk to. Stan went back into the house and brought out a small boom box and grabbed a bunch of tapes to play while he worked. He worked at planting the petunias and marigolds and kept stopping to change the tape to something more his liking. Finally, he found an Elvis Presley tape and slipped it into the machine and went back to work while singing along. He was listening to "Blue Suede Shoes."

A voice joined him in the singing and sounded identical to the one on the tape. Stan turned around, startled. Standing right behind him was Elie singing along animatedly. They both finished the song with a flourish. Then they both laughed and high-fived each other. Elie returned to the porch and opened his book, but you could hear him crooning in the background, just loud enough for Stan to notice that he knew all the words to every song.

Stan got up and came to the bottom of Elie's stoop and looked up, "Big Elvis fan?"

"You might say I'm his biggest fan. I mean, I grew up in Memphis. How could I not be an Elvis fan?"

"You ever saw him in person?"

"All the time."

"What was he like?"

"Nicest guy. Seemed a bit troubled, but a nice guy."

Stan nodded, "Yeah, he was troubled. Tragic life, tragic death. I remember; I was driving upstate on Route 17 near Monticello, listening to the radio when they announced he had died. I got so upset at the news, I pulled over onto the shoulder and sat for a while. I can't tell you why I did that. I liked his music, but I wasn't, into his music, per se. I mean I was into all those folk singers and the Eagles and Fleetwood Mac. But once in a while, I would put on this Elvis tape and sing along. Beautiful voice. Just a beautiful voice."

"I agree. Beautiful voice." Elie looked away as if in quiet reflection.

Stan returned to planting and singing along, and in the background, Elie kept singing along quietly. Stan was crouched planting a marigold plant when it hit him like a thunderbolt.

He whipped around to size up Elie. This was a tall man who, although not fat, was not slim. His hair was cropped short, and he had side curls pulled behind his ears. He had a long full beard that was mostly gray. The nose was long and straight and his eyebrows full but not bushy. When he grinned, his upper lip kind of curled up to the left.

Stan rubbed a hand across his mouth.

"Elie, what's your Hebrew name again? I forgot it."

"What?" Elie looked at him quizzically.

"Elie, your Hebrew name? You know what they call you when you get called to the Torah in Synagogue?"

He got another strange look and then a shrug from Elie. "Elijah Aharon ben Abraham."

"Got it. Elijah Aharon Pressler." Stan knelt and went back to gardening. Something clicked in his brain: Elijah Aharon ... Elvis Aaron. Pressler, Presley. He caught his breath and then fell back from his crouch onto the concrete grabbing his legs, so he didn't hurt himself. With his butt flat on the ground, he scanned his memory. The light bulb went on in his head.

"My G-d," Stan whispered to himself, "He's been hiding in plain sight."

Stanley let out a breath he hadn't realized he was holding. He tried to take some long deep breaths to control himself saying nothing. Sweat poured down his forehead, his temples, and the nape of his neck. Eyes stinging and tearing, he tried to lift himself from the concrete without making it obvious that something was wrong.

"Stan, are you alright?"

Elie looked worried. Stan visualized him younger and without the beard. Should he trust his eyes? He said to Elie, "Yeah, yeah," swiping his handkerchief across his brow, he added, "Got a little overdone in the sun. I'm okay."

"You sure?"

Stan tried not to look directly at his neighbor. It was as if his face melted into the face of a younger Elvis Presley, clean shaven, iconic long sideburns, the upturned lips.

He caught himself staring, so he said, "Sure. Sure, I'm fine. I will take a break and go inside to get some water." Stan went into the house and stood by the kitchen sink. Turning the faucet on, he let the water run for a minute. Dipping his hands in, he splashed his face and arms. He grabbed a glass from the cupboard and filled it. Leaning over the sink, he poured it over his head and then neck, soaking his tee shirt. Grabbing a kitchen towel, He dried off and drew a glass of water.

Sitting down at the table, Stan chugged the cold drink. Head spinning, he began talking himself out of what was swirling around in his brain. He laughed. It had to be a weird coincidence.

But if it was true, it was a reporter's dream. The scoop of a lifetime. Easy street. A book, a movie, lots of green.

Stan muttered, "What a crazy idea." But the more he thought about it, the more it resonated with him. "I'd have to confront him on this, but what if I am wrong? How ridiculous would that be? Elvis Presley. My neighbor? But his last name is Pressler? His middle name was Aaron. Elvis could easily be morphed into Elijah. Close, but different enough to not raise flags. And of course, he grew up in Memphis. Too easy. Got to be coincidence. Must be!" Stan paced around his kitchen musing, "But if it's true, who else is aware?"

He stretched his feet onto another one of his kitchen chairs. Staring into space, he imagined that he was right. Of course, Shoshana surely is in the loop. Or maybe not. She seems so parochial. Maybe Elie never told her. But that can't be, she is his wife. They have kids together. Heck, they have grandkids. But of course she knows if her husband is Elvis Presley!"

Stan went into the living room and clicked on the television. He stood watching golf and drinking his water. Then he went out to finish his work. Elie had gone in. Stanley figured that was probably a good thing. It would take time to figure this all out. Stan's mind kept running all kinds of scenarios. If this were true, then what? And if so, who helped him pull it off? And surely there had to be several people involved?

He went back inside his house and stretched out on the couch. "This is craziness," he thought. Yet, he could not shake the possibility that he was right, and he kept contemplating how it might be true.

Grabbing one of his reporter's notebooks, he started scribbling scenarios and circumstances that might have occurred. He envisioned it as if it were real in his mind. He asked himself a bunch of questions and recorded each in that notebook.

Putting the pieces together would either be the greatest story of his career, or it could be the makings of a great novel. Either way, he married himself to the task of putting it to paper. He took a leap of faith that his suspicions were right. Stan wasn't sure he could handle the embarrassment of confronting the man and being wrong. He might have to move away right when he had gotten comfortable living here. Besides, he had no clue how to confront the man. But he ached to know. As a reporter, there was only one thing to do. Stanley had to arm himself with the facts and then bring them to Elie and see what he says.

Stan drifted off to sleep. The next day in the office, he asked his assistant to find everything in the newspaper's morgue on Elvis Presley. The mental voyage had begun. He hoped it wouldn't drown him.

CHAPTER FOUR

It was after dark when Stan knocked on Elie's door and Shoshana answered.

"Stan, are you okay?"

"Hi Shoshana. Everything's fine. Is Elie around?"

"I think he's out back. I will go get him."

"Thanks, but I can walk around back."

"He is in the basement, not the backyard. I'll get him for you."

She stepped to the back of the house and down the stairs into the basement. Ellie soon came up. Elie wiped his palms on the front of his pants, and the two men shook hands.

"Stanley! My friend what's new?"

"All good. I have to ask you something. When I was gardening this weekend, a thought came to me. I'd like to discuss it with you if you have the time."

"Sure. Let's go to the basement and we can sit down like mensches in my office."

They walked down to the basement and settled into a small, closeted area filled with a small desk and bookshelves teaming with Jewish religious books. They were overflowing onto stacks on the floor. Elie, his eyes twinkling, produced a half-filled bottle of whiskey from behind his desk with two plastic cups. Stan laughed and nodded. Elie poured and they both said L'Chaim and took a swallow. Elie sat behind the desk and motioned Stanley to clear the books from the other chair in the room and sit down.

"So, my friend, what's on your mind?"

"When I was gardening Sunday, it was the first time I have heard you sing."

"Well, you know, I am a cantor. I sing all the time. You should come to Synagogue once in a while. Even though I am retired, they let me sing pretty much whenever I want to."

"I should."

Elie added whisky to both cups. They both sipped.

"Elie, you really know your Elvis songs."

"Been singing them my entire life."

"When did you get into Elvis' music?"

"Ah, I was a teenager, actually, sang for my family when I was just a kid."

"They all must have seen that you had talent?"

"I guess," he said, laughing. "They kept getting me to sing, especially my Mama."

"When you sang those Elvis songs, I am telling you, it sounded so much like Elvis, I could not tell the difference."

"Lots of practice singing those songs." He shifted in his chair, lifted the cup at Stan and knocked back another swallow.

"Elie, you know I am a reporter?"

"Yes."

"Elie, are you hiding in plain sight?"

"I don't understand."

"I think you do!"

There was a pause. Elie took another swallow.

"Elijah Aaron Pressler. Born in Mississippi. Grew up in Memphis, Tennessee. It might be coincidence, but it might not be. Was Elvis your cousin?" Elie sat quietly with his hands folded together across his belly, but Stan noticed he was trembling. "Elie, Pressler could be a replacement name for Presley. Aharon is Hebrew for Aaron and Elijah could be a construct for Elvis. This may sound stupid, but are you Elvis Presley hiding in plain sight?"

Still not a word from Elie. He just sat there behind the desk and then tears rolled down his cheeks. He rubbed a finger across his lips and furrowed his brow.

"I always assumed that someday …!" As his voice trailed off, he scanned the room as if expecting someone to pop in at any moment. He motioned for Stan to swing the door closed. He closed his eyes squelching his emotions. He whispered, "Please Stanley. Shoshana and the kids do not know any of this. You must never tell them. You must never tell anyone. Let this be our little secret."

Stan exploded out of his chair. "Little secret? Elie, I am a reporter! This is the biggest story a reporter could hope to break. My G-d, you're Elvis Presley and you ain't dead!"

Stanley grabbed at the cup of whiskey. He swallowed it in one gulp and motioned Elie for more. Elie refilled the cup. Stan motioned for him to fill it all the way up and then took another long hard swallow. He wiped his lips with the back of his hand, sat down and waited expectantly. Finally, he sat back down. The unbroken silence stretched on, so he took a shot.

"All those sightings! Are they all true?" Stan popped up but was so excited he stumbled over a stack of books. He recovered, fumbling the worn paperbacks and leather-bound volumes into an uneven heap. Plopping back into his chair, he barely escaped knocking them over again. He leaned forward and put his head in his hands. Shaking his head back and forth, Stan looked up at Elie and murmured, "How can I keep this a secret?"

A glazed-looking Elie said nothing. Tears streamed down his cheeks, and he reached for a tissue from the box on the desk.

Stan sighed and caught his eye. "And the most important thing this reporter needs to understand is, how did you do it? How in the hell did you get away with it?"

Elie smiled weakly. Stan held his hand up. "You can't be the only person who knows Elvis is still alive. It is impossible that you just walked away from Graceland without someone knowing!"

Elie was motionless, slumped in his chair. Stan looked at him questioningly.

Stan leaned over the desk and pointed at Elie. He bellowed, "Elie, do you get this? Do you get that everyone believes you are dead, for crying out loud?"

"Shush, everyone in the house will hear you," Elie said, still crying. Shoshana yelled down to ask if everything was all right. Stan opened the door. Elie yelled up to her.

"Shoshana, it's all good. Nothing to worry about. Stan was telling me a sad story."

"Ok. Do you need something?"

"We're good."

Elie looked at Stan with imploring eyes, "Stanley, my life is good here. I am happy, but I am also old and sick. I do not know how much longer I will be in this world." He stopped to wipe his eyes with a tissue, and then said, "You are a fine man and I believe that you would not want to harm my family. I will offer you a deal."

Stan saw his friend's brokenness and relented. He reached for the bottle and poured two fingers into Elie's cup and then into his own.

"What kind of deal? Look, Elie, my goal isn't to harm you, but how can I possibly ignore this? I am a reporter. This is what a reporter lives for. The greatest story that ever will fall into my lap!"

Elie stood and stretched his legs. "I get that Stan. I really do!" Taking a fiery sip, he said, "I'll tell you what. Let me give you the entire story, but do not publish it until I die."

"Elie, that could be years!"

"Or it could be months, probably no more than three or four at the most." Elie whispered to Stan, "I have Pancreatic Cancer. You are the only person other than Rabbi Kaplan who knows. I am not going to tell my family until near the end." He narrowed his eyes. "If you work with me on keeping this secret, the scoop is yours. Exclusively! You can publish it as soon as I die. It will not be a secret to the world anymore and until then, I can live in peace until my Maker takes me home. Will you do this for me Stan?"

Stan sagged back into his chair, shocked at the news. He nodded yes and tears appeared on his cheeks too. The two men got up and hugged.

"Stan, one other thing. Any money you earn from this story, you must share with my wife. A fair share! We will work out the details. Okay?"

Stanley nodded again.

"Good, then we will begin tomorrow. We will go over to Ocean Parkway and sit on the benches, and you can ask me anything. Are you good with that?"

Stan shook his head and wiped his eyes. "Sure, Okay!"

CHAPTER FIVE

"I remember the day I 'died' like it was yesterday."

"Now that was an interesting statement! Elie and Stan were sitting on his front porch in old fashioned cloth folding lawn chairs. Elie was drinking soda from a large glass. He breathed heavily and then just started talking.

"Stanley, let me tell you the story, my way. It's going to sound crazy. Nonetheless, I remember the day I 'died' like it was yesterday. You may ask what I am talking about? But it's all true. It seems like yesterday.

Stan waited, his pen poised over a fresh notebook, and he cocked his head to one side. Elie saw immediately that Stan did not understand, but how could he? He was about to hear a scenario that only crazy people could have imagined. This was the stuff of conspiracy jockeys and the tabloid magazines you found at your supermarket checkout. He would be able to show that so many of the crazy speculations over the years, were true.

"So much preparation had gone into what I'm about to tell you that when I finally did it, well, it was surreal. I just walked out of my life. It seemed far-fetched. After all, how could I just go do that? I had worldwide fame. All these people worked for me, depended on me for a living. I had all these friends, these acquaintances, these wannabe friends, and wannabe acquaintances. The press? They were always around. How could I disappear into oblivion?"

"It seemed impossible to me, perhaps it will seem that way to you as well, but I just walked out of my life. Really! And then I stepped into a more stable, more conventional life instead. A life of peace for me."

"In the strangest way, I never really wanted any of the life I had. I only wanted to sing and make music. I loved singing for my Mama, because it made her happy. That was a great joy. But as it turned out, when the success came, I was still just a teenager. All I had was my fame and all the nonsense that went with it. Sure, there was lots of money, but there was also lots of pressure. That pressure sat right in my gut. Oh, my G-d, I felt it all the time. I would wake up shaking. My chest felt full and fluttering all the time. My neck was so tight I could barely move it from side to side."

Elie appeared to drift to a bygone place. Stan looked at him closely, not knowing where his friend had wandered to in his mind. Elie coughed, shook himself and went on. "Continuing," he said, but this time differently. Not as the soft-spoken Elie, but like a reborn Elvis Presley.

"Oh, that stress. It was constant. I cannot begin to tell you. It was just too much. My chest always felt like it was going to burst. Stanley, I feel it now as I remember it. I couldn't stand still or even sit in one place for more than a few minutes. Forget about sleep. Even when I did, I woke up groggy and dazed."

"As I said, my neck was so tight I couldn't twist my head from side to side. I got massages. I worked on my martial arts, but it didn't give me any relief. I took all the muscle relaxants my doctors gave me. But nothing worked. Well, the muscle relaxants worked sometimes. At first, they worked all the time, but later, not so much. Sometimes I felt that I could not breathe. Lights bothered me, so I had to wear sunglasses much of the time. My skin crawled all the time. My gut locked up like a clogged pipe. Nothing the doctors prescribed helped. When I had a clear enough mind, I could see my life from a distance and wondered how it came to this."

"I needed to get away, to breathe and live! I couldn't even take a piss without someone asking where I was and what I was doing. It was way, way too much!"

"How could I just leave everyone and disappear? Everywhere I went, people followed me, even in my own home. Sometimes I wanted to be alone without someone interrupting me a decision to make. You would think that everyone craves fame and fortune. But by then, all I wanted to be was an average Joe. From the time I was a teenager, fame was all I had. Money, well, I had a ridiculous amount of money, I couldn't figure out how to spend it all. I had cars, motorcycles, houses, ridiculous gifts, but I didn't have a home. Graceland was an enormous old house, but it was never a home for me. A home is where one can feel safe. No siree, I definitely didn't feel that. I never felt safe. I could practice karate all day long and not feel safer. All my guns didn't make me feel protected."

"If I knew then what I know now, well, of course it is easy to say I would never have traveled down that road. But the truth was that I was a young pup, who just wanted Mama to be happy. Then all of a sudden, I was an old dog trying to make everybody else happy. But I was confused, not happy. The truth be known, I was miserable almost all the time. No one around me took me seriously until I acted up. I believe that if I had continued on that path much longer, I would soon be dead. So, in the end, for me 'dying' wasn't hard to imagine."

"And I actually wanted to die! Self-abuse can lead to self-deceit and then to self-hatred. Almost all of mine came from never finding my true self."

"On one level, I wanted to die. but not really. I just wanted to run away. Disappear for a few days, or a week! Go incognito. Have a Big Mac or some ribs without the world watching. I just needed to get away from Graceland and the Colonel and my father. I'd find a cheap motel and sleep. A restful sleep, not the foggy sleep that leaves me still tired. Biscuits with my eggs in the morning. It would be a breath of fresh air."

"So, you see Stanley, dying was as easy as walking into the

bathroom. Or so it seemed to everybody else! Except I slipped out of there and out the door."

"How could I explain this to Ginger or the Colonel or anybody? I felt frantic and wanted out of the limelight for a little while."

"And then I met Anna Rabinowitz."

CHAPTER SIX

Elie came home from synagogue. It was a warm summer evening, so he and Stan sat together again on the porch. His kids flitted in and out of the house, playing in the street, but they were out of earshot. Elie had a cup of tea Shoshana had given him. She regarded him for a moment before opening the screen door and going in.

"Have you told her yet?" Stan asked.

"No, I have some time before it's obvious that I am sick."

"Do you think that's fair to her?"

Elie looked pained, "Probably not, but I'm not going to worry her any more than I have to. Just remember, you promised me that you would ensure that she gets a fair share of the profits from this. Remember Stanley, we discussed this," he said. Tears formed in the corners of his eyes.

"I gave you my word and I will keep my word."

"A substantial share! She will have no other income."

"You don't have to remind me. She will be taken care of." Stanley lifted his soda and touched it to Elie's teacup. He nodded. "So, keep going."

Elie first drank some tea.

"We were playing Las Vegas and had just slipped into the hotel through the kitchen to avoid the crowds. I heard a woman's voice with a thick European accent calling out to me. 'Mr. Presley! Mr.

Presley! I need to talk to you, Mr. Presley!' I saw the kitchen staff running to do their tasks as we threaded our way towards the back elevator to our floor. I focused on a small woman in a waitress' uniform, blocking my path. I hesitated, and one of my bodyguards stepped in front of me to move her.

'Mr. Presley, please don't run away. I must talk with you.'

I focused on a very small woman, in a waitress' uniform, blocking my path. It was something in her eyes that told me to stop and listen. I waved off my bodyguard. 'It's all right. Leave her alone.' To the woman, I said, 'You need to talk with me?'

'Yes, I do!'

"So I asked, 'What's this about?'

'It's very important,' she said, as she raised her index finger at me. 'Important? What do you want an autograph for your grandkids?' I said, smiling.

"She made a face. 'I don't need autographs! I need to speak with you!'

'Me? Why? Do you know who I am?' I tried thinking back if I had ever met her, but I didn't remember. Besides, she had to be at least sixty years old. She spoke with a European accent. Maybe I had met her when I was in the Army in Germany. A maid in a hotel? A cook? She still wasn't familiar to me.

"She answered, 'Of course I know who you are. I called you by name, didn't I?' She leaned close to my ear to whisper, 'It is imperative that I speak to you because a member of your family did an awful thing to my family, and you should know about it.'

"I was still puzzled. 'Do I know you?'

'No!'

'You say a member of my family did something bad? Who? Who in my family are you talking about?' I was too tired for this. 'You're a stranger to me! What are you talking about?'

'What I am talking about is …' She sputtered to a stop. Everyone in the kitchen was watching, and the chef strode over.

"He wrang his hands and said, 'I'm sorry about this disturbance,

Mr. Presley.' He scowled at the woman and said, 'Anna, get back to work! This is not the time or place. Leave him alone!'

"She wagged a finger at him. 'This is none of your business. This is between me and … pointing at me, 'him!'

"I shrugged at my entourage. I really had to get to my room and sleep. It had been a hard tour and a tough show. I was beat.

"But she persisted. For some reason that I didn't understand, I became certain I had to talk with her. Then the string of numbers on her arm caught my eye, and I drew in a sharp breath… The blurry blue numbers, the tattoo. I knew what that meant.

'Mr. Presley, please listen to what I have to say!'

"I held my hands up in mock surrender. 'Okay, I'll listen, but not here.' I looked at my bodyguard and told him to escort her to my room in fifteen minutes. I needed to get my head straight first.

'She whispered to herself, 'Danks Got, he will listen!'

CHAPTER SEVEN

"She sat on the corner of the couch. I was spread out in a chair opposite her," Elie said, staring out toward the quickly setting sun. "She peered at me intently and looked around the suite. The guys were in the other room, laughing and joking as they ate sandwiches and guzzled beer. I was exhausted. Physically and mentally, I had no energy left. What was I doing allowing this old woman to disturb me at this hour?

Stan asked, "What did she say?"

"She said to me, 'Mr. Presley, my name is Anna Steuben Rabinowitz. Rabinowitz is my married name although I have been widowed for many years.'

'How come you never remarried?' I asked her.

'That is for another time, another place.'

"I swallowed hard but did not speak. She continued, 'I come from a small village in Europe called Skalat.'

'Where is Skalat?' I asked.

"Most people would say Hungary. It was actually in the Ukraine. It doesn't matter, as other nations were constantly overtaking us and who knew who really owned the place?" My father was a doctor and we lived a comfortable life until the beginning of the war. The Second World War.'

She looked around the suite again. The boys were having fun and raising hell in the next room. 'May I shut the door?'

"I told her, 'Sure.'

'She got up and closed the door; you could hear hoots and hollers from the guys, who were watching a baseball game on the television.

'It was hard for us during the war, Mr. Presley."

'I bet it was. What was so hard?'

"Her face was thunderous. She hissed, 'It was war, and we were Jews.'

"I squirmed in my seat. Her face relaxed a little, and she said, 'We were hated by all the sides in the war, not only the Germans. But my father was a town doctor, so the people in town protected us from much of the bad things happening to our neighbors. He was lucky. Even the doctors were killed during the pogrom. Do you understand what I am saying, Mr. Presley?'

"I said I did. I was so tired I had to stifle a yawn. She tilted her head and gave me a cool once-over. She didn't believe me.

'Do you really understand, Mr. Presley? It is important that you do."

"I nodded yes. Then I asked, 'What's a pogrom?'

'It was an organized riot, permitted and encouraged by the Germans in which Jews were brutally murdered.'

'When the Germans came, they allowed the local Ukrainians to have a pogrom. We got lucky. We went into hiding with the help of some Polish neighbors. After the pogrom was over, they kept us hidden. They were not Jews, and it was a huge risk for them. We hid in a farmer's hay loft and depended on him and his family to feed us. It was unsafe by day, so they would slip us food at night. But everyone suffered during the war. There was never enough food, barely enough for one miserable meal a day, if we were lucky. The farmer was a kind-hearted man, but if he got fearful, he might not deliver food for a couple of days. Once my mother had to sneak out and tap on the farmer's window to feed us when the German troops were in the area. But we survived. As for the rest of the Jews in town, they were rounding up the remaining Jews not killed in the pogrom and shipping them to concentration camps. Not all at once, but over the weeks, people just disappeared. Many times, my father would say to my mother that we should run up into the hills to hide out, but with five children, two of whom were still babies, it was too dangerous. So, we stayed in our hiding place, hoping against hope that we would not be caught.'

'Were you caught?'

'Yes, Mr. Presley, we were caught. It took several months, and we might not have gotten caught but for one man, who notified the Germans of our hiding place. The result was the farmer was arrested and probably killed and the rest of my whole family ended up in Auschwitz. Of the seven of us, I am the sole survivor.'

"I winced and said, 'What a miserable person to do that.'

'Yes, a miserable person, an animal! Worse still was that he was a Jew himself, just like us.'

"I leaned back, my mouth agape. 'That's crazy!" I said. "One of your own?'

'Shocking, isn't it. But Mr. Presley, who knows why people do the things they do? He might have been scared for himself. Or the Germans might have paid him money, or he did it to escape the camps himself. What does it matter? Will it bring my family back?'

"I couldn't look her in the eyes and just said, 'No.' My voice was husky. I rubbed a hand across my face, trying to wipe away the grim mental images. I sat quietly.'

"Then I said to her, "Why are you telling me all of this?"

"She leaned in, speaking in low tones, "The man who ratted out my family to the Germans was named Mendel Tackett. Does the name Tackett mean anything to you, Mr. Presley?'

"The name sounded familiar. I was not sure where I had heard it before.

'It did, faintly, but I couldn't place it. So, I just shook my head and told her, 'I'm sorry, but I'm afraid I don't know anyone named Tackett.'

'But then I thought back to when my Mama talked about her Great Grandma Nancy whose married name was Tackett. It all began to make sense.'

CHAPTER EIGHT

Elie and Stan sat in Elie's cozy basement office. Stanley had brought a flask of scotch with him. The two of them had already drunk two or three glasses and were feeling loose. Elie acted a bit withdrawn.

"What's bothering you, my friend?" Stanley motioned to the bottle for a refill. Elie poured a splash into Stan's glass.

"Remembering." He sighed. "Just remembering."

"What about?"

"Anna Rabinowitz. She stays on my mind. The night she spoke with me, I could not sleep at all. I sat out on a couch to escape by watching TV. It didn't help. I thought for hours about what she had told me. A distant cousin of mine ratted out his Jewish neighbors to the Nazis. It made me sick to think that I was related to that kind of person. I felt sickened inside. I still do, after all these years." Elie looked at the bottle. Stan passed it over watching him pour some of the brown liquid into his cup. He raised it to his lips and took a searing swallow.

"But I asked myself that night, 'What did it have to do with me? I never knew this person and he was probably dead himself from the Nazis. Why was this weighing on me so heavily?'

"Before Anna left my room, I asked her why she had told me this story. She shrugged but didn't speak. I asked her if I could do anything for her. She shrugged again, but then she said, 'Mr. Presley,

34

I am not asking for anything from you. You are a very famous man, and I am sure you are very busy. I recently became aware of the fact that you were related to Mendel Tackett. I have been searching for him since the war ended, just to ask him why he did this terrible thing. I never heard if he even survived the war. A librarian has been helping me with my research. She discovered that you were distantly related to this man. So, when you came to sing here, I felt compelled to tell you.'

I asked her 'But surely there is something I can do for you?'

'Again Mr. Presley. I am not asking for your help. I need nothing from you. I just wanted to tell you because you are one of this man's relatives. It is not your fault that your cousin did this terrible thing. In truth, it is not even your burden. You seem like a nice man. I am sorry to have disturbed you.' She shook her head and stood up. She looked down at the floor and with tears prickling in her eyes, she said, 'I should not have come and disturbed you like this. It was just important to finish this for my family.'

"She sobbed and then she was gone.

"And from moment on, I was a lost soul dedicated to finding myself.'

CHAPTER NINE

By then, Elie and Stanley were quite drunk and quite sad. The bottle was drained, and Shoshana came down to get Elie and bring him upstairs to sleep. Elie walked Stanley to the front door and stepped out onto the porch with him. The two shook hands. Then, Elie sat down on one of the front porch chairs.

"I'm not done. Stanley, grab a seat." He patted the adjacent chair.

Stan looked at Shoshana and shrugged. She glanced at Elie and said nothing. She went back inside and closed the screen door.

"When Anna Rabinowitz blocked my path that night, something shifted in me. It was cosmic! It was a shift that gave me a purpose and a cause, even if I didn't fully understand then. What would soon become obvious to me was that Mendel Tackett was not me, and his family was not mine. The fact that we shared a bloodline was simply happenstance. I had no relationship with any European Jew. I was just a rock and roll singer from Mississippi who was killing himself inch by inch with drink and drugs and misery.

"Yet this little woman had changed my whole focus, and I spent a long time wondering who I was, why I was the person I am. I pondered what my purpose here on Earth was. Was I supposed to be this rock and roll singer?

"The truth of the matter was that I realized, in many ways, I was Mendel Tackett. Mendel must have been a truly disturbed man to have handed people over to the Nazis. Either he had no morality, or he was just a dog trying to save himself. Either way, I could relate to that. My life had become this huge wave and I was riding it, like a surfer, hoping not to get swallowed up, but fearing it was already too late.

"Mama was long dead, and Daddy knew nothing about my great grandma in this regard. I had asked him about it, but Vernon just shrugged his shoulders and asked why I suddenly cared. I tried to explain about Anna, but he just made a face and reached into the refrigerator for a beer. He popped the top and asked why I was worrying about it. 'She is just some old lady,' he said, tipping the bottle to his lips. He drew deeply on the cold brew and sighed in satisfaction. "Probably scheming for some money or something!"

'I don't know about that.' I said irritated. 'She didn't want money. Just wanted me to know. I don't know why that was important to her. I think she figured that by telling me she would clear her mind.'

"I remember grabbing the back of my neck at that point. 'I sure got a damned headache. We got any aspirin around here?'

"I left the room and went to lie down. I closed my eyes but didn't sleep. I was rehashing this conversation. I got up and called my lawyer and told him the story, and he asked why I called him about this. I told him I wanted him to hire an investigator to look into this.

"I heard him huff, and he said "Hell Elvis, what do you hope to gain from this? It will be awfully expensive and even if it is true, what difference will it make in your life? It's just an old lady letting off steam. And you, being the nice boy that you are, took the time to hear her out. You let her have her moment.' I could picture him while he was saying that, probably gesturing at the phone with a cigar smoldering between his fingers. 'Now, we'll just let her story die a natural death and not worry about it. It's a waste of your precious time.'

Stan wore a small smile. "Of course, you couldn't let it go."

"No." Elie chuckled. "I hired an investigator myself and sent him off to find out the truth."

"Elie, I am going to ask you the same question your lawyer originally asked you. Why did it matter to you then? What were you hoping to find out?"

"I didn't have a clue at that time. I was a mess, all screwed up, crammed full of drugs, my family deteriorating around me. Honest to G-d, I had no idea what I was doing. But something in me said that I had to find out. So, I did."

"Did you get any answers?"

"I'm here now."

"And what does that mean?"

"I am here now because of what I learned about Mendel Tackett."

"I don't understand. What did you learn about Tackett?"

"We'll leave that for the moment."

"Elie! You promised me a story."

"And you'll get it. Okay?" Elie stood up with a wobble. "But I'm a bit drunk right now and should go to bed. So, let's leave this for the moment please."

Stan shook his head. "Wow. This must have blown your mind!"

Memories flashed across Elie's face, and he got up to go inside. Through the screen door, he said. "Stan, we'll continue tomorrow. I'll come knock when I'm ready."

CHAPTER TEN

"I grew up, at least in my teen years, at The Courts," Elie said, putting down his morning coffee. "The Courts was a public housing complex in Memphis. It is now called Lauderdale Courts. We lived in Apartment # 328 from 1949 through 1953. It was a complex of three- story buildings. You could walk to the Mississippi River. We were just a few blocks away. The place was mostly poor to lower middle- class whites. I'm told that today it is mostly rundown. It's become dangerous. The city doesn't take good care of it to this day, not that it did when I lived there. When I hit it big, we moved to Graceland, approximately fifteen miles away. Graceland was built by a doctor in 1939, and I purchased it in 1957. It was my home until 1977, when I 'died'. I'm told it's now the biggest tourist place in Memphis."

"Ever miss it?" Stan asked. pausing in his notetaking to sip from his own coffee mug.

Ellie shrugged. "Not really. Well, sometimes I think about it, but mostly in sadness. It's not who I am now. In truth, I was showing off to Mama. She loved all the glitz. I mean, I liked living there. But the place lacked a moral compass, and it dragged me down. Lots of fun, but mostly sad memories."

"I went to Humes High School. I was the shy outsider who brought his guitar to school every day. I liked school but believe it or not, I failed music. Never learned to read music. It's all by ear for me.

"I was a twin, born second of twins. My brother, Jesse Garon, passed away either in early infancy, or was stillborn. Mama would never tell me exactly which. A cousin of mine once told me a story of visiting the house in Tupelo. Someone had died. I suspect it was Jesse. The family sat on low chairs and the mirrors were covered. "It was years later," she told me that she learned, "that these were Jewish traditions.

"Mama always told me I was Jewish, even though we went to church regularly. She was proud of her Jewish roots. I once asked her how she knew we were Jewish. She pursed her lips and looked up while she retrieved the memory. I must have been about seven or eight. Then she said, 'Well you was born and grew up in Tupelo, Mississippi. We lived in a poor area known as "That's what the locals called the home of the "rag trade."

"I asked her what that was. She said it was an industry that up here we call the shmatta business. It is still going strong even today. It was worked mostly by Jewish immigrants who repaired and resold secondhand clothing."

Stanley nodded, scribbling some quick notes. He was familiar. "Our family tradition goes way back to a time when Jewish immigrants settled in the South bringing the rag trade with them," Elie said. "My maternal great-great grandmother was a woman named Nancy Burdine. She came from a family that had traveled to America from Lithuania. They say they probably immigrated around the time of the American Revolution. I never verified that, but Mama insisted it was true. Nancy married a man named Abner Tackett around 1850. We always said Abner may have been Jewish himself, or at least half- Jewish. The Tacketts had two sons, Sidney and Jerome and a daughter named Martha, who grew up to become my great grandmother. Martha married a man named Whitey Mansell. They had a daughter, Octavia, whom they nicknamed Doll, and she was my grandma. Doll married Bob Smith and they had nine children. Their fifth child was a girl they named Gladys Love. She was my mama."

Elie had a fond look on his face. "Now my Mama was so proud of her Jewish roots. When she died, I told the stonemasons to inscribe a Star of David and a cross on her tombstone. Later when her body was moved to Graceland, they put up a new stone with only a cross. I couldn't do anything about that at the time without giving up the secret of my disappearance.

"Getting back to Memphis, we lived in a cheap cramped apartment. Above us lived a Jewish Rabbi and his family. His name was Rabbi Fried. I liked visiting him and his family. They always fed me. I loved that chicken soup and those matzah balls." Elvis licked his lips and patted his belly with a chuckle.

"I would listen to Jewish music with the Rabbi and the wailing and crying sounds grew on me. I came to love it. It reminded me, in some strange way, of the blues I heard on Beale Street."

Stanley could tell he drifted into memories of music and concerts past, but then Elie continued. "I was their Shabbos goy. I never told them of my Jewish side, so they thought I was one hundred percent gentile. I would do the things that were forbidden to them on Shabbos, such as lighting a stove or turning on the lights. Rabbi Fried tried to pay it, but I always said no. I enjoyed being there so much. I somehow acquired a skull cap, which I always kept in the back pocket of my pants. I think I had found it in my Mama's drawer. Not sure why she had one, but from then on it was mine.

"Mama, as I said, never hid her family tree from me. I also learned I was part Cherokee Indian and was proud of that. But she always warned me not to share my Jewish stuff outside the family. Anti- Semitism was a big problem in the South in the '40's." Elie shook off that depressing reality, and then a faint shadow of that famous lopsided Elvis grin skimmed across his lips. "But I loved the Frieds and was glad to help out whenever I could."

CHAPTER ELEVEN

Avner Tackett was done with it. Just done! He stood in the middle of the small synagogue in Hanover in what is now Germany. The year was 1841 and Avner was seventeen years old. He was an apprentice tailor. It was a job he despised along with everything else in his life. He hated being tucked into a traditional Orthodox Jewish life and yearned for freedom from conformity.

But that morning as he put his phylacteries away and prepared to go to work, he decided he has had enough. "No more," he thought to himself. "I am going up north to Hamburg and sailing to America." He dreams of a new life, new fortunes, free to be whatever he wanted, no matter what.

Leaving his entire family, his community, and his legacy and going to America was something Avner had been pondering for some time. He had no use for the tailoring business, but he had a knack for buying and selling. His patron, Reb Elimelech had come to rely on the boy to choose the best quality materials when they went to the fairs to buy and he was skilled at negotiating the best prices from the sellers of cloth, particularly the gypsies. Smart, with a quick wit and slight smile, he was well liked by most everyone. He came from a family of workmen who were highly praised in the community. Most of the men were carpenters, masons, or merchants. Not well off, the family managed to get by.

Avner's immediate family lived on the outskirts of the Jewish section of Hanover. His father, Mordechai Tackett, was a dairy merchant. His mother, Elka, ran a household of seven children. Avner's older siblings were Menachem Mendel, who was twenty-one and married to Sara. They had a little boy, Aaron. His sister Shoshana was Nineteen. Younger than him were David, Gila, Bella, Reina, and the baby Moses. Avner was the classic middle child, lost in a big family, feeling ignored and put upon.

"They won't even miss me," he grumbled. "I am just another mouth to feed." He was a voracious reader and a brilliant student. But as time went by, he was reading books that his parents would have been troubled by and he yearned to travel and get away. His father, seeing that he was such an antsy kid, set him up in an apprenticeship to tailor with Reb Elimelech, who had a dry goods and cloth store in town. He hoped this would calm his son's wayward spirit and set him on a responsible path. While Avner never outwardly showed his dissatisfaction, it was obvious to his parents that he felt restrained by life in the Jewish Quarter. They sought out a matchmaker. Although he was rather young to be married, they hoped that finding him the right girl would calm his wayward spirit.

The matchmaker came over on Friday and had an extensive talk with his parents. On Sunday morning, his father and mother left their house, dressed like it was the Sabbath. They went to the home of a local merchant, Reb Yehuda Rapoport, and met with him. They met his daughter, an eighteen-year-old named Chana. Chana was a slightly plump girl on the throes of womanhood with a pretty face and a quick wit. She had a sarcastic and sharp tongue, but today when she met the Tacketts she showed the sweetest disposition. The fathers agreed to the match and the men scheduled the engagement announcement, for Sunday in the Rapoport home. The whole synagogue would be notified by word of mouth and an announcement from the pulpit by the Rabbi. They shared glasses of schnapps and congratulated each other with a mazel tov.

The next morning the announcement was made in the synagogue to the astonishment of Avner. As men came up to him with congratulations on what was new to him, he felt shaken and annoyed His world was closing in on him.

He was not ready to get married and he had no idea who his bride- to-be was. He looked to the back of the synagogue and met his father's eyes who nodded briefly at him. Avner gathered his things and brushed past him on his way out. He prolonged his walk home, dressed in his work clothes and headed out to work. Reb Elimelech congratulated him with a handshake and patted him on the shoulder. Avner grunted his thanks and went to work sewing pants. As the disgruntled and secretly panicking young man looked up from his work, his patron brought over a small flask with two glasses and poured him a drink. They toasted and clinked glasses, and Avner returned to his work.

He stewed all day and when he got home, his parents pulled him aside and talked about him getting married. Avner had nothing to say, kept his lips pressed shut and shrugged when they asked his opinion. They told him the wedding would be in a month and that he would have great blessings from such a match. Her father was well to do. Money would not be a problem. And if he didn't like being a tailor, his future father-in-law could bring him into his business. It would all be fine; they assured their son. He smiled tightly but still said nothing.

That Sunday evening, he dressed in his Sabbath clothes and went with his family to the Rapoport home, where they made the formal announcement. He met his future wife for the first time and coldly assessed her. She wasn't exactly his type, but she wasn't heaven forbid, ugly. She, in turn, sized him up quickly as someone she would be able to control. She weighed his looks, and a wisp of a smile lifted her lips. Avner was tall and thin, with dark eyes and hair; he was nice looking. In her mind he would be a quiet compliant husband. She was satisfied.

They barely swapped words for the rest of the night but stood side by side as praises from the Rabbi and family members washed over the couple. Avner spoke a few words, and everyone mingled, had some cake, and schnapps, and then it was over. Everyone went home and Avner and Chana were engaged.

CHAPTER TWELVE

The month flew by so fast, Avner had no chance to catch his breath. The Rapoports sent fine gifts to him and his family. Reb Yehuda, as he was known, invited Avner to his office, where the older man with earnestness about his daughter and the impending wedding. Avner was not talkative, nor did he have to be. Reb Yehuda was most loquacious and even if Avner had wanted to speak, he couldn't get a word in anyway.

On the Sabbath before the wedding, they met in the synagogue for a celebration by the groom's family. After the service, they all shared wine and some cakes and congratulations all around. They went home and prepared for the wedding which would be that Tuesday night.

Avner was caught up in this whirlwind of activities and was numb to what was going on around him. On Tuesday morning, he got up before dawn and ate a small breakfast, reasoning that since today was his wedding day he would have to fast from sunup until after the service under the wedding canopy, the Chuppah. He moped as he got ready for the morning service, left the house with his father and walked to the synagogue.

There he was once again revolted by his new reality. "I'm done with this. Just done!"

It struck him this time like a lightning bolt. "I am completely done with this! This is not what I want. I am not going to do this.

No. No. No! I am not going to do this!" It was unimaginable that this was the way his life was going to go. "No, not like this. I can't endure this." He gritted his teeth and sat down to regain his composure. His father was praying. looking serene and happy. He glanced at his son, and his face lit up with a smile. Avner's heart sank. He dropped his eyes to the prayer book, but only saw scribbled ink on a page. Tears welled up. He was doomed! He couldn't hurt his family.

He stood under the Chuppah and watched his bride walk toward him. She circled him seven times as was tradition. They drank the wine. Avner placed the ring on Chana's finger. Then he broke the glass, and they were married. He danced, drank, and ate all in a daze. Finally, the party was over, and he went with his new bride to their new home.

The two joined as man and wife, and the next morning, Avner was gone.

CHAPTER THIRTEEN

No one initially noticed that Avner was gone. Chana thought he had slipped out to go to Synagogue. When Avner didn't show up there, the rest of the town assumed he was enjoying the time with his new wife. In fact, nobody acted concerned at all until around four in the afternoon, when it was obvious that he couldn't be located. They all waited around for hours assuming he would be back for the first night celebration, the Sheva Brochos (Seven Blessings) meal. They waited several hours.

As it became painfully clear that something was wrong, the men organized a search party, but since it was dark, they realized that they would only be able to search local buildings. To search the roads, that could not start until dawn. They did not find him in any building, so at dawn several men on horseback traveled around the roads. They found nothing.

Avner, however, was far down the road on his way to Hamburg. He had sneaked out of the house as Chana slept and had gone to the tailor shop of Reb Elimelech. He opened the shop and went to his workbench. Under the table, he gathered up a box in which he had been collecting things for the past month that he knew he would need to escape. In the box, he had assembled a duffel bag and some clothing and had hidden everything under his tools.

When he entered the shop, he stuffed the duffel bag with his clothes and some rolls that he had pocketed from the wedding feast, locked the shop, and hit the road under the cover of darkness.

He plodded ahead for several hours until a horse cart came alongside him with two horses and a heavy-set man driving the cart. The driver was clearly not Jewish but offered him a ride. He jumped aboard.

"Where are you going?" asked the driver.

"Hamburg."

"Long way to walk."

"Yes, it is. Thank you for giving me a lift."

"Not a problem for me. Did you plan to travel on foot all the way?"

"If I had to! But I am hoping to find people driving in my direction and maybe pick up a ride or two along the way."

"Ah!" the driver said. "You're running away."

Avner nodded.

"From what or whom?" the driver asked.

"From my wife," Avner replied.

The driver laughed, "Aren't we all?"

Avner laughed as well.

"Seriously?" the driver asked. Avner nodded again.

"You are so young to be married! How long have you been?"

"I got married last night." A storm of emotions swept across his face. He swallowed hard and looked at the man, he said, "Listen, it's a big mess. I am not really ready to talk about it."

The driver tapped a finger on his chin and pondered. Then he said. "Young man, in a strange way, I understand." He returned his gaze to the horses in front of him and reached back to shake hands. "Herman is my name."

"Avner," he said, returning the handshake. "Thank you again."

"No need. You're Jewish?" Avner tipped his head again to indicate yes.

"Don't worry. I won't bite. This may be your lucky day, young fellow. I happen to be going to Hamburg myself to buy supplies for my shop. You can ride with me. But you have to pay for your own lodging and food." He shrugged. "So, if you want to go with me, you can."

Avner again thanked the man who snapped the whip over the two horses. "We are going to have to put some distance between you and all the people who will be beating the bushes for you. Hold onto your hat, my boy, because here we go!"

CHAPTER FOURTEEN

Avner had been in Hamburg for three days before he found a small ship which would take him. He travelled in steerage to Liverpool, England where he disembarked. Not speaking English, he nevertheless was able to find the small Jewish community there. He was put up for a few days with a family who spoke Yiddish as he did.

He explained to his new acquaintances that he wanted to go to America. They said that their cousin had gone there a few years ago, and an ideal place to go to was Charleston, South Carolina.

Charleston had a decent sized Jewish community, and he could expect to be sent in the right direction once he got there. There were many packet ships that regularly crossed from Europe to Charleston, and he should have no trouble finding one to embark upon. Packet ships carried mail and regular supplies between England and the States. They were reliable and decent to travel in.

Avner was able to secure a place in steerage on a small packet sailing ship after a week in Liverpool. He boarded the "Sanctity" and crossed over the Atlantic, landing in Charleston. The Charleston he arrived in was a vibrant pre-Civil War city full of people bustling around. He found his way to the Jewish section of town and was directed to Kahal Kadosh Beth Elohim, the main synagogue in town. Although the synagogue was Sephardic and Avner was a German

Ashkenazi Jew, they quickly accepted him and arranged for his room and board.

Avner found a job with a millinery company and quickly distinguished himself for his ability to discern fine fabrics and to buy and sell them for a handsome profit. By early 1842, his English skills had improved, and despite his accent, he was becoming a successful merchant. Never divulging that he had been married, he was the subject of many families' attempts to fix him up with the local girls, but he demurred for the most part although there were one or two young ladies who captured his attention. He told everyone he was twenty-one rather than his real age of eighteen. Although he looked young, they accepted him at his word.

His employer, Mr. Simon Isaac, liked the young man and decided he should go to New Orleans to scout out and buy bundles of cotton cloth at the best prices. Mr. Isaac had just received a contract from the Army to make uniforms, tents, ammunition bags and the like. It was a very lucrative contract, but the South Carolina cotton was too expensive for the contract to be really profitable. Also South Carolina cotton was rough and not the best quality when processed. Cotton entering New Orleans from Texas and Egypt was of a high quality and was selling for dirt-cheap prices. Unable to go himself, and convinced that Avner would do right by him, he sent the young man by boat to purchase cloth for him in New Orleans.

Avner was thrilled at the opportunity to go and took full advantage of the boat trip to perfect his English and to enjoy the surroundings. He ate whatever was served on board and dropped all vestiges of his Jewish heritage.

He renamed himself Abner and as the newly minted Abner Tackett, the first thing he did when he got to New Orleans was purchase clothing that was more in keeping for a Southern gentleman. He thus abandoned the clothing that had marked him as a Jew all his life. He didn't pretend he was a Gentile; he just never mentioned his religion. When someone asked him his nationality, he told them he grew up in Germany.

He purchased a large amount of cloth for Mr. Isaac and arranged for its transport back to Charleston. He stayed in the city for a few days, enjoying the restaurants and the inns and the music. Abner decided that rather than returning to Charleston by boat, he would go up the Mississippi River to Natchez and then go across overland. He boarded a steamer upriver, and within days landed in Natchez.

As it happened, he arrived in Natchez at an auspicious time. A year earlier, the first Jews started settling Natchez in earnest. A man named John Mayer and his wife came from New Orleans to Natchez and settled there. At first, he worked as a tailor and then became a successful merchant whose business thrived for many decades. Following the Mayers over the next few years were merchants Simon Adler, Solomon Bloom, Aaron Beekman, Isaac David, and Joseph Tillman. They all came to live in Natchez and established a Jewish community. Within a few years, their businesses began to boom. Their stores became famous throughout the South, such as Schatz's, producing ladies' ready-to-wear clothing. Schatz sold ladies' garments into the early twentieth century. By 1858, eight out of twelve Jewish businesses in Natchez traded either in clothing or dry goods. It was probably the right time and the right place for an enterprising young man from Germany to settle down and grow his own business.

Abner wrote to Mr. Isaac that he was staying in Natchez but offered to be his agent in New Orleans and make several buying trips a year. Mr. Isaac accepted the deal and arranged with a bank in New Orleans to provide the credit for making purchases. Soon, other merchants in Charleston heard about the arrangement and contacted Abner to work as their broker to purchase supplies for their businesses as well. It wasn't long before he was buying corn, wheat, leather, dried meats, firearms for the Army and also purchasing whatever he felt he could safely handle.

By 1850, he was wealthy and a very eligible man. He was twenty-eight and had purchased a large house and owned several slaves. He traveled throughout Mississippi, Tennessee, and Alabama, scouting out new opportunities. On one of those trips, he went to Tupelo, a small town in Mississippi. There he met an attractive Jewish girl named Nancy Burdine. He let on to her that he was also Jewish. It turned out that Nancy's family had originally come from Lithuania, and they all spoke fluent Yiddish, so he was able to speak in his mother tongue once again. They fell in love in short order, and he married her. Unbeknownst to her, he was already married back in Germany. But he said nothing, and no one was the wiser. In 1851, Nancy gave birth to Sidney and then in 1853 the couple had Jerome. A daughter named Martha, came in 1857. By then, inklings of war were getting louder and louder. Abner kept prospering, and the couple hoped that their blessings and good fortune would continue.

CHAPTER FIFTEEN

Meanwhile, back in Hanover, all hell had broken loose. Nobody knew what had happened to Avner nor could people make sense of his disappearance. Initially, the local Jews suspected something terrible had happened to him. He could have been kidnapped, but no ransom letter was ever sent. Or he might have gotten sick. He could have had lost his mind and wandered off alone, without knowing who or where he was. G-d forbid, he might have even been killed by some locals or a wild animal.

They looked high and low but found not a trace of him. Not even a clue. They sent letters to the surrounding towns and to relatives as far away as Bohemia and France. It never occurred to them that he had willfully just left, as it would be an unbelievable to think of that. Why would he, after all, he had just gotten married. The Rapoports and the Tacketts were at first both in shock and fearful. As time passed by, it became obvious that Avner was not returning any time soon. He may have simply died somewhere and was lost to them.

Chana, having spent only one night with her husband was now a trapped woman. She was neither a widow nor a divorcée. She could not remarry under Jewish law, even if she wanted to. Her initial response to Avner's disappearance was bemused concern. No histrionics from her. She was far too cynical for that. She suspected he had simply run away but never said so to anyone. And of course, she was right.

Unconcerned for the moment, the spotlight was on her. She proceeded to go through the motions of the stricken young wife, but that ran thin for her after a short time. She yearned to go away and decide for herself what to do and how she would now live. She was young and pretty. She hoped Avner would pop back up and she would divorce him and move on with her life. All that might have been possible, but she missed her period the first month after the wedding. She dismissed her fleeting worry for the month. A second month passed with no period and then a third. It was obvious she was pregnant.

She had returned to her father's home right after Avner had disappeared. Now she came downstairs, gathered her parents, and told them the news. They were stricken. Reb Yehuda listened to the news, felt a sharp pain in his chest and collapsed from his chair. He was dead before he hit the floor.

After another six months she would give birth to a son she named Yehuda in her father's. She would never hear from Avner again, and she remained in limbo until she died of consumption when she was fifty.

Yehuda would grow up to be a Rabbi. He would marry a woman named Fruma in 1860, and they would have five girls and a boy named Boruch. The son would grow up to be a merchant and would move to Bohemia and marry twice. His first wife Sara would die in childbirth after delivering a son, Moses, in 1882. His second wife Rebecca would have five boys and three girls. By 1900, Moses was a strapping young man who married Lina and had a son they named Mendel.

They moved to the Austro-Hungarian Empire into a town in what had once been considered part of the Ukraine. The town was Skalat. Mendel grew up to be a lawyer. He was living when the Second World War lurched into motion around him.

CHAPTER SIXTEEN

It was a warm humid evening to sit out on the porch, but Elie preferred to sit out rather than go into the air-conditioned house. He would not say it, with cancer he felt cold all the time. The summer heat seemed to revive him, in contrast to Stan, who sat there, sweating rivers.

Stanley retrieved some cold beers from his house and handed one to Elie. He smiled at the beer and although he knew he shouldn't have it, he reached greedily for the bottle opener. Elie popped the top and brought the bottle to his lips drinking joyously with his eyes closed.

"L'Chaim to you, Stanley."

"You too, my friend."

Stan sat, and Elie resumed his tale.

"So now you know Avner's story. His relevance to this story will become clear soon. Jumping ahead, let me tell you a bit more about my dear friend, Rabbi Fried. I loved that man." He took another sip and looked out upon the street. Shaking his head, he said, "Yes, my dear friend Rabbi Fried. How I loved that man. We would sit sometimes and listen to records of these old time Cantors on the Victrola. Great voices. There was this one guy, Yoselle Rosenblatt. I imitated his voice and did a pretty decent job at it. Rabbi Fried was impressed. Told me if I were Jewish, I would be a good cantor." He chuckled, "He would have never guessed that someday, I would be one." He thought about that quietly for a moment.

"Of course, I doubt he envisioned that I would be a rock "n" roll singer either. But later on when I was a big star, we met in the street one day. He gave me a big hug and a kiss and shook his head saying, "My Elvis, my little Elvis. Look at you now. Such a success!" He was beaming, but then he looked at me more closely and his face fell. He grabbed both of my shoulders and looked me right in the eye. I tried to look away but couldn't. He said, "Elvis, are you happy?"

Stan's pen stopped moving, and he looked up. "What did you say to him?"

"I looked away. I felt sheepish. He was like a father to me, and he was asking a question a father would ask his son.

"Am I happy?" I teared up behind my sunglasses. He saw the tears running down my cheek."

"I see you're not so," he said, patting my arms. You miss your Mama and all the money in the world cannot replace her. Elvis, you have such a gentle soul, and you are so lost. I see it.'

"I told him he was right. He said, 'Of course.' He could tell that I wasn't all right, that I was not happy.

'Elvis,' he said. 'You can always call on me. I'm still in the same place. You should always know that. Don't be afraid to reach out.'

Elie and Stan shared a smile, and Elie continued. "I never expected to see him again, but life is never what you expect it to be."

"What do you mean?"

Elie waved a hand. "Let's just say that the hand of G-d plays out in mysterious ways and with the most unusual people."

Stan huffed, frowning. "I don't understand. Was Rabbi Fried involved in your great escape?"

Elie's lip curled up. "Maybe he was the escape!"

"What? I don't understand."

Elie's smile broadened into a grin.

CHAPTER SEVENTEEN

"It would be ten years or so before the next time I saw Rabbi Fried," Elie said. He glanced at Stan, who had finally stopped sweating and was looking comfortable in the evening's fading heat at last. "I never sought him out in all that time. He never expected to see me again and was surprised when I just showed up at his door early one evening, all by myself. By then Priscilla and I had divorced, and I was falling apart. I was studying all this Eastern religion stuff, trying to find meaning in my life. It wasn't helping but was so interesting.

"I couldn't focus on anything. I was doing all this karate and meditation, but none of it helped. My head was always hurting. And I was constantly on the road to support this big Elvis machine that required endless dollars to keep everyone working. My television special had returned my career to star status and the Colonel was pressuring me to tour all over the place, to rake in as much money as possible, in the shortest time imaginable. I don't know how I did it. In the end, it cost me my marriage and my daughter Lisa Marie.

"I was never home - and when I was home, I was constantly working on upcoming tours or the next special the Colonel wanted to book. It was no life, now I was alone with a house full of people dependent on me for their living. I started dating again about six months after Priscilla left. She was a beauty queen named Linda Thompson. She was my companion for over four years. I was not good to her. I was drugged most of the time. She tried hard, but she had to compete for me with my 'Memphis Mafia' as they were called. There were six of us, mostly boyhood pals, Sonny West, Red West, Billy Smith, Marty Lacker, Lamar Fike and myself. We hung together. We drank together. They loved me like brothers, and some of them tried to look out for me. But man, I was so hard to deal with.

"One evening, I drove myself back to the old neighborhood. I had disguised myself so no one would recognize me, and I skirted around the building so no one would see me. I went up to the Fried's apartment. I wasn't sure they still lived there or whether the old Rabbi was still alive. I nervously knocked on the door and heard footsteps inside. The peephole darkened for a moment as someone looked out the peephole in the door. Then I heard Mrs. Fried's hesitant voice on the other side asking, 'Who is it?'

"I steeled myself and stood up straighter, 'Mrs. Fried, is that you?' "She repeated, 'Who is it?' and I recognized her voice.

I removed my sunglasses and whispered, 'Mrs. Fried, this is Elvis. Elvis Presley.'

"I waited for what seemed like forever before the door chain rattled and the lock unclicked. She cracked the door open a couple of inches. Then she recognized me and cracked the door open wide. She pulled me in and gave me a big hug. Rabbi Fried shuffled over from the hallway. He was wearing slippers and a red sweater over a white T- shirt and black pants. His skullcap was perched on the top of his head and his reading glasses were at the tip of his nose as always. He smiled broadly and shook my hand. He had grown old and frail looking. She looked worse for wear as well. But he really looked tired and worn.

"He stood aside for me to come in and said, 'Mamale, please make Elvis a cup of tea. Elvis, come into the living room and sit on the couch. What brings you here?'

"He looked at me closely and saw that I was a real mess. I had grown so fat, and my face was pasty white. He could tell I wasn't well.

"Mrs. Fried brought in tea and a plate of cookies that she remembered I liked as a kid. She and her husband shared a look in that unspoken way that long time couples communicate. She retreated to the kitchen, leaving the Rabbi and me alone to speak. 'Son, you look terrible.'

'I know, sir.'

'Trouble?'

'I believe so, sir.'

'What kind of trouble, son?'

"I started to cry, and he let me cry for a long time. Here I was this big star, bawling on the couch in a little apartment in the projects where I grew up. I could not believe that I was even there, and I was not sure why I came. But I have come to believe that G-d sent me to him then and that through him would be my saving.

'Elvis, you want to tell me what's going on with you? I'm not sure if I can help you, but I will certainly listen.'

'Rabbi, I am just a mess. My life is a disaster, and I am in over my head about what to do.' I stopped and tried to pull myself together. 'I'm asking for help sorting it all out. It is so complicated, and I do not know where to turn. I just can't make sense of any of it.' I sobbed again, embarrassed for myself.

Rabbi Fried got up and rested his hand on my shoulder. He sat by me on the couch.

'Son, take a breath. I am here to listen. But you need to take a breath and get yourself together. Whatever it is, it can only be solved calmly.'

I tried to stuff down my feelings and stop crying but couldn't. I was coming apart right in front of him.

'Miriam dear, please get me a glass of whiskey,' the Rabbi called out to his wife. She came in a few moments later with a glass of ice and a bottle of Canadian Club. The Rabbi poured a little into the glass and handed it to me.

'Here, take some sips.'

"I slowly sipped on the liquid courage. Rabbi Fried waited

calmly motioning me to take a sip every few minutes. I started to feel more in control. I yawned loudly. The Rabbi went into the kitchen, and I heard them having a quiet conversation, although I couldn't tell what they were saying.

"The Rabbi and his wife asked me if I had eaten recently. I shook my head no. They brought me into the kitchen and she made me a turkey sandwich with potato chips and some seltzer. They watched as I ate.

"She said to him, 'Some color is coming back into his face.'

"The Rabbi looked over at me and then nodded agreement. Then he said, 'Elvis, we are going to put you up tonight and maybe for a few days. My wife will put healthy food into you, and you can rest and get your mind straight. That is, if you wish. We will talk and map out a plan to help you. That's all I can do. The rest is up to you. Call your home and tell them you are taking some time away. Please don't tell them you are here. I don't want a whole circus of people trying to reach you here. It would disturb my wife very much. Let's take a day or two to help you figure this out. Can we agree?'

"I felt like a great weight was lifted from my chest. I agreed, but my car was parked in front of the building. The Rabbi made a telephone call. A young man from the Yeshiva came over about an hour later. He took my car keys and told me he would park the car in his home garage, so no one would see it. When I was ready and wanted it back the Rabbi would call so he could bring it back. He was a young man in a black suit with a fedora. He told me I could rest assured that he would tell no one, not even his wife. 'She never goes in the garage anyway and even if she did, she's unaware of who you are, Mr. Presley.'

Stan was slack-jawed by this point, his notes forgotten in his lap. Elie broke off his story and asked, "You have a question?"

"So, you just disappeared and no one came hunting for you?"
"Oh, I wish it were that easy. No, there was a bit of excitement at Graceland. The Colonel apparently got all mad and talked about sending out private investigators to scour the neighborhoods. But Red

convinced him I was just exhausted, and wherever I was, I would be home in a few days, rested and ready to work. The Colonel calmed down but told Red that if I wasn't back in three days, he would have his investigators smoke me out."

"How long did you stay with the Frieds?"

"About a week."

Stan was taken aback. He asked, "And did the Colonel do what he said he would do?"

Elie rolled his eyes. "No, I called him and said I was in California and would be back soon. He got all sore with me and was yelling as usual. I told him I was holed up with a girl and that he should leave me alone. I suppose he decided that was all right, because when I returned to Graceland, he was all nice, joking with me about my 'good time' in California."

"Amazing. . ., you got away with it."

"Yes, it was. It was amazing. And I learned something. For the first time since I was a boy, I could get away and hide. I figured that out from spending the week away from Graceland. And it was the beginning of a plan that started growing in my head. Oddly enough, it was Rabbi Fried who would help me to make it happen."

"What?" Stanley doubled over. "A Rabbi helped you escape?"

Elie smiled. "No," he said, "Not him alone. Actually, there were two Rabbis who helped me!"

"Two? Who else helped you pull this off?"

"Not so fast. I haven't told you how we did it. Tomorrow is a new day. That's for tomorrow's conversation."

With that, Elie got up from his chair and went into his house.

CHAPTER EIGHTEEN

Stanley had something to stew on when he got in bed that night. Ever since figuring out that Elie was, in fact, Elvis Presley, he had wondered how the whole escapade had been pulled off.

Stanley remembered that on the day Elvis "died," there was a body found in Graceland. So, he reasoned that clearly there was a conspiracy to get Elvis out of Memphis and to safety. This place of safety had to be a place where no one would suspect him to be this huge international star.

There had been supposed Elvis sightings for years, and Elvis disappearance conspiracy theories multiplied every year. In speaking to Elie, Stan had to consider that instead of these being crank sightings, some of them may have been real. It was evident that real people had actually seen Elvis and, in the end, talked themselves out of it.

He opened and closed his hands, wincing at how cramped they still were from so much notetaking that night. He laughed to himself, forgetting the soreness as he treated Elie's story like a mental puzzle. How had Elie done it?

Part of Stan's thoughts revolved around a tight-knit group of people who knew what was going on and helped him pull it off. These must have been people like the Memphis Mafia who could be trusted not to spill the beans. But now thirty-five years had passed and seeing how Graceland and all the Elvis paraphernalia were so profitable, it would be natural to assume that someone would have revealed the secret to cash in on it. Yet so many years had passed without a peep from Elvis' closest companions, so Stan had to discount that group of people.

Stan also reasoned that Elie would have gone back to Priscilla, because of their history and the fact that they shared a child. He quickly discounted the notion. He recognized that after the "death," Priscilla had grown the whole Elvis enterprise into an enormous money-making machine. Her being the mastermind behind the disappearance didn't figure into his equation; she had been the grieving ex-wife with a young daughter who would never again see her father. But Stan wondered "Maybe Lisa Marie was told years later and then had contact with her father?" Stan sat up in the bed. He decided this theory was nonsense. "Lisa Marie had been married to Michael Jackson. He was a huge self-promoter. Would he have kept the secret if he had been told?" He reasoned not. "No, Priscilla couldn't have been a part of this. Surely not."

Another round of conjecturing hit Stan. "Could Linda Thompson have known? After all, she had been with him for at least four years. She loved him and had tried so hard to take care of him. Interesting possibility. After she left Elvis, she married former Olympian Bruce Jenner in 1981 and had two sons with him. She divorced him in 1986. She then married David Foster, the composer, in 1991 and was married to him for almost fifteen years until they divorced in 2005.

He rejected that idea. It became clear that the more people involved, or the more Elie interacted with other people, the more likely the story would have gotten out." He dismissed the notion of Linda Thompson being a participant.

He immediately dismissed Ginger Alden, the fiancée after researching her online. As he read the various articles, he grunted out loud. "Ginger was just a kid. twenty years old at the time and Elvis was forty-two. Nearly everyone around Elvis disliked her too.

But then he recalled that it was Ginger who had found the body.

"She had to have known" he mused. But why would she have been so willing to give him up after she had agreed to marry him? Maybe that was the missing piece.

"She might have gone along because she saw how miserable he was and how she would never belong in the Graceland world." That thought stuck in Stan's mind, but the concept was riddled with holes. In the end, he realized it was all mindless speculation. He shook himself.

"I really just need Elie to tell me how he did it," he said out loud.

CHAPTER NINETEEN

Rabbi Fried sat at the kitchen table sipping on a cup of tea. Elvis had been sleeping for at least twelve hours. The Rabbi got up and woke him.

Elvis shuffled into the Fried's kitchen clutching his head. Miriam Fried, seeing this, reached into a cupboard and handed him a bottle of aspirin. He shook out three and downed the pills with the glass of water she provided. He sat at the table while she fried three eggs and buttered some toast. She placed it in front of him silently. He mumbled his thanks and began eating quietly while his eyes stayed glued to his plate. Rabbi Fried watched the meal, and his wife. Mrs. Fried placed a cup of tea in front of him and he drank it up greedily.

"Would you like another tea, Elvis?'

Looking up at her, he smiled weakly, "Yes ma'am that would be nice."

She made him another tea and he sipped slowly. "Would you like more eggs?"

"No ma'am, but some more toast would be nice."

She headed to the toaster. Soon, she placed the warm freshly buttered slices in front of him.

"Thank you, ma'am."

"It's no problem, Elvis. Last night when you came here, we were worried sick about you. I will leave you and the Rabbi to talk. If you need anything, just ask." With that, she swiped a towel across the counter and left the room.

Elvis ran a hand through five o'clock shadow and said, "I am so sorry to have bothered you. I'll finish up and get out of your hair."

"Where are you running to, son?" Rabbi Fried asked. "Where do you have to go that's so important?"

"Well sir, I have rehearsals and I have to get ready for my upcoming tour."

The rabbi lifted a shoulder. "If you missed today, would it make a difference?

"I suppose. But probably not."

"Then where are you running? You're safe here. Why go looking for trouble? I am frightened for you, my boy. How old are you now?

"Almost forty-two."

"Almost forty-two! And look at you. Is this the way you want to live your life? You look so sad. The Holy Book, the Mishna, says that he who doesn't take the time to learn in wealth, will not take the time to learn in poverty. You see Elvis, life is one big circle. Sometimes you are on top of the circle and other times, you are on the bottom. Those times are clear to a person. But as you ascend the circle, life seems wondrous, but you don't understand why. As you descend the circle, you pick up on it, but you refuse to accept it until you are at the bottom. It seems to me that you are on the descending side of the circle. But you don't have to go to the bottom. Even if you do, you don't have to stay there for very long. But you do have to acknowledge where you are and work on changing the things that are weighing you down. Do you understand that?"

"I think so. Mostly."

"Well, clearly you came here because you recognize what is dragging you down. What you don't know is how to fix it. So, Elvis, why are you so distraught?"

Elvis then told the Rabbi about his encounter with Anna Steuben Rabinowitz and how it had moved him.

The Rabbi's brow furrowed. "You said her name was Steuben?"

"No, Rabinowitz."

"That was her married name. Steuben must have been her maiden name. My wife had cousins named Steuben back in Europe. Where did you say she lived?"

"She said it was town named Skal-something. I can't remember it exactly."

"You must mean Skalat. Did she say she was from the Ukraine?"

"She said Hungary or Ukraine. She said the borders kept changing."

"I know about Skalat. I grew up in the next town over, which was Grzymalow. So, she said you had a relative named Mendel Tackett. It means you have some Jewish relatives in your family tree."

"Rabbi, I think I am actually Jewish. Mama always told me I was." "How so? I remember you and your mother always going out to church on Sunday mornings."

"True, true But Mama always talked about my Great-Great Grandma Nancy Burdine. She was Jewish from Europe. She married a guy named Abner Tackett, who came from Germany."

"Abner Tackett must be how you're related to Mendel?"

"I suppose.".

"But that was a long time ago, why did your Mama think she was Jewish? For that to happen, all of the women in your family line had to be Jews as well."

"Well Nancy had a daughter Martha, my great- grandmother. Martha married a man named Whitey Mansell. Their daughter was Octavia. Everyone called her Doll. She was my Grandma. Doll married Bob Smith and their fifth child was a girl they named Gladys Love. Gladys was my Mama."

Rabbi Fried sat stunned. "Well, Elvis, if all that's true, you are Jewish. One hundred percent! That's amazing."

He got up and went into the other room. Elvis heard some murmuring between the Rabbi and his wife. They came into the kitchen together. She sat at the table and considered Elvis' appearance sadly. She took his hands in her own.

"Elvis, is it true? You're one of us?" She held a finger under his chin and perused him with her lips pursed, gently turning his head from side to side. She dipped her head decisively and snapped a glance at her husband. "Of course, it's true! David, look at him carefully."

The Rabbi shrugged. He was not so sure.

She observed their guest again.

"Elvis, I grew up in Skalat. I knew Anna Steuben. She is a distant cousin and a childhood friend, and I am so glad to learn she is still alive. You must tell me where she works so I can get in touch with her. She took a deep breath. I was also familiar with your relative Mendel Tackett."

She tilted her head "It's such a sad story. Skalat! Elvis, I can tell you the story of Skalat. Maybe it will help you understand why it was so important for Anna to speak with you. Tell me, do you want to know? Because I can tell you. But only if you wish to hear, it dredges up many hard memories."

Elvis opened his mouth but closed it without speaking. He watched Mrs. Fried's familiar face, and there was an intensity he had never seen in her eyes before. He remembered her as she was when he grew up. Always smiling, always welcoming, she would sit him down in the kitchen, feed him and schmooze. She was so vibrant then. At that moment, she seemed just old and tired from life.

Sitting in the small world of the couple's apartment, he had no background to comprehend what she had gone through in Europe or what her life had been like before Memphis.

His gaze bounced around crowded room and settled back on her face. He raised both shoulders and said, "If it's important to you."

She shook off his tepid response. "Elvis, it is not a pretty story. Anna didn't tell you all of what went on, and she told you her story alone. Clearly, it has affected you badly. What I will tell you will shock you even more. Are you sure you are ready to hear this?"

Elvis huffed out a deep breath and nodded firmly. She got up and poured a glass of water for herself and sat back down.

"It was 1939. Of the approximately 8,000 inhabitants in my

town of Skalat, some sixty percent were Jews. Most of us lived in the center of town. We consisted of some craftsmen, businessmen, small traders, and a few professionals. Some of us Jews were minor local officials. There were also a few Yeshiva students learning the Torah. We, of course, also had some full-time beggars and the ordinary unemployed, reluctant to work. We also had a high rate of unemployed Jews, whose circumstances meant that they simply were unable to find a decent job to support themselves and their families." She shrugged.

"In all respects, Skalat was no different than any other typical shtetl. Jews started settling there as early as the 1500s or even earlier, making it one of the oldest Jewish shtetls in the part of Europe known as Galicia. Jewish life thrived in Skalat. Jewish organizations took an active part in the town's social, cultural, religious, and political activities. On the surface, Skalat was an Orthodox (for the most part a Chassidic) town; the younger generation often strayed from those values and often pursued a secular education in addition to their religious instructions. All of the politics of the day, from the extreme left to the extreme right, exerted their influence on the young Jewish people in the town. Modern clothing, modern music, and modern mores and values were infiltrating the minds and the lifestyle of the young people. Otherwise, our shtetl life was not that different from other Eastern European towns and villages. The people of Skalat occupied themselves in the constant daily struggle for existence and human dignity.

"In 1941, the Germans occupied my town. It came with tragic, terrible consequences. When the Soviet Russians returned ultimately in 1944, the town was without a Jewish population.

"Germany attacked the Soviet Union on June 22, 1941. The war had been going on for two years with the Russians and the Nazis carving up Poland. Skalat had been under the control of Poland for a long time. Now as a result of the war and the dividing up of Poland, Soviet Russia took power in Skalat.

"The Soviets' presence introduced a certain calm and order

throughout their twenty-two-month rule of Galicia. Life in Skalat was fairly ordinary and normal. Day-to-day activities went on much as they had always. Life did not significantly change for the townspeople. The Poles, who formerly controlled the land, now were defeated and divided. The Ukrainians, who had for centuries dreamed of again ruling this land, saw their dreams dashed once more. Their response to the Soviet rule was virulent hatred. But outwardly, they appeared to accept the Soviet regime.

"Soviet rule in Skalat put the Jewish population in a very precarious position. At first, they adapted to the new regime, but they feared how their Gentile neighbors would view this adjustment. For several generations, quiet but powerful Anti-Semitism had been engrained into the souls of their non-Jewish neighbors." Mrs. Fried's expression darkened. "With the Soviets in power, it would seem that this Anti- Semitism would break out into the open, having found a fertile soil to flourish in as the Soviets were no friends of the Jews either. With the coming of the Soviets, the fires of the Jew-haters had the fuel to erupt into the open, in quiet ways. The term "Commie Yids" was an old slogan in Polish politics. Now the Jews were perceived as being chummy with their old buddies, the Bolsheviks. The Ukrainian nationalists used this for their Anti-Semitic rationalizations.

"Under the Soviets, everyone could find work. Despite that, daily life was both good and bad. In a strange way, the Soviets in charge of Galicia trusted their Jewish population over the local Ukrainians. The Jews had survived over so many centuries of political upheavals that it was quite understandable they were able to conform more readily to the new regime than their gentile neighbors. The Jews- therefore the workers, artisans, and the working intelligentsia were able to assume leading roles in the economic and social life of the town. Many held important posts in the cooperatives as well as in communal and public institutions. For the Jews, it appeared that no other group could have adjusted better to the Soviet occupation than they did.

"This was a radical change in the social and economic structure that had previously left a great deal of the Jews without a way to earn a living. Among them were businessmen, small traders, and craftsmen. There were new opportunities to work for the formerly chronically unemployed. In our typical provincial town, Skalat, the number of prosperous Jews was tiny.

"Jews were desperate to obtain formal positions, because one of the clear distinctions of the new order was: *One who does not work does not eat.* Additionally, the middle class along with the former house owners and traders, made sure to find employment in order to obtain a work-card. This protected a person from being deemed 'non- productive,' and thereby exposing themselves to various troubles. That might include exile to Siberia, which no one obviously wanted. Whether it was out of necessity or simply as a ruse, the previously non-working Jewish population exerted the effort to work and be productive. The changing social standing seemed to happen overnight. This trend undoubtably had some positive value in the social, egalitarian restructuring of the Skalat Jewish everyday existence.

"For the local Ukrainian populace and the Poles, who mostly lived as farmers on land of their own, they did not experience a noticeable disturbance in their lifestyles. As they already were 'productive,' they had no reason to find new employment or other sources of income. Peasants did not stop being peasants.

"They also had seen regime changes many times over their history. 'Our people left; our people will return' was a familiar, meaning-filled folk saying among them. The particular tragedy for them was of an ideological, nationalistic, and certainly a territorial quality. Peacefully living, waiting for better times, and hoping for improved conditions, they had lives that were essentially static. With a Soviet power in place, the Ukrainians and Poles were weak and powerless. This did not bode well for the Jews as powerlessness draws out hatreds bred over centuries. The result was a spreading of the Anti-Semitic poison. This sowed the soil for the eventual slaughter.

"And when it came, it would be quite powerful and almost obliterating. Despite their Gentile neighbors' own national tragedy, germs of envy which were mixed with ancient hatreds and traditional Anti-Semitism grew into such a powerful force that it confused the minds and consciousness of both the masses and their leaders.

"So, the local populace could hardly wait for the inevitable German invading forces to arrive. Among the Poles, the popular opinion was 'better the Germans than the Soviets.' The Ukrainians flatly loved Hitler and saw in him a savior, one who would help them create an independent Ukraine.

"From the first days of battling in Europe, Skalat was gripped by a rough, edgy, and raw mood. It was as if instinct told them to brace for the upheaval that was soon to occur. Radio stations kept broadcasting alarming reports: A German force under General Von Runstedt was successfully advancing through Galicia and Wolin. Soviet authorities, knowing that it was inevitable that they would have to retreat, tried maintaining the calm of the civilian population, even as they themselves prepared to evacuate the region. In the early days of July 1941, the Soviets began an orderly withdrawal from the town.

But they didn't go alone. Foreseeing disaster, they were accompanied by about 200 Jews. They were mostly workers, craftsmen and some who simply had common sense and saw the writing on the proverbial wall. My father was one of them but his friends talked him out of it. Where we should have gone with the Soviets, we didn't. We learned the hard way. That in itself was another type of trial for us, for we were in danger either way. Russia was not much better and was enduring a terrible beating by the Germans that summer."

She shook her head. "If the truth be told, there weren't many of the town's Jews who fully understood the danger that awaited them by staying. No matter how fatally foolish it may now appear, there were some Jews, mainly among the more affluent, who thought it might be easier living with the Germans than with the Russians. And again, where could they run to? Russia proper was being devastated by the war. That was how some Jews assessed their situation. The reality was that, as the war drew closer to them most thought, 'How can we leave our homes and go off into exile? And where to go?'

"Again, that questioned loomed heavily. So many Jews left their fate in the hands of God and hoped for the best in the future.

"On the third of July, the Soviet civil administration, police, and armed detachments left Skalat for good. With just a few soldiers remaining to carry out specific assignments, the town was left without a government. The town descended into chaos and disruption. The underworld of the town and various peasants from the neighborhood took advantage of the new opportunities for robbery and other acts of disruptions.

"It became obvious that the German war machine was approaching Skalat. People could see the seeds of agitation and turmoil beginning, even before German jackboots began their march into town. It started with a peasant named Hilko taunting some Jews, 'Wait. Just wait, you kikes. Hitler's coming and we'll slaughter you all like chickens!' A Soviet soldier, hearing of the incident, got outraged and tracked down the peasant. Catching him, he dragged him off into the fields, leaving him there, dead. The executed peasant was venerated a 'holy martyr' by a local priest. This action infuriated the already animated peasants and served as a pretense for the peasants to carry out acts of vengeance on a few Jewish families living nearby. Murdering them all in a horrific way, they blamed Hilko's death on the Jews.

"Now the peasants in town were all stirred up. They prepared their knives for the inevitable carnage when the Nazis took over the town. By midnight on Friday, July 4, they heard continuous sound of machine guns and exploding grenades. At two in the morning, the first German patrol roared in loudly on motorcycles. We were all startled awake and peeked out our windows, and then their loudspeakers boomed, "All of you, our Ukrainian brothers, awaken!"

"The Ukrainians were already wide awake and fully ready to help the Germans. The Jews were already fleeing for their lives in all directions. By Saturday, July 5, the regular German troops arrived and encamped. The Ukrainians were delighted. They got dressed in all of their holiday clothing, some fully decorated with ribbons in the blue and yellow of their Ukrainian national colors. Ukrainian flags and red swastika flags were draped in front of their houses. Bearing flowers and gifts, singing loudly, the Ukrainians came to greet their German liberators. They danced in the streets, kissing and hugging as if it were a party.

"Since it was the Sabbath morning, some Jews walked openly and unhesitatingly to services. They carried their prayer shawls, as though nothing had happened. There were others, very few, who went off to look at and admire the German military equipment. Some of the local Jews were convinced that the Germans, a cultured society, would not harm them. Some believed that, in fact, now they would be more secure. While before there had been danger from the enraged townspeople, many Jews now thought the Germans would impose law and order. From today's perspective, it seems incomprehensible. We were afraid, but we held out hope.

"And at first, they seemed right. The German military harmed nobody. In fact, they were friendly to the Jews, boasting of their swift heroic deeds against the Soviets. While some Jews remained frightened and alarmed by the German presence, this group of Jews who had interacted with the soldiers later argued with the others saying, 'Fools, what are you hiding for? Are they harming anyone?'

"Some of the affluent Jews, though not all, naively thought that if the worst were to occur, it would only affect the impoverished among them who couldn't buy their way out. They reasoned that the Germans themselves realized knew that the prosperous were also victims of the Soviets. Maybe the new rulers would return their land, their confiscated wealth, maybe even their nationalized houses. Such was the reasoning of the deluded. They would be disillusioned quickly, but for the moment such foolish optimism clouded their minds.

"At around ten in the morning, several battalions came to a

halt in the Shtetl. Other German troops continued their 'triumphal march' eastward. The commander of this SS brigade gave the order, 'Tzen minuten shlachten Juden!' *(Ten minutes for killing Jews)* so that his troops might 'have some fun.' Passing the order on to each other, the troops jumped from their automobiles, tanks, and other armored vehicles and ran to the center of town. With animal like ferocity, these troopers ran about firing their guns everywhere with random abandon assaulting any Jews they came upon in the streets. The first victim was Mendel Dienstock, whose beard they cut off along with part of his face. Miraculously, the bullets they fired at him missed. The German troopers were in such a hurry, they left their victim, who fainted, onto the ground.

"Peasant children ran after the troopers, pointing out, 'Jude! Jude! (Jew! Jew!).' The whole of Skalat was in turmoil, and panic gripped the Jews. The Germans ran after the fleeing Jews, shooting at them continuously. One man, Mordechai Wolf (the milkman) and his wife were chased down the riverbank and then driven into the water. The Germans fired at both of them until their bodies sank, leaving red stains on the surface.

Mrs. Fried looked nauseated but cleared her throat and continued. "Then some of the Germans, led by the Ukrainian peasant children, started running among the houses, shooting at each Jew the children pointed out. Other soldiers broke into homes on the pretense that they were searching for weapons and hidden Communists. They robbed, defaced, and destroyed the contents of these homes in the most outrageous way."

She sat silent for a long stretch, unable to continue. Then she shook it off. "At the end of the allotted ten minutes, Skalat had been turned upside down. Twenty Jews were killed and an equal number wounded. Some were only slightly wounded and others gravely injured. The Jews sought hiding places wherever they thought they might be safe. Their homes, left open and unguarded, were ransacked by Ukrainian peasants and the Polish town hoodlums. They rioted for hours afterwards. They stole whatever they could. They beat, without mercy, any Jew they found out and about.

"But this was merely the prologue to the butchery that would follow the next day. This event was organized and perpetrated completely under the direction of the newly appointed Ukrainian 'administrators.'

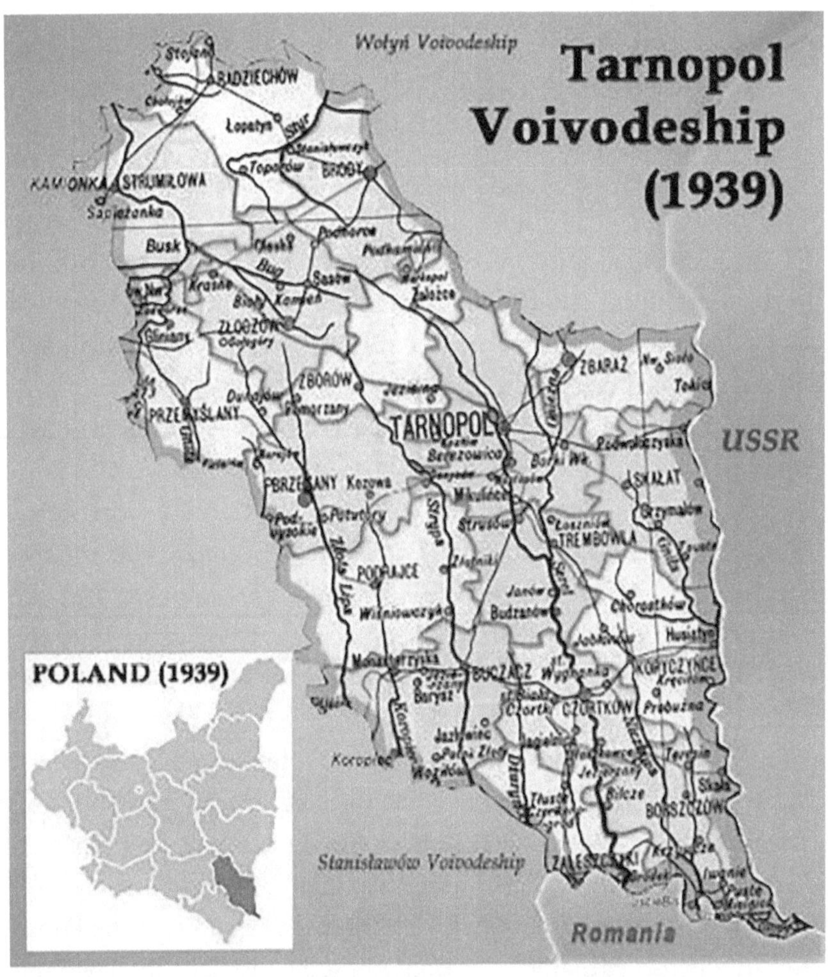
Wołyń Voivodeship
Tarnopol
Voivodeship
(1939)
Stojanów
RADZIECHÓW
Chołojów
Łopatyn
STOJ
Stanisławczyk
Toporów
BRODY
KAMIONKA STRUMIŁOWA
Sapieżanka
Busk
Olesk
Ponikwa
Podkamień
Bug
Sasów
Zalozce
Krasne
Biały Kamień
ZŁOCZÓW
Gliniany
Ostogóry
ZBARAŻ
Nowe Sioło
Todica
ZBORÓW
Jezierna
PRZEMYŚLANY
Dunajów
Pomorzany
TARNOPOL
USSR
SKAŁAT
Berezowica
Borki Wk.
Płotycza
Grzymałów
PBRZEŻANY
Kozowa
Mikulice
Podhajce
Strusów
Łosiniec
TREMBOWLA
Podh.
Potutory
Wysokie
Ustnki
Złota
PODHAJCE
Janów
Chorostków
Lipa
Wiśniowczyk
Budzanów
Jabłonów
Husiatyn
Monasterzyska
KOPYCZYNCE
BUCZACZ
Wygnanka
Krecowce
Baryż
Skała
Czortki
CZORTKÓW
Probużna
Jazłowiec
Koropiec
Połej Złoty
Teretyn
Koźłów
Worwolince
Tłuste
Bilcze
Skała
BORSZCZÓW
Stanisławów Voivodeship
ZALESZCZYKI
Iwanie
Puste
Romania
POLAND (1939)

CHAPTER TWENTY

lvis seemed to be overwhelmed by the unfolding story of the atrocities perpetuated against the Jews of Skalat. Mrs. Fried had more details to provide, but she stopped to ask, "Should I go on, or this more than you can handle right now?"

His mouth was open and he wasn't speaking, but he gestured for her to keep going.

"As strange as it might seem Elvis, the Ukrainians, the Poles, and the Jews had lived together in Skalat for centuries in relative peace. Over the generations, the Ukrainian part of town and the Jewish shtetl had relatively friendly contacts. After all, why would the Jews stir up conflict?" Mrs. Fried exchanged a weary look with her husband. "They had no territorial designs in the area. The Ukrainians had suffered almost as much as the Jews had under the Polish rulers. Oddly enough, this tended to unite the two groups in a common struggle for minority rights and the ability to preserve their national identities. Often, the leaders of the Ukrainian folk movements spoke out in sympathy with their Jewish brethren. In elections to the Polish Sejm (the Polish Parliamentary body) in some districts, the Jews and Ukrainians often ran jointly. In other districts, the Ukrainian press would at times urge its readers to vote for the Jewish slates.

"So, who would have predicted that these same Ukrainians, who had lived in peace with their Jewish neighbors for centuries, would turn so savagely against them? Well, these hideous deeds were in fact carried out, not by unenlightened individuals among the Ukrainians, nor by fascist terror groups. Rather, these acts from hell were the work of none other than the UNDO (Ukrainian Nationalist Democratic Organization), the main Ukrainian political organization in Galicia and its official representative for many years.

"The UNDO organized, controlled, and coordinated the first pogroms in most of the towns and villages in Galicia. They involved almost all of the Ukrainian community in these massive, bloodstained events. With few exceptions, the balance of the Ukrainian population of that time shared the full burden of guilt for destroying Galician Jewry. It is notable that a small group among the older generation found the savage behavior of their children to be disgusting and would not participate.

"It was mostly the Ukrainians, not the Germans, who murdered their age-old neighbors. Without a doubt, the Germans permitted it and let the savage behavior run wild." She slapped a hand to the tabletop, startling Elvis. "But the established facts, copious documents, and the multitudes of eyewitness testimony proved that the Ukrainians wielded the hands of death. If one were to create a chronological review of events in this single shtetl of Skalat, it stands as a testimony and reveals similar behaviors of the Ukrainians in other Galician towns. Wherever Jews were killed, it was the Ukrainians who actually carried out the mass murders. The same criminal hand was at work in all of these places throughout the Ukraine."

Her face was flushed, and Elvis noticed a tremor in her hands. She sniffled, needing to catch her breath or her thoughts. Her mind obviously was spinning over the painful memories. Rabbi Fried seeing her distress, got up and brewed her a cup of tea. He poured a smidgen of whisky into the teacup and stirred the contents for her. She sipped and made a face but relaxed slightly. She cleared her voice.

"Already on that Friday evening although some say it was after the Sabbath evening, the Ukrainians in Skalat had held a secret meeting to consider their new situation now that Hitler's troops were in the town. All the elite of the local Ukrainian townsfolk attended.

In fact, every segment of the Ukrainian population was represented, from the priest down to the peasant.

"They opened the meeting with the singing of the Ukrainian national anthem, 'Shehe Ne Vmerla Ukraina' (*The Ukraine is alive*). The conversation flipped to matters of state. They discussed organizing a Ukrainian militia as well as choosing persons for public positions and institutions. They became absorbed in speculating about the nature of their work, and how they looked forward to the fulfillment of their aspirations in the future. They wanted a return to a Ukrainian state. They bandied opinions about how they should treat the Polish population in the town. After all, there was real enmity between them and the Poles. But the most important question was what to do with the Jews?

"One person after another took the floor, quoting Alfred Zweigberg as well as whole pages from Hitler's Mein Kampf. They vowed to give the Germans their total support; they were the true liberators.

"People said things like, 'We must gain the Germans' confidence,' 'Hitler is right. The Jews are a menace to the world,' and 'They are like a bone in our throats as well, so let there be an end to them!'

"A majority of the assembly voted for a pogrom against the town Jewry. Understanding, that they were obligated to request the Germans permission to act on this proposal, they sent a three-man delegation to the military command in order to obtain permission. Their goal was a slaughter of the Jews for a twenty-four they could annihilate the Jewish presence in Skalat in that one-day period.

"Their ringleader was a big man about town: Canon Onuferko, the Greek Catholic priest. He had a long and rich history of many business dealings with the town's Jews, having been involved in countless matters with them. He boasted of having been a Judeophile all his life and he spoke Yiddish fluently.

"Local Jews, however, would say of him, 'A hen that crows and a priest who speaks Yiddish should both be sent to the chopping block.'

This folk expression was quite on point. In addition to the priest and his wife, others at the meeting were Judge Politila, a Maruszszuk (a blacksmith); a Bilyk; and fellow notables Jaromiszyn, Chruszcz, and Wilczynski. All of these were unofficial leaders of the Ukrainian community and were prominent people in Skalat and nearby towns.

"The next day, the Ukrainian delegation led by Canon Onuferko, went before the German general staff. They presented a signed petition requesting permission to carry out an anti-Jewish pogrom. The commander, an aged general, considered their demand and weighed it against other considerations in his head. He approved the slaughter but felt it should be done in a planned and orderly way. His first thought was to use the Jews for physical labor. This would be useful to his military machine. But after further thought, he allowed the pogrom. He did not agree to a full day of killing. He limited it to only eight hours and specified that all of the women and children should be spared. The delegation thanked him, bowed deeply, and went home satisfied.

"The Ukrainians promptly called a general meeting of all their community activists. This included their newly organized militia. They decided to begin the necessary preparations to execute the pogrom.

"The General sent a report to Berlin, enclosing documents that showed a 'justified' local hatred of the Jews. That petition was released sometime later to the press by the German ministry of propaganda, along with hundreds of similar petitions from Ukrainians in various other cities and villages. This was to show the world that it was not the Germans who were slaughtering Jews; rather local populations were demanding the right to carry out their own gruesome bloodbaths.

"On Sunday, July 6, 1941, at about eleven o'clock in the morning, the pogrom in Skalat began. Ukrainian organized gangs set about moving through the town. The new militia armed with rifles, as well as civilians carrying sticks, went house to house, calling Jewish men and youths out to work. While German soldiers stood and watched the scene, these gangs of militia and townspeople cursed, shouted at, slapped, and pushed these men into the streets. The wailing of women and the cries of children could be heard from Jewish homes.

"These Jews, having been drawn out, were forced to perform sadistic and fruitless tasks. The first group was ordered to uproot small trees with their bare hands. Since they could not, they were beaten to death. Another group was ordered to crawl on all fours and gather stones in their mouths. Then they were to crawl further and place the stones into pots. Others were forced to clean outhouses with their bare hands. A third group was forced to sweep streets with their hats and to perform other senseless tasks.

"All this time, they were tortured by the gangs and then put to death. Some of the Jews were assigned to the German military units, where they worked while being bashed with rifle butts. One Jew, Chaim Kaczer, who had been badly beaten, was thrown to the ground and run over by a truck, which crushed his bones. He writhed in pain, and a soldier finally shot him through the heart.

"At the water pump in the marketplace, some Ukrainians forced the spout of the water pipe into a Jew's mouth and kept pumping the water until he drowned. Another Jew, Levy Cohen, an imposing man, tall and handsome with a silver-grey beard had his legs broken by assassins wielding iron rods, and they placed his head under the pump for a 'cold shower' as they laughed. Levy pointed to his heart, as he could no longer speak, pleading wordlessly to be shot to end his suffering. Wild, crazed bystanders chortled and called for his killers to ease up, letting him live a little longer to prolong his suffering. The mob ripped his hairs, one by one, from his beard. Near dead, he was again placed under the waterspout. They pried his mouth open and pumped water into him until he drowned."

Mrs. Fried had her eyes squeezed shut by then, but she continued the litany of terror. "Rabbi Judah Wolowicz was tied behind a horse. Germans, Ukrainians, and other peasants, standing on the sidewalks whipped the horse into a gallop. The Rabbi at first tried to run but soon fell down and was dragged as far as the towers. Bloodied and tortured, he died there. At the tower, his body was tossed onto a growing pile of corpses. Similar was the fate of a Jonah Steuben (son-in-law of a tinsmith from Grzymalow), who was tied behind a car and was dragged through the streets until his body was unrecognizable.

Mrs. Fried clenched her hands together to strengthen her resolve and to keep going. "Dr. Leonard Simon was dragged to the public outhouse near the bathhouse where he was ordered into the cesspool and shot. Many Jews shot by Ukrainians had their clothing, shoes and other personal effects ripped from their bodies. While this was going on, village peasants roamed the streets of the Jewish sections, ransacking and robbing houses.

"In the center of town stood the four old towers that were part of the old Skalat Palace. It was there that the worst of the bloodbaths occurred. The Ukrainian police led Jews in groups of thirty or forty to the tops of the towers and ordered them to jump. While the victims were flailing through the air the police shot at them with automatic weapons. The men died in pain crying the Shema Yisroel as they fell. While this was going on, the Germans photographed the ruthless murders and later sent the captioned photos to Berlin to prove it had been the Ukrainians killing the Jews." She sneered, an ugly expression unfamiliar on her kind face. "They wouldn't have wanted it said that Germans had killed anyone. All told, at the towers more than 300 people were brutally murdered, including some thirty children and youths." She paused to let that number sink in.

"At the cemetery, new horrors. Groups of Jews were forced to bring the dead to the cemetery and bury them. Then they were shot to death themselves. I heard of Isaac Lerner, son of Zvi-Nuty Lerner, a butcher, who, among tending to other corpses had to bury his own father. While reciting the Kaddish for his father, he was cut down by a bullet, falling on top of the fresh grave. Approximately 150 people were destroyed at the cemetery alone. By three in the afternoon, the total death toll in the town had reached 500. We can only speculate about how high the victims count was that day. But right in the middle of all the killing, Soviet bombers attacked Skalat from the air." She laughed bitterly. "This caused the killers to scatter across the fields. Had it not been for the attack, the synagogue would have been attacked by the mob. The bombing caused a break in the murdering.

"For several hours, it was quiet, but then the mob returned to finish what it had begun. Although the permitted eight hours was over, the killing went on for two more days, but on a smaller scale. Additional scores of Jews fell as the Ukrainians let blood. Wednesday morning, Ukrainian militiamen dragged out the three Klastorin brothers and Loma Goldman and shot all four, claiming they were communists.

"All of the remaining slaughtered Jews were still lying around the towers where they had fallen. The Ukrainians dragged the surviving Jews out of their hiding places and ordered them to haul the gory bodies to the cemetery. Using horse carts, the Jews carried the corpses, wrapped in blood-stained sheets and prayer shawls. Blood dripped the entire length of the route to the cemetery.

"Deep sorrow permeated the town. The remaining Jews tried to observe Shiva. The surviving Rabbi proclaimed a community day of fasting and ordered the wearing of sackcloth and ashes as a sign of mourning for the martyred dead. Surviving Jews sent a delegation to the German commander. He promised to restore the calm. Military authorities issued an order for the population to return all stolen items. Of course, nothing was returned, nor could the 500 lives lost in the pogrom be returned.

"Meanwhile, similar tragic reports began to trickle in from the surrounding areas. The Ukrainians had conducted a pogrom in the neighboring shtetl of Grzymalow. That is where my husband was from. Luckily, he had left the town, having been conscripted by the Red Army. In his town, some 500 men, women and children had been driven into the river and all were machine-gunned to death. For days, the river ran red with Jewish blood. In the village of Chmielisko, the Ukrainian peasants buried alive some thirty of their long-time neighbors. In the village of Turowka, the local Jewish doctor had his legs broken and was then impaled on the tines of pitchforks. In

Tluste, a smaller town near Skalat, the Ukrainians slaughtered all of the Jews.

"The Rape of Skalat was over. But the great tragedy of my town had just begun. Many of us hid in the forests, and many fled towards Russia. Over the next year or so, the Germans rounded us up and sent us to work camps and finally to concentration camps. When the Soviets returned in 1944, there was hardly a Jew left in town."

She stopped speaking and looked at Elvis. Tears streamed down his cheeks, matching her own. He reached for a napkin to wipe his face. She looked at him. "That is why Anna Steuben wanted to speak to you. Her father was the Jonah Steuben who was dragged behind a car to his death. He had already gotten the rest of his family to safety. He had befriended a Polish farmer, and this farmer hid his family. On the day, the pogrom started, Jonah went back into town to collect food and clothing. The Ukrainians caught him in the street."

The Towers of the Old Skalat Palace

The Old Ruined Cemetery of Skalat

CHAPTER TWENTY-ONE

"After the pogrom ended, the Skalat shtetl was in complete shock." Mrs. Fried said. She looked at her guest and registered the devastation on his face. It was reflected in her own heart, she thought. "Jews could not recover after the unspeakable horrors. The Germans let the Ukrainians be the masters of the town. Their brutal behavior terrified the Jewish population daily. Hundreds of Jews were dragged off each day to perform hard labor and throughout this process they were beaten mercilessly and degraded.

"The Ukrainians naively believed that this was their time. They had somehow won, and the 'liberation' they sought had come to pass. Under the protective wings of the German forces, young and old rushed to join the militia and other administrative offices of what they perceived to be the beginnings of the future free Ukraine. Once established in their new positions, each strained to outdo the others in patriotism. They expressed this in an active and thorough hatred of the town's Jews and through public beating and kicking of them, their neighbors and former friends. In this way they hoped to gain favorable status in the eyes of their German 'liberators.'

"Nikolaj Bilyk was chosen from among the local Ukrainian activists to rule over the Jews. Two weeks after the pogrom, he authorized a former cattle dealer, Leibisz Degen (with whom he had a business relationship) to form a provisional committee. This temporary body consisted of twelve members. Bilyk would demand that Degen provide a designated number of Jews for forced labor.

"The required number of workers would assemble early each morning at the marketplace to await their assignments. Jewish men and women were chosen to sweep streets, clean toilets, and wash floors in various government offices. Some were assigned to local farms in the surrounding villages. Additionally, a store was established in the marketplace for Jews to obtain goods." She sighed.

"Four weeks after the pogrom, an order arrived from the German Security Service (SD) in Tarnopol to establish a Judenrat (Jewish council) to serve as the liaison between the German authorities and the Jews. The Ukrainians asked Jacob Weiderman to undertake the task of establishing the Judenrat in Skalat. He refused. No one among the professional intelligentsia would accept the 'honor.' After a number of days of indecision, Mendel Tackett, the local lawyer, was placed in charge of the Judenrat.

"So, you see, Elvis, I knew Mendel Tackett. Or at least who he was."

Elvis got animated at the mention of Tackett. "Really? What was he like?"

"I was a young girl at the time. The adults knew him better. He had a neutral reputation at that time. He had survived the pogrom by escaping into the forest at the night when the Germans first entered town. Where he went and how he survived, nobody knew. He showed up a few days after the pogrom was over. He avoided most of the trouble with the Germans and the Ukrainians that the rest of the Jews had encountered. Otherwise, he fell into line with what was happening to all the town Jews.

"As the head of the Judenrat, he was extended a certain amount of protection from the Germans. But I tell you, your cousin became a terrible man. I am sorry to say that to you, but it is the truth."

Elvis seemed shocked but said nothing. He was having trouble processing it. Mrs. Fried left the room and returned shortly with a group photograph of young girls. When the picture was taken, they were all dressed for school and were sitting outside. It was a bright sunny day. It looked like a picture, taken anywhere, of young people with their whole lives ahead of them. She showed it to Elvis while standing behind his chair.

She pointed at one of the girls, "That was me. We were so hopeful at the time." Then she pointed to another girl who was standing behind her and to the left. "That's Anna Steuben."

Elvis lifted the picture up closer to his eyes. He looked closely at Anna. "That's amazing! I recognize her. She still has those eyes and that pointy chin. My gosh, how old is this picture?"

"This picture was from the spring of 1941. It was taken a month or so before the Germans marched into town and the troubles began. Anna was a sweet, shy girl. We were friends. She was in the same group of girls that shared classes together in school. I slept over by her once. She came by occasionally when she was near my house to say hello. We were not what you would call close, but we were friends. I always wondered what had happened to her. I wondered about a lot of the girls. Some I knew never made it past the war. But I never knew about her. I just assumed…" She became quiet for a moment and looked towards the ceiling.

"I always thought that I was the only one of us to survive. It is nice to learn that she lived through this too. I hope she is well."

Elvis answered her. "She was working as a waitress, so I assume she was healthy enough to do that. It is hard work. But I don't know more than that. She was thin, and she looked so tired. But it might have been because of what she had to say. Tremendous burden to bear. I did not understand at the time and I'm not sure I even understand it now. It is so unbelievable to listen to. It blows my mind."

They sat quietly. Elvis looked at the picture again and then handed it back to her. He breathed in deeply and said, "Tell me whatever else you know about Mendel Tackett. How come he became such a terrible man?"

She sighed. "Are you so sure you want to dig up all this?"

Elvis shrugged.

"There is much to tell. What a chazer (pig)! Here is what happened in Skalat after he took over the Judenrat."

He looked over at her as she sat back down at the table.

"Go ahead."

CHAPTER TWENTY-TWO

"At first, it seemed to some that it might be possible to live with relative normalcy," Mrs. Fried said. "For the most part, the Jews were allowed to tend to their own affairs. Some Jews dared to joke that, 'We have a small Jewish republic, here under the sheltering wing of the Germans.' It was impossible to imagine then that soon the Judenrat would devolve into a tool of the German regime.

"The Judenrat's main function in its early days consisted of providing between 200 to 300 workers daily to the German and Ukrainian authorities. They also had to feed the Jewish population via a bakery that was made available to them. They organized the activities of all of the newly established administrative functions to keep the 'peace' with the Germans and Ukrainians." Her upper lip curled with disdain. "They were also required to provide 'gifts' for the Germans, who extorted money and property from the Jews daily. They found it necessary to set up a storehouse for items to be surrendered to the Germans on demand. This storehouse quickly filled up with clothing, furniture and tableware collected by members of the Judenrat, These 'collections' often resulted in a fight from the Jewish population. Soon a sense of resignation fell over the population.

"Orders came from Tarnopol on Saturday, July 19, that the Jewish population of Skalat had to pay a ransom of 600,000 rubles must be paid by Thursday, the 24th. Tragic consequences would result if they failed to meet this demand. All Jewish affairs in Tarnopol were then under the control of a German named Faulfinger. The Judenrat was summoned to the regional command office where they received this harsh order in Faulfinger's name: the Judenrat was to provide, by the same deadline, lodgings for twelve Germans. These lodgings were to be equipped with pots and pans, furniture, linens, and whatever else the German's might need or want.

"Faced with these demands, the Judenrat created a large committee to comply with the order. First of all, they needed to raise a large sum of money. That would not be easy, but Jewish tradition requires the 'rescuing of souls.' Often- times in Jewish history that was enough to overcome the impossibility of the situation. The committee chose to tax those who were rich among them, and with the help of the ordinary Jewish citizenry, they hoped to succeed. Working feverishly day and night and in consideration of the danger the community faced, the goal was accomplished. Tackett, as the chairman of the *Judenrat*, worked tirelessly to organize and bring the effort to success. When the appointed day arrived, the required sum, as well as a surplus amount, had been raised.

"The delegation took the funds to Tarnopol, but the surplus amount was kept, serving as a reserve in the Judenrat treasury. The lodgings for the twelve Germans, fully equipped as per the order, were provided."

Elvis looked at Mrs. Fried. "He does not seem so bad from what you've told me." She grimaced and continued.

"During the same period, on July 16, the Germans ordered the Jews to wear white armbands marked with the Star of David on their right arms. The members of the Judenrat were to print the word 'JUDENRAT' in large letters on their own armbands. The Jewish *Ordinungsdienst* (Jewish police) were ordered to wear yellow armbands marked as such.

"Jewish houses were required to show Star of David signs. The Judenrat was required to pay the Germans a high fee to obtain them for each house. After that was in place, life in the shtetl fell into a routine. With the exception of minor changes, life continued this way until the beginning of autumn."

Mrs. Fried took a long, deep breath. Another horrible part of the story was coming.

"Just before the start of the High Holy Days, the *Judenrat* announced that all the town's Jews were to report to the marketplace at nine o'clock the next morning. No one seemed to know why they were ordered to gather. Tackett came forward. He explained to all of us there that we had no reason to worry; it was simply that a certain number of them would be used for labor. The German Kommandant of the Skalat *Schupo* (Security Forces), a man named Schneider, designated 200 young people to be sent off to Maksymowka to perform heavy labor on the rail line. The conditions there were brutal. Most of these young people returned by the end of the month when they were ransomed from the Germans for a large sum of money.

"The Germans then established a camp for Russian prisoners of war in the nearby village of Borki- Wielkie until they were ragged. These inmates were worked extremely hard. Their substance was a single daily ration of watery soup. Their treatment from the Germans was subhuman. The Russian POWs in the camp were broken in spirit and exhausted, and an increasing number of these men died daily. The Jews, feeling pity would help them as much as possible. In secret, they would toss them pieces of bread, other foods and cigarettes. When the Germans discovered these actions, they punished those Jews with beatings and occasionally by shooting. Over time, the camp systematically starved these prisoners, unfortunately, were systematically starved to death. When this shrank the workforce too much, the Germans filled their ranks with transports of Jews from Lwow and Stanislawow. The Skalat Jewish labor office was also forced to supply Borki-Wielkie with 200 Jewish workers each day. These workers were returned home by train in the evening.

"On Christmas Eve 1941, the Germans murdered all of the remaining Russian prisoners. That is when they established the forced labor camp exclusively for us Jews. Starting that day, the 200 Jews from Skalat no longer returned to their homes. They were simply prisoners of the new Borki Camp.

"Seeing the situation in Borki-Wielkie, the *Judenrat* in Skalat organized a Women's Committee. Their task was to bring aid to the Jews in the work camp. Every other day, the women would travel there to bring food, mainly bread. During the winter of 1942, it was extremely cold. The Women's Committee tried to supply warm clothes, gloves and even straw to stuff into shoes as insulation against frostbite.

"By early 1942, a camp in Kamionka was established. This camp was filled with Jews from Czortkow, Kopyczince, Trembowle, Mikulince, Chorostkow, and Grzymalow. New camps were formed in Stupka and Romanowka. Food packages were being sent to the Jewish inmates there through the connections of the Skalat *Judenrat*. So as the camps around Skalat consumed so many lives, it became the duty of each city in the Tarnopol area to supply a monthly quota of men, primarily youths, to replace the ranks of dying workers.

"There were people in town, who talked to the Germans. The various Judenrat from towns and villages around the Tarnopol district connected through these peoples, to conduct transactions such as ransoming of people. Often, this meant trading poorer inmates for wealthier ones. The Germans found a way to financially gain from all that was happening.

"Over time, the Skalat *Judenrat* became the main point in the trade of human lives, and thus they began to sink deeper into a vicious swamp of lies and deceit. While the leadership was trying to be of help to the population, it faced life-or-death choices and soon became the arbiter over whose life was spared and those who would face death. In an effort to preserve local lives, the Judenrat organized a home for the elderly and a soup kitchen for workers. Whenever possible, children received extra food rations, even if it was only extra milk and cereal.

Officially, the ration per person was supposed to be one hundred grams of bread, a few hundred grams of grain, and a couple of kilos of potatoes." She shook her head. "Believe me, these were starvation rations. If you had money, you could purchase extra food on the black market. In that way, some families were even able to manage a small reserve. But the poor suffered. Deprivation, hunger, and starvation became the normal way of life for those without money."

She glanced around her kitchen, recalling the groceries the couple had stored in their cabinets, fridge, and pantry, as well as the tidy balance they had in their savings account. She knew how blessed they were in the present.

Shaking her head, Mrs. Fried explained, "The main food sources were bartered with the village peasants, who took advantage of the situation when they traded with the Jews for clothing and other goods. The Judenrat social aid group helped out, when possible, but their financial resources were minimal at best. The population endured collections of various goods and funds, but you cannot draw blood from a stone. They had limited success in accomplishing this goal.

"Things seemed as bleak as possible, but then the Tarnopol SD issued an order in January of 1942 for the Jews to surrender all fur coats they might own. They had three days to comply under pain of death. For fur coats!" She held her hands wide in disbelief, then let them rest back in her lap. "But by the deadline, the warehouses were filled. The higher German functionaries chose the best coats for themselves. In a matter of a few days, two wagons were loaded with furs for the 'Winterhilfswerk.' This was a campaign to provide warm clothing for German troops inside Russia over the winter of 1941- 1942. Specifically, they were designated for the German troops fighting deep inside Russia. Some of the Jews burned their furs, rather than surrender them to the Germans. Many turned in the fur collars of their winter clothes. Thus, these Jews' outer garments were left with collars of raw buckram. They looked ridiculous. As crazy as it might seem, the Judenrat instituted an ordinance that the collars be covered with dark cloth because of their concern with the appearance of the people in these coats.

"February and March of 1942 were quiet in Skalat. Then in April, the Jews were ordered to evacuate their homes on the main streets of the town. Their homes were assigned to selected Ukrainian families. Over the next eight days, scores of Jewish homes were emptied and transferred to these Ukrainian peasants. The expelled Jews moved in with people in the back streets of Skalat.

"The first 'action' occurred in Tarnopol in May. This consisted of a quota of the aged and sick rounded-up for extermination in Belzec. These victims were predominately people from the hospital, the old- age home, and some of the children from the orphanage. This dreadful news from Tarnopol brought panic to our shtetl. It was clear to everyone that disaster was close at hand."

CHAPTER TWENTY-THREE

"We were getting near the planting time," Mrs. Fried said. "All of the villages and rural estates nearby were short of farmhands to help with the crops. The Judenrat's labor office was assigned a daily quota to provide five to six hundred Jewish workers to these farms. They left town to their workplaces guarded by the Jewish Ordinungsdienst. When the Jews began to receive authorized work-passes with German and Ukrainian signatures, those bearing the documents hoped they were in some way protected against eventual dangers.

"The passes were arranged through the Judenrat and those working papers were like gold. They also became available to those who did not work if they could pay the high prices. The feverish rush to get these passes gripped the entire Jewish population in Skalat. We assumed that possessing a pass assured our very existence. But everyone was running around like chickens with their heads cut off. The passes were good for only about two weeks. After that they were worthless. Anyone could and would be shipped off to the work camp at Borki-Wielkie at any time.

"In July of 1942, the Judenrat was told to supply thirty girls a day to the tobacco plantations at Jagielnice. I was terrified they might pick me, but I was too young." Mrs. Fried's eyes looked haunted as she recalled. "These young women worked under atrocious conditions. It took a while, but eventually, most of their parents were able to ransom them home. This was a miracle in itself as within a few days 400 other girls were brutally shot to death there.

"So life went on in Skalat for these so-called 'calm' days from July of 1941 to August of 1942. Contrasting with what came shortly thereafter, that period could almost be called the 'Golden Age,' as if that were possible under the German regime in Skalat."

Elvis asked, "How did Mendel Tackett fit into all of this? It would seem that he was trying to work in terrible conditions and faced difficult choices. You can hardly blame him in having to decide like that. They could have just as easily killed him."

Rabbi Fried interrupted to answer, "Son, it is true what you are saying. I had escaped from the Red Army and returned home. I lived through the bloodbaths in the Tarnopol district. Having come home, I saw with my own eyes that, as sometimes happens, the people who are straining to control the situation, simply break. Then they become like their captors, and sometimes they become much worse. They take on the airs of their captors. What originates as a survival technique now becomes a terrible habit for them. They come to love their petty powers and believe that their captors will not betray them in the end. They morph into horrible murdering people themselves, willing to sell souls to protect themselves. Cowards really! The Germans cultivated those people. Many of the capos in the concentration camps were Jews themselves and often were much worse than the German soldiers."

Mrs. Fried paused. "I have told you a lot of terrible things, my dear Elvis, but there is much more to tell. Do you want to hear the rest?" She looked him in the eyes. He seemed weary and troubled. She worried that this was too much for him. Eventually, she said, "I think you know you should hear the whole thing. I promise you that it will give you some of the answers you seek. But it will bring you no peace. That I can assure you of. It will bring you only pain and you will not like it. Should I go on?"

Elvis got up and paced around the table, holding his forehead. The Frieds shared a curious look. The Rabbi motioned to his wife that she should leave, and just as she rose from her chair, Elvis took his seat again.

"By G-d, he was my relative. I should at least know the story." He laid his head on the table to get his composure. He looked up at her. "Please go on!"

CHAPTER TWENTY-FOUR

"It had been a year since the first pogrom of July 6, 1941, but the wounds had not healed," Mrs. Fried said. "During the year, under profoundly difficult circumstances, our lives were controlled by the Judenrat. Tisha B'Av came, the saddest day on the Jewish calendar, when both the temples in Jerusalem were destroyed. It is a very difficult day even in the best of times. In our circumstances, it was almost unbearable. Afterward, the Judenrat leadership seemed to be particularly dejected. They announced to us, 'Fellow Jews, things are bad. There is an evil hanging over us and may G-d be merciful.' This sadness spread like wildfire throughout the Shtetl. For many, there were sleepless nights. People were depressed and despondent with the lack of control over their future security. Every day, a new fear permeated the community. What was about to happen? When?

"The Judenrat held daily meetings, racking their brains, looking for a way out of this crisis, recognizing that while the Germans were in charge, nothing would change.

"For lack of other real possibilities, they decided to raise a large fund of money. Its purpose was to bribe the Germans in hope of averting the obvious imminent jeopardy. The Jews contributed whatever belongings they still had.

"Within two days, the leaders had filled two valises with cash, gold and silver jewelry and implements, and any other valuables they could think of. The committee chose a delegation, led by Tackett, to rush to Tarnopol and meet with the Gestapo. How much of the treasure was actually relinquished to the Gestapo is a mystery, but the delegation returned seemingly encouraged and satisfied, although the encounter was somewhat traumatic for the delegation. Tackett was missing some teeth, and the other delegates were badly bruised by the SS.

"The delegates believed, nevertheless, that they had accomplished something for the common good. They told their fellow citizens, 'It was worth it. We have saved the town.' They believed in some magical way that having met with the Germans in Tarnopol, they had accomplished a great feat. They truly believed that going forward, no further evil would befall Skalat. In their imaginations, they believed that the gift to the SS was so successful that this delegation had saved the day."

Mrs. Fried shook her head. "These tales of wonders and miracles helped to calm the nervous Shtetl, which was so desperate to believe all this was true. But wishful thinking, is just that. These leaders, these 'protectors of the community' soon came to doubt the success of their mission. They held daily secret meetings. No one understood why they were always meeting, but eventually the whole story came out. In truth, to the dismay of the Judenrat, the Germans intended to carry out an 'action' against the sickly and the old. The bribe had been worthless.

"The Judenrat delegation to Tarnopol tried to deal with the matter themselves, telling the Germans, 'You need not come to Skalat.' They pleaded with the SS. 'We will carry out the "action" ourselves. Just set the quota for us.' The chief of the Tarnopol Gestapo, an Obersturmbannfuhrer Muller, let the Judenrat pick the five hundred souls to be delivered on August 31, 1942.

"So, on August 30, 1942, the residents of Skalat strolled about the town with no thought of any ill winds. At five in the afternoon, the Judenrat set out in pairs, carrying prepared lists of names and accompanied by the Jewish policemen. They entered scattered houses and dragged-out aged grandfathers and grandmothers, elderly parents, orphans, and bedridden children considered to be too sickly to ever recover. They also captured the so-called 'useless' Jews, the relief cases. All of the people who had been selected were led to the synagogue which was used as the collection point. These khapers (catchers) deceived their victims, saying there was nothing to fear, they were simply meeting at the synagogue. They told them it was a matter of state. Those who resisted were asked, 'Would you rather have the Germans drag you there?'

"It was useless to cry or protest. One had to go! Those who refused to go peacefully were taken forcibly by the militia. Unable to walk? You were carried. Heart-rending scenes took place when the sick were brought out of the hospital."

She stopped for a minute and got up to pluck a tissue from the box on the counter. She rubbed her eyes as the tears flowed down her face. Elvis reached over and touched her arm. She gathered herself together, and with a will of steel, continued.

"It is difficult for me to talk about all the awful scenes from that evening. In the end, the Judenrat was successful.

"With Mendel Tackett in the lead, the Judenrat members went around all night, looking for even more people, even searching in holes. They looked in cellars and attics, forcing the aged and sick to the synagogue. By then, everyone knew what was going on. Almost no victim succeeded in hiding. When a calamity engulfs a community, hiding is useless. The 'catchers' were determined to fill their quotas. If a designated person could not be found, another family member took their place. Every 'catcher' had to meet his quota. The Germans had successfully instilled in them discipline and order.

"Those not directly affected by this misfortune were saddened and confused. Hadn't they been assured that they would be safe? What was happening here? Unfortunately, people react strangely to tragedy. A segment of the Shtetl reasoned that if people had to be sent to their deaths, maybe it was better the aged were picked. After all, they had lived out their years. This rationale, though wrong and immoral, helped influence the supporters of the Judenrat. In their minds, these men were doing the best they could on behalf of the community in a terrible situation."

She stood up and bent over the sink, sobbing. Rabbi Fried stood up to comfort her, but she motioned him away. Elvis stood up as well, but she told him to sit. He did so without a word. She reached for a towel, wet it with cold water and wiped her eyes and face for a while before returning to the table. She sat down again.

"I always wondered how such a twisted idea arose from the Judenrat members and their supporters. I think that the tremendous pressure warped their minds. In some cases, they had smothered their thought processes to mimic the Germans. The overwhelming majority of us were too weak to resist and powerless to do anything about it. All we could all do was watch the bloody happenings with horror.

"By nine o'clock that evening, most of the victims were already in the synagogue. The building was surrounded with an enlarged guard of the Jewish police to prevent escapes. They were most concerned about overnight when new victims were brought in.

"After all of this, incredibly, the Judenrat members came together to review the day's 'accomplishments.' Liquor and cake were placed on a small table in the Judenrat headquarters, and they congratulated each other, believing they had rescued the town. They believed that 'if not by us, it would have been done by the Germans.' They rationalized that if the Germans had made the arrests, there would have been a bloodbath. I heard that one of the councilmembers, Meyer Leopold, was given a cash prize from the Judenrat for being the first to round up all the people on his list. This payment was authorized by Chairman Mendel Tackett himself.

"After they celebrated, they telephoned the Gestapo in Tarnopol reporting that the job had been completed. The Gestapo came the next day to handle the transport.

"All of this may seem hard to believe, but the surviving witnesses saw it themselves and reported it. No matter how painful the truth, it really happened that way. My mother, who was in the synagogue on that tragic day, took the place of her mother, my grandmother, whom she hoped to save. Miraculously, she was able to escape in the confusion of the next day.

"But she told me, and I will always remember her eyewitness account. She told me and I quote, 'On the tragic day of 31 August, I was able to hide my mother, Freida Perel Kaczer, age eighty-seven. My mother was a treasure. She was well-read in the *Tzena Renah* ("Let's Go and See" - a book of prayers written in Yiddish and read mostly by women) and other books of Torah. She had borne five sons and three daughters. Some thirty years earlier, three of the sons had gone to America, and from them, she received regular support until war broke out. In Skalat and in Tarnopol, she had two daughters and a son, whose families included about twenty-five grandchildren and great-grandchildren. On Sabbath days, my Mamale was always trying to decide which child or grandchild she should visit first. Most years, one of the American sons would visit her and see to her needs.'

"My mother's story continued: 'On that fatal day, we said, "Come, Mama. We will hide you. We won't let you go to the hangman!" She trembled like a leaf. Mama still wanted to live. "Dearest children, don't leave me," she said and went into the hiding place on unsteady legs.'

"'I'll just summarize the rest for you," Mrs. Fried said, her posture slumped and tired looking. 'The Judenrat officials ran about looking for her everywhere. They were furious asking how the old Kaczer woman had not been crossed off the list yet? In their warped minds they justified their anger by saying outright, 'Can you imagine the gall of such a conscience-less family, to hide away such a broken old woman? No, they won't get away with it!' The militia came to Mother with an ultimatum demanding: 'Are you turning over your old mother or not?' 'I don't know where she is,' she replied.

"They shouted, 'If you will not turn her over, then you have to come with us. You will bring harm to all of us! We require the total number of people - don't you understand?' No. She did not understand. She felt it was better to go herself than to deliver an aged mother to her death. She screamed, went faint, cried, and then fought with these awful men, refusing to go. But it was to no avail: they dragged her off to the synagogue as a hostage.

"The synagogue was crowded and suffocating. There were screams and sobs. Old people moaned, or coughed, made a fuss or just fainted. Not even a drop of water in the heat. The Judenrat figured we would all be dead within a day, so why waste time providing food or water. Some of the aged and sick, lacking stamina, had already died.

"One of the old-timers, Hersh Solomon stood at the pulpit and recited Psalms in a tearful voice. A teacher, he had become penniless and was supported by communal funds. So, he ended up on the list of the 'useless' and, as such, he, his wife, and their three children, were dragged to the synagogue.

"The time passed, and hours flew by. Nothing is heard; nothing is seen. No rescuers appear by night and new victims are brought in regularly. They are surrounded, being asked what is happening in town. Faith in any kind of rescue weakens. Fear of death assaults one's thoughts. What a night the other Jews and my mother spent trapped inside there! I cannot imagine that a night in hell could be worse. When the dawn arrived, the red, blue, and green panes of the tall synagogue windows let in the daylight, which revealed the frightening reality.

"Everyone was knotted with fear awaiting whatever the coming hours would bring. My mother had lost hope, no longer believing that she would be rescued. Meanwhile, my old grandmother had found out what had happened. She experienced the ultimate dilemma. How could she permit her daughter to be lost? She wove together the strands of Fate and Divine Providence. G-d knows what He is doing.

"She did not sleep all night and barely survived until morning to ransom her daughter from the murderers. 'My daughter. I have come!' Mother was surprised to hear her mother's voice in the background. 'You will not die. I alone will be the sacrifice for the family. Go home. You are younger than I, and I have lived a long life,' she said. Into her daughter's hand she pressed a gold coin worth twenty dollars, and whispered in her ear, 'Maybe you will be able to ransom me.' She looked at her daughter with love and a small smile. 'You never know?'

"My mother did not want to go. Tears choked her as both of them, mother, and daughter, stood there frozen and mute. Finally, my grandmother pushed her away, 'Go, my daughter. Before it is too late,' my heroic eighty-seven-year-old grandmother warned. 'But remember me. Perhaps you may yet be able to ransom me.' She so wanted to live. Their embrace went on and on. A policeman led mother outside. She was barely able to stumble out. My dear old grandmother remained in the Synagogue."

"At four o'clock on Monday afternoon, a group of the SS came to get the victims. Led by Obersturmbannfuhrer Muller, they arrived from Tarnopol with eight empty trucks to transport this 'live contingent.' After the first truck stopped at the gate of the synagogue, Chairman Mendel Tackett and his cohorts appeared before the SS. They were servile and obsequious at the feet of the Germans.

"How many have you gathered here, you shitty Jews?"

"Mendel Tackett stammered the number. This enraged the German, who replied with a wild shout, 'What? So few? Damn you! Another hundred Jews in a half hour or we will shoot you like dogs!' There were supposed to have been 500 people, but they had only 480 people in the building.

"Somehow, twenty people had disappeared. One of them was my grandmother. It was said that one of the policemen had let that many people ransom themselves and slip out the back door during the night. He figured that if the Judenrat let people ransom themselves or replace their relatives with other people, why couldn't he do the same?

"A scattering of Germans and the Jewish police spread out across the town. They grabbed anyone they could. In that half-hour chase, an additional eighty souls were added to the 'live contingent.'

"*Obersturmbannfuhrer* Muller checked his watch and waved his hand to indicate that they had enough people. The hour was getting late. The doors of the synagogue were opened and everyone inside was loaded onto the trucks by the Germans and the police as if they were handling freight. People were jam packed in to accomplish the fullest load. All this occurred while the Germans cracked their whips overhead. Feeble older people were carried and loaded with significant effort.

'Move them out!' the *Obersturmbannfuhrer* shouted, and the trucks began to move, to the sound of sobs and wailing. The 560 victims were taken to Tarnopol, and then, from there, some to work camps, but most went on to an extermination camp. One of those victims was Anna Steuben. I never expected her to still be alive. I assumed she was one of the victims who ended up in a concentration camp. That was the story my mother told me when she got home, and I have never spoken about this until today."

Elvis looked at her, unable to say anything.

CHAPTER TWENTY-FIVE

Stanley looked over at Elie, who had stopped talking and was weeping. Stan said, "That's a remarkable story. How do you remember it all so well?"

Elie looked up at him as he dried his eyes with a handkerchief. "When Mrs. Fried told me this story, it was as if I became a part of it. I felt this all so vividly. I was a part of it, not because of my cousin's presence in these terrible events, but because I felt that in some measure, I was one of those victims whose life was dust. I was one who was being destroyed because my cousin was a wicked coward and because, at the time I heard the story, I was also a coward. I may have never killed anyone, but I wreaked havoc over people's lives and did it with wanton disregard. This was not who I wished to be and if I was to continue doing the same things, well...I would still be the worst piece of crap. I finally knew my truth and could not look at myself in the mirror. Both inwardly and outwardly I despised who I had become. Simply put, I could not be Elvis Presley anymore!"

With that said, Elie got up and went in to go to sleep.

CHAPTER TWENTY-SIX

Stan and Elie reconvened the next day on the porch. Elie looked tired and pale. When Stan asked if he was up to it, Elie started talking like he had a mission to get his story out.

"So, you see, I stayed with the Frieds for several more days. I told Mrs. Fried what information I had on Anna Rabinowitz. Working like a detective, she quickly found Anna and got her on the telephone. They spoke for hours, it seemed. Mrs. Fried cried most of the time she was on the phone. At one point, she handed the phone to me. I had no notion of what to say to Anna. But she made it simple.

'Mr. Presley, thank you for not forgetting me. Thank you!'

'Anna, how are you? Since we spoke last in Vegas, I have not stopped thinking about you.'

'Really…why?'

'Something switched on in my head. I could not put my finger on it while we talked in my hotel room. You were talking about my cousin as a horrible person. I had never heard of him and I felt no connection. Nevertheless, I felt very lost after speaking with you about him. My first thought was that if he was a relation of mine, he couldn't have been so bad. But, Anna, I was wrong about that. Really wrong! I apologize for what he did to you and your family. That may help you or not, but I am so sorry for the way he treated you.'

"Anna didn't speak on the other end of the line. It was an awkward silence. I was about to hand the phone back to the Rabbi's wife when she said, 'Elvis, you are not Mendel Tackett and I never wanted that to be your burden. I only wanted you to know the whole story, to absorb it about him. It would seem that Miriam told you more about your distant cousin than I could. It was a horrible thing that happened to the Jews of Skalat. Miriam and I were lucky to survive and come to this country.'

'What happened to you after you left Skalat?' I asked.

He heard a groan on the other end of the line. 'It was very difficult. We arrived at a work camp by truck. That is, those of us who survived the trip. Those healthy enough were sent to farms to do backbreaking work all day away from the camp. Eventually, after the harvest was over, we were returned to the camp. One day, trucks came and hauled all of us who were relatively healthy to a railway station. We were herded into boxcars, like cattle, but worse. There was no room to move, no food, no water. People vomited again and again. There was no privacy. Not even a place to take care of your bodily functions except in a couple of buckets. We could not see light except from the crack of the doors. We traveled for many days. There were many who died on the trip and two women gave birth on the train. Then the train came to a stop. The door screeched open. We were at Auschwitz."

CHAPTER TWENTY-SEVEN

"Stanley, after I got home to Graceland, I was deeply depressed. I knew what had to be done in my life, but I was afraid to do it," Elie said. His voice was gloomy unlike the peaceful tones Stanley usually heard from his friend. "Life kind of returned to what had been normal before I went to the Fried's. The Colonel was booking tour locations, and I was back on the road. Las Vegas was a particularly useful place to play with all its distractions, and I settled back into my previous numbness.

'But this powerful feeling stuck with me. My stomach was a mess, and I couldn't sleep. Visions of Skalat haunted me. Struggling so much, I had my assistant go to the local library and get me any and all information available about Skalat. The librarian contacted the Library of Congress, and within a few weeks, I received a large box filled with eyewitness reports from the Germans and the Jews of the events that Miriam Fried had described. The Germans were crazy. They snapped pictures of everything, as if they planned to rewrite history when they won the war. I saw for the first time, pictures of Skalat from the earliest days of the twentieth century through to the present. Skalat had cleaned itself up pretty well. From the look of it, they had transformed into another pretty European village, like I remember in Germany from my army days. Kind of a sanitized version of themselves. I saw pictures of the four towers where all the killings had happened. It was deceptive, as they looked to be nothing special. I could not imagine how it must have looked the night of the first pogrom."

Stan interrupted, "Elie, stepping back for a moment. Did you see Anna again when you returned to Las Vegas?"

"No, actually not."

"Why not? She obviously had forced you to look differently at your life. Weren't you at least curious what had happened to her?"

Elie stopped for a heartbeat. "Stanley, I really don't understand why I didn't reach out to her. I wish I could tell you that Vegas caused me to go into a mental fog. That would be an easy excuse." He looked up at Stan blankly. Then he got up and went inside. After a lengthy wait, Stan got concerned and knocked on the door. Shoshana answered it.

"No, I don't know where he went," she said. Hold on, I see if he is in the basement." She soon returned and motioned him to follow her. "Elie asked me to send you downstairs."

"Stan took the stairs and went down into the basement. Elie was not in his office, but in the corner of the basement was a closet where he kept some bottles of whisky and liquor. Behind that was a false wall. Stan helped him move all the bottles. Elie tried to shove the false wall, but he didn't have the energy to get it to move. Stan got it unstuck and helped him pop the wall out of position. Behind that wall was a large box. Stan helped him carry it out, and together they brought it into his office. They replaced the wall in the closet and returned the bottles to their place.

Back in Elie's office, he opened the box and removed pictures and papers all about Skalat. Digging through the box, he would grab a picture or a document and pass it to Stan to look at. He looked at them for quite a while. His blood ran cold as he read through some of the documents. The pictures the Germans took were frightening and unnerving."

Stanley sat in front of the desk and paused before speaking. "Elie, somehow, I don't understand all this. Sometimes, I think I do. But not really. Why is this Skalat stuff so important to you? Really my friend, what has any of this got to do with you leaving Graceland to live here?"

Now Elie sat as well. He leaned forward and said, "Stanley, my dear friend, this is me. It's why I decided to give up my whole life as Elvis Presley. This may be hard to understand, but I left my old life to make amends and the only way I could do it was to return to my real roots as a Jew and start a new life - to make things right."

"Elie, make amends for what? All this has nothing to do with you, yet you cling to it as if you lived through it yourself. To whom were you able to make amends? Anna? Mrs. Fried?"

He leaned back in his chair and played with his beard. Refusing to look directly at Stanley, Elie quietly repeated, "I needed to make amends."

Stan asked again, "Amends for what? For what Mendel Tackett did to all those people?"

Elie said in a whisper, "Maybe?"

"Elie, do you realize how absurd that sounds? Has this life you have led for the past thirty-five years brought you the peace you so desired?"

He looked at Stanley with an intensity that he had never shown him before. "The life I have now is a blessing. I have a wonderful wife, a terrific family, and I get to say Kaddish every day for all the people who died because my cousin was such a coward that he was willing to sacrifice all their lives. Hundreds of lives, thousands actually. I get to make those amends, and when I meet them in heaven, they and the Master of the Universe will know I tried to right a wrongful part of my family's history. It may not be enough, but it is something. I will be able to rest in peace with that thought."

CHAPTER TWENTY-EIGHT

Vernon stomped behind Elvis and swatted his head. "Boy, what the hell is wrong with you?"

"Huh? What are you talking about?"

"Man, ever since you came back from California, you've been moping and yelling and acting like a total A-hole."

"I have not!"

"Yes, you have! Ask anyone around here. Hell, you shot out another TV the other day, and you're holding a pistol now. What the hell is wrong with you? Give me that gun. You are scaring the heck out of everyone around here, especially the help."

Elvis reached for the nape of his neck. He rubbed at it hard. He looked down at the kitchen table and shook his head. Then he slammed his fist on the table, knocking over the salt and pepper shakers and the bottle of ketchup. Vernon's cup of coffee, which was sitting across from Elvis, spilled all over the place.

Vernon yelled at him some more. "Have you gone crazy, boy? Look at this mess. Geez!" He grabbed a towel to clean up the spilled coffee. He sat at the table and looked at his son.

"What the hell happened in California? You came back a different person. Come on boy, what is going on with you? Did some broad screw you over?"

"I wish!"

"Well, what is it, Elvis? Lots of people depend on you and you're acting like a damned crazy man. So what gives?" Vernon snatched a pack of cigarettes from his shirt pocket. He shook one up and drew it out with his lips. He grabbed a match and lit the cigarette. He drew a lungful and blew the smoke out into the air above him. Elvis watched the smoke curl above Vernon as if it were a cloud changing shapes in the sky.

"Daddy, I didn't go to California."

"You didn't? Then where the hell were you?"

"Here in Memphis."

"The whole time?"

"Yeah."

"You are full of crap. You expect me to believe that you hid out in "*this*" town. The minute you hit the street or anyone saw that big old Cadillac of yours, everyone would have recognized you. Come on, boy. If you weren't in California, where the hell were you?"

"Really. Daddy. I was in Memphis."

"Yeah? Tell me where?"

"I went back to the old neighborhood. To the Courts."

"To the Courts? That place is a dump. Why would you go back there, and where the hell could you hide in that G-d forsaken place?"
"Rabbi Fried still lives there. Same apartment and everything. I stayed with them."

"Rabbi Fried? You mean the couple who lived upstairs from us? They're still alive? He wasn't so young when you were growing up there. How old can they be?"

"In their eighties, I suppose."

"And they remembered you?"

He nodded.

"And why would you go to see them? Were they expecting your visit?"

"No. When I went to the building, I wasn't even sure if they still lived there. But they were there, and they took me in for the week."

"I don't understand, Elvis."

"I had run into them about ten years ago. The Rabbi had

followed my career for some reason. I believe they really liked me. After all, I was their Shabbos Goy."

"Their what?"

"Their Sabbath gentile. I handled the things they were not allowed to do on their Sabbath. Lighting lamps, adjusting the thermostat and so forth. You've probably heard that Jews can't do those things on Saturday."

Vernon raised his eyebrows. "Crazy. I didn't know that. You did that for them all the time?"

"No, just on their Sabbath and holidays."

"That explains why we couldn't find you on the weekends. So, you went back there?"

"He said when we met back then that if I ever needed help… well, I knew where they lived."

"So you went over there, not knowing if they were even going to be there? Because you needed help? And how were they going to be able to help you? Explain that one to me?"

Elvis squeezed his eyes shut and rubbed his scalp.

Vernon looked at him in amazement. "You could have gotten help from us here. And exactly what kind of help did you need? Because I got to tell you, whatever help you got, well, you came back a bigger mess than before you left here."

"I know it seems that way, Daddy. But they did help me. I hate this life. It doesn't work for me at all. It is killing me, just killing me."

"How can you say that? Look around you. You grew up in a dump in Mississippi. Then we moved to those damned projects here in Memphis. We couldn't rub two nickels together. And now look at how you live. Man, this is luxury. Luxury, G-ddamnit! What could be better than this? What are you, on drugs? Well, get a damned doctor and get yourself straight. Whatever it takes. Get yourself straight."

Vernon stopped to compose himself. He sat down at the table, looking at his son. His early adult life flashed across his eyes. He remembered his own insecurities.

"I picked up on the fact you hated doing those stupid movies, but they sure paid the bills around here. Those concerts too. They pay your alimony to Priscilla and the child support for Lisa Marie."

"I know. I know."

"Yeah! What are you going to do anyway, just run away somewhere?"

Elvis was silent. Vernon looked at him in disgust.

"You do want to run away! My gosh! You are one stupid person. Agh! You must have Jell-O for brains, boy. Where in the hell are you gonna run to anyway? You're Elvis Presley! Where in this whole damned world could you hide? Do you think that no one would look for you? And where you dumbass, where? You think you could just disappear somewhere, and that Colonel wouldn't have an army of private eyes looking all over for you? They'd drag you back here so fast, you wouldn't know what hit you. We have contracts. That's right, contracts! Contracts that have to be fulfilled or we will lose everything. You don't think they would take us to court? You think those boys in Vegas wouldn't want to get a piece of you if you didn't show up at their hotels? These are not nice guys, Elvis. Definitely not nice guys. I'll tell you: they'd leave you for dead and they'd grab everything. The house, the cars, the money. Everything. You'd be better off dead. Wake the fuck up, you stupid spoiled baby. You would end up on a street corner with nothing. Nothing, I tell you!" Vernon was screaming at the top of his lungs. He ran out onto the porch slamming the door.

Elvis groaned. The maid came in and asked if everything was all right. He nodded that he was fine. He cupped his hands under the kitchen faucet and took a drink of water. Then he went upstairs, swallowed some sleeping pills, and went to bed.

CHAPTER TWENTY-NINE

"Vernon was really pissed off at you, huh?" Stan looked at Elie.

Elie chuckled and said, "He sure was, but I can't blame him. Daddy had a hard life, and now he was living it up. Mama was gone. She died of a heart attack on August 14, 1958. She was just forty-six. I was crushed. She was my everything. He remarried two years after Mama's death. He married a younger woman named Davada Stanley. He called her Dee. I hated her. They stayed married seventeen years. They divorced right before I 'died'. Miserable woman! But with Mama gone, he had his freedom. Nice cars, all the booze he could drink, and all the cigarettes he could smoke. As Elvis' father, he could find a woman everywhere he went. And so, he found her. It was a good life for a man who had nothing growing up and had gone to prison as an adult. But that's a side issue.

"Getting back to Vernon. How we kept the family together was a miracle in itself. And the fact that Mama took him back? She did it for me so I would have a daddy in the house. He was impossible, but she was so strong willed that he buckled under to her. I understand it now. At the time, I was simply happy to have him home. Vernon was in many ways a complex man."

"How so?" Stan asked.

"Well, he always was difficult."

"Tell me about your dad, Elie. What was it like, growing up with him?'

"Stanley, do you know anything about him?"

"Not much. I didn't find much about him when researching your family."

"Really? Well, we were close. He was impossible at times, but he was a really great guy. You will see that, without him, I wouldn't be sitting with you today."

"How so, Elie? Are you telling me that Vernon helped you escape?" Elie grinned, "We're getting way ahead of ourselves right now. First, I'll tell you about him."

Stan got up from his chair and walked around for a second. "I knew it. I couldn't figure it out, but of course Vernon would be the one to help you. I just knew it! I looked at all the possibilities, Priscilla, Linda Thompson, Ginger Alden, the Memphis Mafia. But the name that kept popping up in my head: – Vernon. I'm right, Elie. Am I not?"

"Stan, I said we are getting way ahead of ourselves. Let me tell you about Vernon, and maybe you can figure it out."

"You mean it wasn't Vernon?"

"Stan, let me tell the story!"

"Okay, okay, talk to me." Stan sat back down.

"As I said, Vernon was a complicated fellow. He was born in Fulton, Mississippi, on April 10, 1916. My grandparents were Jesse and Minnie Mae. His full name was Vernon Elvis. I ended up with Elvis as part of my name. When he was around sixteen or seventeen, he met my mama Gladys, at church. She was five years older than him, but somehow, they got together and fell in love. Since he was seventeen and Mama was twenty-two, they couldn't get a marriage license and would not have been allowed to marry. But when they filled out the papers, they switched their ages and were married in Verona by the Pontotoc County Clerk on June 17, 1933.

"Daddy, his brother Vester, and his father Jesse built a house for Mama and Vernon to live in. It was really a two-room shack. Mama gave birth to me and my twin brother Jessie, who died, in the house. That was January 8, 1935.

"My father worked at whatever job he could get. It was the Depression, and work hard to get. Daddy worked manual labor and whatever odd jobs he found, but we barely got by. We were a loving family and would sit around an old piano we had acquired, and we would sing mostly gospel songs.

"Daddy got into trouble with the law when I was three years old. Daddy had sold a pig to our landlord, a man named Orville Bean. They had argued over the price of the pig until Orville told him to take it or leave it. Needing the money, Vernon took the check. But he was furious. He always had trouble keeping a job, most likely because he drank health. Anyway, he altered the check and got caught. He served nine months in Parchman for forgery. When he left, he told me to care of Mama. I remember crying and crying. But he was gone to prison.

"Things got much worse during that time for Mama and me. We lost the house and had to move in with relatives. I was so upset by all this that I started to sleepwalk, scaring Mama half to death.

"Mr. Bean felt sorry for us, and he spoke with the judge and somehow got Daddy released after nine months. Mama wasn't so glad to see him, and Daddy's family piled on him for having gotten into trouble. It was not a great time for us. We moved from place to place. Sometimes we lived with relatives for a while, and then we were back out looking for places to live. Food was always a problem. There was never enough. We were always one step ahead of the creditors. Daddy worked odd jobs, and then ran moonshine. He never made enough money to take care of us, and he never stayed with a job for long.

"I remember after Daddy got home from Parchman; he gave me a spanking for doing something. I must have been about four years old. I don't even remember for what. I decided that was it for me and I was going to run away from home. I packed up a couple of sandwiches for myself and slipped out the door as soon as Mama and Daddy went to bed. I was scared. It was dark and cold, but I was going to teach my folks a lesson. So, I kept on walking the dark road. It must have been fifteen or twenty minutes before I heard an engine in the distance. I moved to the side of the road, so no one would see me. A truck pulled alongside me and stopped. It was Daddy's truck. He scooped me up into the truck. I was hungry, so I ate one of the sandwiches and gave the other one to Daddy, who laughed when he saw it. He ate it on the short ride home. Mama was waiting for us outside, nervously playing with her apron. "Thank G-d you're home safe," she said to me and looked up at Daddy. I got spanked another time but, I hugged and kissed my folks and promised not to do it again.

"Now Daddy was not afraid to use the strap on me when I misbehaved. Here is a funny story, looking at it as an old man. The first time I remember committing a sin, I must have been seven or eight at the time. I stole two empty cola bottles off the porch of our neighbor, the Harris family. When Mama asked me about the bottles, I told her where I got them from. She asked me if I had asked their permission. I said no, them being empty bottles and all, I figured no one would care. But back then, you would buy the bottles and pay a penny deposit. So, in reality, I wasn't just filching a couple of bottles. I was costing the Harrises the deposit money. A penny went a long way during the Depression.

"Well Mama was so mad that she dragged me back to the Harris home. I was so ashamed to return the bottles. I said I was sorry to Mrs. Harris. She smiled weakly and told me I was forgiven. She closed the door, and we went home. She talked to Daddy that night and then told me I would have to confess my sin at church the following Sunday. She was going to teach me a lesson about stealing that I would never forget. Well, when Sunday came around, I pretended to be sick. I suddenly got better when Daddy showed me his strap. When we got to church, Mama pushed me up to the front and ordered me to confess in front of the entire congregation. Crying and looking down at the dirt floor, I whispered my sin and then ran out of the building, still in tears. But I never took another thing without permission. Hard lesson for a hard time!

"Daddy was away a lot and Mama and I got close. I learned to be the man of the house. I sometimes called my parents my 'babies' because I did everything, and Mama could always count on me.

"I learned to really love music in church. We might have been dirt poor, but we still went to church. In our case, we worshipped at the Assembly of God church in Tupelo. They were Pentecostals and if you know anything about Pentecostals, they love to sing. Our preacher would bang away on the piano and get sweaty and hoarse but letting it all hang out as he sang along. There was no dancing in our church, but singing? Let me tell you, you could hear us out in the street. We were swaying and singing with a choir and all kinds of commotion. I loved it!

"My musical talent was first recognized by my fifth-grade teacher, Mrs. Oleta Grimes. Mrs. Grimes was the daughter of Orville Bean, who had caused so much trouble for us when I was a young one. She was so moved by the way I sang this sad old ballad called 'Old Shep' that she mentioned it to my school principal. He had me sing it to him and decided to enter me into a talent contest at the Mississippi- Alabama Fair and Dairy Show. I wore a cowboy suit and stood on a chair. Without a guitar or a piano to sing along with, I sang this sad old song about a boy's love for his dog. It was great, and I won second place. The prize was a free pass to ride all the rides at the fair.

"I was dying for a bicycle, but there was never enough money for anything so special. Shortly after the fair, I asked again. Mama always said no. She worried I'd fall and get hurt or get hit by a car. But the real reason was we had no money. Instead, she arranged to buy me a second-hand guitar. The preacher from church, some of my family and some of Mama's friends pitched in to give me informal guitar lessons. I got good really quickly and I was also learning to play the piano as well. When I started seventh grade, I brought my guitar to school every day, and at recess I would practice and play it.

"As for Vernon, we lived a hand-to-mouth existence in Tupelo, because he couldn't keep a job. It was hard to always be moving about and not have a steady place to live.

"Soon after I started High School, Daddy moved us from Tupelo to Memphis, Tennessee. This was in November 1948. We left in the middle of the night with all our belongings tied to the top of our car. That is, except the furniture. Daddy figured he would have a better chance at a steady job in Memphis, which was a real city, not an overgrown town like Tupelo was then. We found an apartment in a housing project known as the Courts, and I was enrolled at L.C. Humes High School or, as it was known around Memphis, Humes High School. I did okay as a student most of the time, but my shyness meant I never fit in. When I was a Junior, I decided to mix things up. I let my hair grow out and grew long sideburns. I found the wildest, most flashy clothing in all kinds of weird stores. I wore dress pants and would wear a scarf like an ascot." Elie snorted, "I wanted to look like a movie star. People thought I was really weird, but I loved it. I figured that if I didn't fit in, I would stand out.

"In my senior year, I took a job at the MARL Metal Products Furniture Makers from three to eleven o'clock at night. We didn't have enough money and I intended to pull my weight. But it was too much. I would fall asleep in class and Mama was afraid my grades would suffer, so she made me quit. The money was nice, but I was getting totally burned out.

"Later that year, I appeared in a school talent show. I sang a song called 'Til I Waltz Again with You.' After that performance, boy, did I become popular! My crazy looks suddenly were cool, not weird.

"I graduated from Humes on June 3, 1953. Now what to do with my life?

"I called Daddy into my room one afternoon soon after graduation and told him, 'I want to be an entertainer.' Daddy said to me 'Well, I don't know much about that sort of thing, but you've dealt with quite a few people in the business. Why don't you talk to some of them to see what you got to do to get into it." I was most interested in singing gospel, quartet singing. I tried out for two or three different young groups, hoping to get in with one of them. The groups were either full or they didn't think I had what it took to sing gospel. Isn't that crazy, Stan? They didn't judge me good enough to sing gospel. Ha! They did me a favor by not letting me sing with them. Soon, I would blow by all of these groups in no time flat. But at the time, I was so disappointed. I went back to Daddy for advice. He told me to go record a song, something I was afraid to do. I had once recorded a song for Mama at Sun Records, but that was for her. I had been singing with some groups doing gigs in local places, but you never have the confidence in yourself at first. By late summer, I mustered up the nerve to go to the Memphis Recording Service, where I recorded two songs: 'My Happiness' and 'That's Where Your Heartaches Begin'. I don't know all about what happened, but it was a success for me. After I made this record, a lot of the quartet groups begged me to join them. I talked with Daddy again about what I should do, telling him, 'I can get into quartet singing now, the gospel field.' His reaction was, 'I wouldn't do it. I'd keep what you got. You tried that before, and they wouldn't accept you. My advice is to just stick to what you got.' So, that's what I did, and it was the best advice about my singing career that I ever got.

"Then in 1956, I got a chance to go to New York and the rest is history. I realized then and still recognize it today, after Daddy has been gone all these years: although he might not have been the brightest fellow when it came to working like plain folks, he was a downright genius when it came to my music career."

CHAPTER THIRTY

fter listening to Elie talking about his father, Stan started to suspect that the real mover and shaker in Elvis's life was his old man. What the reporter was wrestling with was whether Vernon had or had not been involved in the escape to Brooklyn. Vernon had a lot to lose if Elvis 'died.'. So, the odds of him doing something to facilitate this process began to seem remote in Stan's eyes. Vernon had died less than two years after Elvis's 'death.' He had a longtime heart condition, and he died of cardiac arrest at the age of sixty-three in Memphis.

He was remembered for sobbing bitterly at his son's death. It appeared to be a genuine shock to him that Elvis was dead. Stan was unconvinced that Vernon could have been a part of spiriting Elvis away from Graceland to a new life. Besides, Vernon was the executor of the will. This was a wrinkle that Stan would have to chew on, because in a strange way, it reopened the possibility that Vernon might be involved.

Stanley kept mulling over Priscilla or Ginger Alden. In his mind, Priscilla emerged a viable suspect. She had joined the Church of Scientology and was an active member. Because of her fame, the Church of Scientology probably had a financial interest in the Presley family. Besides, Scientology was a super secretive organization, employing drastic tactics to silence their members about church goings-on. In many respects, they would be the perfect vehicle to pull this off. In fact, they could have successfully spirited Elvis out of the country until the furor subsided and then set him up somewhere else.

"It had to be Priscilla! Maybe Vernon as the executor was also involved? Who knew? Elie was the one who might confirm if any of this conjecture was true. Of course, Elie might have pulled it off in some completely different and unique way. He did hint that two rabbis were involved. But how were two rabbis able to pull something like this off?"

Stan pondered the possibilities. "Two rabbis? Ridiculous. There was a dead body found. Ginger found a dead 'Elvis!' There had been an autopsy, a toxicology report and everything. How complicated did this conspiracy get? What rabbi would have gotten involved in that?"

Stan worried at the breadth of all this. The only one with all the details was Elie, and he was dying. Stan hoped to be able to get the whole story from him in time. Elie still looked all right, but pancreatic cancer races through the body, and he might miss the opportunity to get the whole story pieced together. He was going to have to push Elie to move the story along. How he would do that was anyone's guess.

If all else failed, he could reach out to Priscilla, although the chances of her coming clean after all these years would be practically nil. Besides. having built the Elvis brand into a major moneymaking enterprise, she would be risking way too much to expose her own role. No, he would have to push Elie to get to the meat of the story, soon or the whole thing might go up in flames with no story to tell. He could not let that happen. That was not a thought he wanted to ponder. He had to act. Elie loved to talk and talk. And Stanley was fascinated by the whole thing. He was amazed that he had discovered this great secret and that he was talking with the great "King of Rock 'n' Roll." But Stan was going to have to be the old tough beat reporter and not the glassy-eyed fan to get this story. Otherwise, there were too many variables to string together into a coherent story.

Stan pieced together several potential conspiracy theories to press Elie on. The Priscilla angle. The Ginger angle. Maybe the Memphis Mafia was in on it all the time. Vernon? It was conceivable that Elie went to Linda Thompson for help. But that did not resonate with Stanley. He wasn't sure why. But it didn't.

He sat at his kitchen table, drinking coffee, and looking at his notes. Questions kept bubbling up. He knew for sure that Elie had pulled off the great escape. He was also certain he could not be the only one who knew about it. Stanley hoped his friend would live long enough to spill the beans on how he did it and who helped him. The bigger question in his mind became, how did Elie get to Brooklyn?" More important than that was the question of how he managed to live in plain sight for all these years without someone else, anybody else, putting two plus two together. This inflamed Stan's mind. Elie had lived for thirty-five years in relative obscurity in Brooklyn. He had married, had a family, and sat on his damned porch every day and not one person had realized that Elvis Presley lived among them?

Stan rubbed his eyes. His head was hurting. Tomorrow would be here soon enough, and he needed to clear his mind, so he could work then. He turned on the television and watched the Mets lose another one and dozed off on the couch.

CHAPTER THIRTY-ONE

"Okay Elie, how in the hell did you do it?" Stan blurted out the next evening as they once again sat on the porch to talk.

"Do what?" he replied.

"Come on Elie, stop playing around. How did you pull off the great escape? I couldn't sleep last night, running possible scenarios on how you pulled it off. I've guessed at hints from you. I've speculated about the people in your life who might have helped you. Any one of these scenarios, in my mind, is possible. Let me say it better: they are all plausible, but only you know the truth."

Elie laughed out loud. "How do you think I did it, Stanley? Since your mind seems to be running wild, what are your ideas?"

Stanley shifted uncomfortably in his chair. "Don't play that game with me. I could envision a hundred different ways you pulled it off and still be wrong. My friend, and I am going to be perfectly straight with you. You're dying. And you know it. You might be feeling all right now, but tomorrow it could change in an instant. You could wake up much worse and go quickly. Then, Elie, your story never gets told. Your wife and kids will never hear that you were once this great world-famous person. Any monies that can be made from this story would be lost, and your family would suffer. So stop kidding around and spill it!"

Elie sat in his chair, stroking his beard and looking out onto the street. Some boys were riding their bicycles in front of his house. He sighed out a loud gust of air.

Stan looked at him. "Unless, you really don't want to have your story told? Maybe you really want to take it to the grave. Is that what you want, Elie?"

Elie kept stroking his beard and looking out at the boys in front of him. "I sure wish I had a bicycle at that age. I never really learned to ride one, even after I grew up and could afford it. I learned to ride a motorcycle, for sure. And that was great fun. A real rush. A girl and I would go for a ride. Great fun." He grinned and turned to Stan. "Almost, a guarantee I would get…well you know. I would end up in bed with her. But gee, I would have loved to have a bike. Ride around Tupelo wherever I felt like going. That would have been real freedom for a kid like me. A guitar for a bicycle. I know Mama was always worried I'd get hurt. But as much as I loved that guitar…ah, a bike. She was right about the guitar. She knew the music was in my blood. But really, Stanley, a bike! Did you have one as a kid?"

"Not sure what that has to do with my question, Elie. But sure. At least until it got stolen when I was about ten. Remember I grew up in Brownsville. That was a tough neighborhood."

Elie smiled. "So, you understand."

"I think so. It did give me a sense of freedom to come and go as I pleased."

"Exactly! You see, Stan, for me running away from Graceland and all that it meant was like a little boy exploring his world on a bike. No one to bother me. Time was all mine. I could wander and be free. Getting there was a long journey, but now I have all this." Waving his arm at the front window of his little house, he added, "It's certainly not Graceland, but it is the home to me that Graceland never was. In many ways, I never stopped being the little boy in my daddy's two room shack in Tupelo, Mississippi. This is certainly no shack, but it's small and intimate. When the kids were young and crawling all over the place, I would stand in the foyer in amazement and imagine how they would react to Graceland. It was an entirely different world. So abstract, so crazy. My little sixteen-foot-wide house with its two tiny bathrooms and hardly room to move means more to me than Graceland ever could.

"I gave up all those beautiful, sexy women for my sweet Shoshana. You have to admit Stan, that she is something entirely different."

"I wouldn't say that Elie."

"Of course. But what I mean is that compared to Ann Margaret or Cybil Shepard or even Priscilla, Shoshana is no match to them physically. Shoshie is so thin and pale and so quiet. Sometimes, we can sit together for hours and not say a thing. And it's all right. It really is. I mean, she would never get on the back of a motorcycle and ride with me."

"Are you so sure, Elie? Maybe deep inside her heart is a burst of adventure that you don't know is lurking there. Maybe she is just living the life she was expected to live by her parents and family. Maybe, she wanted more. Maybe, she needed more. I think it's likely she wants to know that she is the one who managed to tame the great Elvis Presley. You think that's possible?"

Elie shifted uncomfortably in his chair. He pursed his lips and stroked his beard, and a tear trickled down his cheek. He brushed it away with his shirt sleeve.

"You could be right. But it's too late now. I cannot upset the apple cart. It would be a terrible shock, and I will soon be gone. Won't do it to her. Love her too much!"

Elie got up and went into the house. He reemerged with his wedding album. He opened it and started to explain the pictures. After he had left Graceland, he had lost a tremendous amount of weight. Except for the beard and his cropped hair, it was clear to Stan that the man in the pictures was Elvis Presley. Shoshana was in a white wedding dress typical of Orthodox Jewish brides, high necked and long sleeved with a simple crown and veil. In the photos, Shoshana had a beautiful countenance that belied her everyday existence. Thin and tall with red hair and a face that normally looked gaunt, she wore makeup that filled out her face and showcased her best features. Elie was obviously older than her in those pictures, but he looked genuinely happy. She looked happy too but had a somewhat worried look that remained with her through all the years of marriage. Now Elie looked filled in, as age and married life tend to make a man fuller in the body. But Elie also was now clearly showing the signs that a disease was working its way through his body. His hair had thinned out and his beard flowed down his chest, whiter than Stan remembered. Elie's paunch was melting away. The cancer was showing its ravages in small but definitive ways.

"I can't do it to her, Stanley, and I won't. I will tell you." He said with strength in his voice. "So that you can tell her."

"Me?"

"Yes. Promise me you will tell her everything before you publish this book. She should have no surprises."

"Don't you think she will be surprised if I tell her? I think she'd be damned mad at me, and she would be terribly hurt that you shared a life with her without telling her your secret. I can't do that, Elie. That's not fair."

Elie looked even more serious and took a deep breath. "Yes, you are right. I am a chicken about this." He peered out at the street. The streetlights were just starting to turn on. There was a weird glow around him. He exhaled and shook his head. His expression collapsed.

"I am sorry, but I can't tell her about all this. I may be a coward about it, but I would rather it be a story from the grave than to face her with it. Stan, this is a big deal to me. It's a long and complicated story. I did things to live this life that I am not proud of. I got help from people who were entrusted with this secret, and they kept their word not to spill the truth. For all of them, I am deeply grateful, they kept an oath to me, and I kept an oath to them. Stanley, in the Torah, when Joseph's brother sold him to the Egyptians, they swore an oath not to reveal the secret to Jacob. For twenty-three years, they kept that secret. Even Isaac knew about it and kept the truth from his son. Joseph himself, long after he was named viceroy and could have easily let his father know, even he did not reveal he was alive, until the moment the oath was ready to be revealed. I also swore an oath with the people who helped me. They have kept their word. When some of them died, they took my secret to their graves. Who am I to speak out now? An oath is an oath and I will keep it until I die. Heck, I would not have ever told you, except you figured it out. I realized it would be better to tell you than have it leak out from you in speculation. But I agonized over this. I determined that you are a truthful man. You are trustworthy and you've respected my wishes to guard my secret until after I die. So I ask you to understand that it has to be you who tells my wife before the story goes public. Will you do that for me?"

Stanley was so flooded with conflicting emotions that he was speechless and that is rarest of things for a writer. He got up from his chair, went into his house, and closed the door.

CHAPTER THIRTY-TWO

"The next morning before he went to work, Stanley knocked on Elie's door. When the door opened, he saw Shoshana ushering the kids out the door to the school bus that was pulling up in front of the house.

"Hi Stanley," she said as he opened the door and the kids ran out waving at their mother. She threw them air kisses and faced Stan.

"Hi Shoshana. Is Elie around?"

"He's at synagogue." Looking at her watch she said, "But he should be home in a few minutes. Can I give him a message?"

"No need. Do you think he'll be here soon?"

"Probably another five minutes or so."

"I'll wait, then." He sat on one of the chairs on the porch.

"You're sure?" He nodded. She shrugged. "Would you like something to drink? A coffee or something?"

Stan waved her off. "No, no, it's all right. I'm fine. Thank you for asking. I'll just wait."

She smiled and just said, 'Okay.' Then she closed the door.

Stan looked down the street and saw the lumbering shape of Elie coming toward the house. He climbed the first step to the house and looked up at the chair. He looked quizzically at Stan.

"I see your point, Elie. I don't agree with you, but I see your point."

Elie nodded. He took his hat off and climbed the remaining

steps to the porch. He sat beside Stan. They were silent for a spell. Finally, Elie placed his hand on Stan's shoulder and whispered, "Thank you."

They shook hands. Stanley got up and walked down the street towards the subway.

Elie shook his head. He got up and tapped on the door. Shoshana let him in.

CHAPTER THIRTY-THREE

Vernon sat on his bed smoking a cigarette. As he blew smoke into the air, his troubled expression grew darker. "That boy really wants to run away somewhere. Incredible! All that talent and no common sense. He's not stupid. Either he really is a spoiled selfish man, or something is eating him to the point where he has gotten this out of control. I wish I could figure out which."

He went to the bathroom and looked into the mirror. "He'd never be able to run away. And why would he try? He has the pick of any woman he would want. And there's so much money. Heck, he is a virtual money machine."

He looked again in the mirror carefully. The reflection he saw in his mind's eye was a younger Vernon. The man who could not sit, a man attracted to his vices. Deep inside, he hoped to be a more stable man. Managing his son's life had given him a sense that he was a responsible adult. And he was proud of how he had changed. He was a man of substance now.

Vernon frowned in the mirror. He also saw that there was another side to his becoming responsible, there was still a dark side within him. For one thing, he had finally gotten rid of that damned woman, Dee. "I should never have married her. She was an anchor around my neck. Elvis was right about her: she was just mean. Her three boys were decent, though, and I always treated them like they were my own. Elvis treated them like brothers for the most part. But she was a mean, bitter woman. It's crazy how we lasted for seventeen years, but I am so glad to be rid of her."

He entered the bedroom and snuffed out the cigarette in an ashtray. He reached for the pack to take another one and thought better of it. He tossed the pack on his bed and went downstairs. The boys were playing pool and drinking. He strode past everyone, and went outside, and got into one of the cars. He had no particular plan in mind and drove aimlessly.

At some point, he realized he was near the Courts. Vernon had not intended to go there when he started but realized that Providence was guiding his hand on the wheel. He parked his car and went up to the old apartment. He looked around at the dingy hallways and was disgusted, although it wasn't that different than when he and Gladys had lived there. It was only older and less well kept.

He was saddened that there was a time in his life when this was the best he could do for his family. They were scarcely able to scrape by. Living on government support and working when he could find something decent, they had managed to survive. But Elvis was why they were able to break out of this. Without Elvis, he probably would still be living here, or he'd be dead already. Maybe that would have been the end of the story.

But Elvis had been successful beyond their wildest dreams. Their lives were turned around so quickly that they never had a chance to savor it. Hell, Gladys hadn't made it to her forty-seventh birthday. All so fast. One day their son was singing in some club in Memphis, then appearing on Ed Sullivan, then drafted into the Army. It was too much for her. Her heart couldn't stand it.

He returned to a familiar mental loop. "Well, I did my best to keep Elvis on the ground. With all the success, he was flying so high that you never knew what he was doing. Priscilla! Me letting that go on was just crazy. She was a little girl, for G-d's sake. I was still the boy's father. I should have put a stop to that on the spot. But I was riding the Elvis rollercoaster as well. The lights were too bright. The noise too loud. The women too pretty, and the booze flowed freely."

He pondered it all as he turned around and looked at the hallway. "And now look at him. My son is a lost man- a drugged-out, overweight forty-one-year-old man-child. I've never been able to help him with any of that. Maybe now?"

He took a breath, found the Fried's apartment and knocked on the door.

CHAPTER THIRTY-FOUR

When Vernon returned from the Courts late that night, his thoughts about his son were profoundly changed. He had sat at the Fried's table and listened to them talk about Elvis. It dawned on him that he had never understood his son. What drove his son to succeed and what was driving him to his inevitable breakdown and failure finally came into focus. He learned a lot, listening to the Fried's talk. It was not normal for a man to shoot out televisions, and Elvis did it out of boredom and frustration. He let himself go physically out of severe discontent while he searched for meaning in his life. He explored karate and Eastern mysticism. But that gave him no relief: his actual existence was the complete opposite of what they espoused.

Vernon, of course, understood none of this inherently. He only understood that his son was searching for a way to survive. That, Vernon understood instinctively: searching to survive. But it had always been about having a job and enough money. For Elvis, it transcended money, because his talent meant there was so much money around. Giving Cadillacs to strangers was one of the ways he acted out to find acceptance. This was the world in his head, he couldn't accept his life as it was. All Elvis had was the numbing of his brain through drugs and alcohol. This was how he coped when he saw no other way out.

Vernon left the Fried's apartment, determined to find a way to help his son. Time was not on his side, and Elvis would self-destruct like an atomic bomb going off. While Elvis was hoping to ditch everything, Vernon's concern was about the contracts and losing everything. Now *that* was sensible. Vernon had grown up poor and spent most of his adult life perilously close to being unable to support his family. He remembered packing up in the middle of the night and moving to Memphis. He had no job and they had not a stick of furniture. All that was left in Tupelo. They had packed everything, tied it to the top of the Plymouth, and driven all night, without a plan for where they would live or how they would manage.

He feared returning to that kind of existence. He was too old for it. But that was going to happen in some form if he didn't get Elvis some help, away to get his life back on track.

As the car rolled along the road to Graceland, weighed all the options. He reached into his shirt pocket and pulled out a cigarette. He pushed in the car's lighter and waited for it to pop. Touching it to his cigarette, he took a deep drag and held the smoke in his chest. He blew a plume out of the window and drove. He watched the faint red glow dangling from his lips as he looked through the windshield. By the time he pulled into Graceland, he knew what he must do.

CHAPTER THIRTY-FIVE

For the second time in two days, Stan asked the question, "So Elie, how the hell did you do it?"

Elie laughed. "Seems like we've been down this road once before." "I guess we have." Stan laughed as well. "But I have a better understanding of what you need for me to do with your story. I don't necessarily agree, of course. But I get it. The problem is that I am just as reluctant as you are to break the news to Shoshana and your family."

"It will be hard for you, but you will do fine. I trust you more than you know, my friend. Maybe I shouldn't trust so much, Stanley, since we've been friends for such a short time. But I've also floated through this phase of my life for thirty-five years. I never expected to get away with it for so long. When the doctor gave me the news about the cancer, I was scared and then actually relieved. The story would go to the grave with me. But then somewhere deep within my heart, I realized that I did not want to die without telling how my new life had been put together. For the past thirty-five years, I've looked over my shoulder plenty of times. I always feared that I would run into someone from my past life on the street. They would recognize me, and the gig would be up. I imagined the headlines, "ELVIS IS ALIVE!" Crowds of people showing up at my door, scaring Shoshie and the kids. All that I loved would be wiped out. I would never have another real place to hide. People would want me to sing in public again, and that isn't who I am anymore.

"When you discovered that I'm Elvis, I already knew my cancer was terminal. Somehow, I felt safe with you. That you were a person who would respect my privacy. But more important to me was that you weren't just some stranger who had stumbled upon this and would blab it to the world. You are a journalist, and I had read your column for years before I met you. I always sensed a great integrity in you. And you have shown me that. You could have run with the story, and the last days of my life would have been a media circus. Now I believe my story will be told with respect and kindness, even though it is not a kind tale. To get to the here and now took great deception and I am not proud of that. Great people helped me, and they had tough decisions that must have really stressed their moral compass. I believe they chose a greater good because they saw the greater good in me."

He shifted in his chair, to look Stanley fully in the eye. He stopped twirling his beard with his fingers and placed his hands squarely on the armrests of his chair. "Stan, there are people who helped me who are still alive - people you will be surprised were involved. Please respect their privacy when you tell my story. Most are now dead. Please respect their reputations even though they are gone. They have families who would be shocked. Change the names and muddy the story up enough so that they may rest in peace.

"Others you will be able to talk about. Some might be willing to talk to you in person if you approach them in the right way. Others – no. Everyone who helped me did so because they loved me. They helped a helpless man to build a whole new life, apart from my previous existence. Some never met me. Some barely knew who I was. Some simply helped me as a fellow Jew in trouble. I left a lot of wonderful people behind when I did this, so remember Stanley. Remember this for me when you tell the story."

Elie looked up. A bird was flying overhead. He followed the bird with his eyes as it flew from one tree to perch on the tree in front of his house. He grimaced slightly and turned his attention back to Stan.

"So how the heck did I pull this off, exactly?" He smiled warily, chuckled slightly, and lifted his hands off the chair placing them out in front of him with his palms cupped upward, praying. "Master of the Universe, I knew there would be a time when you would command me to tell this secret. I am willing, but I am afraid. Guide me. Place the right words in my mouth. Let me be truthful and fair to everyone who will soon know my truth. It is your truth, and it must always come out either in this world or the world to come. I am ready. Help me to be ready. Help me, my Master!"

Stan whispered, "Amen."

Stan looked at Elie, "That was pretty dramatic!"

"Would you expect anything else? I am, after all, Elvis Presley."

CHAPTER THIRTY-SIX

"It would be easy, Stanley, for me to assume I have the whole story about how we pulled this all off," Elie said. "The truth is, like a true military operation, not all the players understood their role in the plan. As the man who needed to be moved, I probably know the least, believe it or not. I was so messed up with drugs and people were afraid to fill me in for fear I would screw it up. And, Stanley, I made huge mistakes that almost blew my cover several times. It is truly a miracle that we got away with it. I came close to blowing it years after I was settled here in Brooklyn. Luckily, it flew under the radar due to the help of someone you would never expect to have been involved."

Stanley yawned. "Elie, all that is very tantalizing, but come on, get on with the story."

Elie stared at Stan. "It may sound strange, but I am not exactly sure where to start."

"Elie, it's not like it's a murder mystery. Just say what happened. Unless it is a murder mystery? Is that why you're so reluctant to tell me?"

Elie laughed. "No, no. Nothing like that!"

"Well, Elie. Look at it from my point of view. There was a body and there was an autopsy. And you are sitting here in front of me, so you can understand why I might ask."

"We can thank Daddy for that."

"What, Vernon killed somebody?"

"No, of course not! But anyone who guessed my old man was a dumb country bumpkin would be sorely surprised."

"How so?"

"Because without Vernon, no Elie."

"Yes!" Stanley jumped out of his seat and turned to Elie. "I got it right that your father was involved." Stan shot a fist into the air before he could contain himself. "Damn, I knew it. I just knew it!"

"You mean you guessed it."

Stan reclaimed his seat. "Yeah. You know what I meant."

"I get that."

Stan leaned back to relax in his chair as Elie added, "Why are you surprised? I mean, he was my daddy."

"Oh, I am not surprised at all. But how was he involved and, more important, Elie, why? In a sense, he had everything riding on you."

"Darned right. He may have had the most to lose of anyone, even the Colonel."

"Huh? What has the Colonel got to do with this? Did the Colonel help you?"

"If the Colonel had known, he would have tied me to a chair and kept me locked up until right before each performance. Heck, no! The Colonel was the one person Daddy and I had to hide it from most of all."

"So, what gives, Elie? Spit the damned story out already!"

Elie inhaled sharply. "Well, on some level, you got it right. Without Vernon, none of this would have worked. Daddy worked real magic for me."

"But why? How did you convince him?"

"Didn't have to."

"What? You didn't have to convince him? Explain that?"

"He was my daddy. He knew that if I kept on my current path, it would kill me. He was the one who convinced me."

CHAPTER THIRTY-SEVEN

"When Vernon pulled into the drive at Graceland, he had figured it all out. The hardest thing would be to convince Elvis. He knew his son was a drug addict. He knew that Elvis also was someone who insisted on immediate gratification. This was going to take time, he had to make Elvis understand that. But his son had a volatile personality.

"Damn it, Gladys spoiled the boy. If we didn't have money for something he asked for, she'd give him food or something else. She could quiet his temper, but he could control himself about whatever he wanted. When I tried to teach the boy some patience, she would yell at me and give him something to shut him up. Those two, they were as thick as thieves. They shared stuff they never told me about. G-d, I let her turn him into a big ol' mama's boy. I should have put a stop to that. And he's still a mama's boy, but his appetite for things is not just for a banana and peanut butter sandwich or some pancakes. Now, it's…whatever he can get his hands on. Man, now I got to live with it."

Despite his irritation, Vernon saw the pain his son was genuinely going through. He had a plan, a crazy one, even to him. But Vernon was far smarter than anyone thought he was, and this kind of crazy might just work. But he had to pull all the pieces together. As he had sat across from Rabbi Fried and his wife that evening, the ideas had started to pop in his head. He developed a strategy. They told him the same story they told Elvis. He looked at the older couple and realized they were probably the only people in the world whom Elvis inherently trusted. The only skin they had in the game was seeing Elvis happy. They could not care less about his money. And they had a track record with him. He had disappeared from Graceland successfully into their tiny apartment. Vernon saw their fondness for his son and now understood Elvis' attraction to the couple. He got why Elvis hung out at their place as a teenager and why in Elvis' deepest moments of confusion, as a grown man, he had returned to them for their advice and help.

Vernon sat down at the kitchen table with a cup of coffee and lit a cigarette. He stretched out his legs in front of him as he smoked. It was late and quiet in the kitchen. His mind rummaged through many different scenarios, but one plan stayed in the forefront of his mind. There was one glitch: for this plan to work, Elvis had to "die" so, there would be no one coming after the estate. The income stream would dry up from the touring, but Elvis' records would still generate revenue. The Colonel would have to pack up his operation and leave. The hangers-on would all go. The boys would all disperse so they could earn a living elsewhere. For this to work, the world had to be convinced that his son was dead. That would take some real effort. But if it worked, Elvis could have a new life, but only if he cleaned himself up. And most important of all, only if he really wanted it.

CHAPTER THIRTY-EIGHT

"Now you see, Daddy had a plan," Elie said to Stan as he tipped a generous portion of scotch into his friend's glass. They were in Elie's basement office, and the door was closed. Stan lifted his glass, said, "L'Chaim," and took a healthy sip.

They had adjourned down there because it had started raining heavily outside, and the basement offered some privacy. What Elie was about to describe would surprising. Stanley would be shocked at the sheer audacity of it. Elie himself, after all these years, remained surprised because he couldn't believe it had worked.

Elie sipped from his glass and sat behind the desk. "Gosh darn, Stan, daddy was a genius! If he had only gone to school…but that's a different story. What he figured out in his head, well, no general in the army could have. This was like a CIA operation. Really, one man's claim to fame would forever have to be secret. But Daddy was okay with that. He loved me, and I would never have cleaned up my act without him. He passed a couple years after that, and of course I couldn't go to the funeral. Couldn't even say Kaddish for him as he was not Jewish. But I sort of sat Shiva for him. Miss him badly, even now. After Mama died and he married Dee, I felt abandoned by my family. But no matter what, and despite the woeful woman he was married to, he always was available to me."

Elie poured himself a splash of scotch and pointed the bottle at

Stan who lifted his glass for a refill. They clinked glasses, took a sip, and shared a sad look. Elie sighed.

"I was really wrung out at that point, both physically and emotionally. I started a tour in the middle of March in 1976. We toured continually until the end of June in 1977. Crazy, but in less than sixteen months, the boys and I spent a total of 141 days touring the country. And that didn't include performances for ten days in Lake Tahoe and eleven days in Vegas. Brutal!

"Throughout the spring and the summer of 1976, I worked a punishing tour schedule with occasional breaks. I was sick and exhausted and was ingesting pills to help me sleep and then more pills to help me wake up. Whatever breaks we had were far too short to get me back to full health. My weight, which had been getting bad, well, forget about it. I got so fat that I couldn't fit into my outfits. My heart wasn't in touring, my voice was a mess, and really, I couldn't care less. Thousands of people were paying good money to hear me sing, but I left the stage as quickly as I could. Not every night, mind you, but a whole lot of them. I was physically present but not 'there' in any other real way. The drugs were so bad, it was hard for people to understand me. I mumbled to the audience. I forgot words to songs I had been singing for years. It was obvious, especially to the press, who were pitiless in their reviews. Looking back, they were right. I had no business being on stage."

Stanley asked, "Where was Colonel Parker during this time? He must have seen his meal ticket self-destructing."

"Well, in all fairness to the Colonel, he was well aware of what was going on with my health and emotional stability. He enlisted Daddy and the boys to get me some help. But I was my own worst enemy. I pushed them away. There was nothing the Colonel could do but try to shield my true condition from the press. After my appearance in Charlotte, a reporter wrote a story saying I had a touch of the flu and my fans shouldn't worry. I would be all right for years to come.

"My health did not improve, but I continued to go onstage,

although the performances sapped all my energy. The night after Charlotte, we went to Baton Rouge. I couldn't go on. I was so sick. We had to cancel sold-out shows in Mobile, Macon, and Jacksonville. On April 1, I went home to Memphis and was checked into Memphis Baptist Hospital. I was exhausted and whacked out on drugs. They sent me home after four days. By April 21, the Colonel had me back on the road for shows in eleven cities over the next twelve days.

"At my last concerts in May and June 1977, I was a disheveled, uninterested person, barely surviving my nightly ordeal on stage. It wasn't fun for me, and I am sure the fans were not happy, given the boos I was getting when I left the stage early and couldn't perform. What I needed to do was to stop touring. I had to concentrate on regaining my physical strength and improving my mental state. But I was my own worst enemy. I wouldn't quit, even knowing it was killing me. Daddy said I was doing it deliberately, hoping to die. I am not so sure about that. I don't think I wanted to die; it was a scream for help. On June 26, 1977, I played my last concert at the Market Square Arena in Indianapolis. The concert officially was scheduled to begin at eight-thirty at night, but I didn't perform until ten. We had warm-up acts of brass bands, soul singers, and a comedian before I went on. I sang for about an hour and a half. Among the songs I sang were my classic tunes like 'Jailhouse Rock' and ' to rev up the crowd. I sang some slow and sad songs like ' and then I did a cover of Simon & Garfunkel's 'Bridge over Troubled Water.' I closed with 'Can't Help Falling in Love with You,' one of my favorite ballads.

"I was exhausted by that time. I told the crowd, 'We'll meet you again, G-d bless, adios,' and I left the stage. The crowd was happy and seemed to enjoy themselves. I felt that performance was one of the better ones I had performed in a while. Now I had six weeks off before I had to go back touring again.

"It was Daddy who finally had a conversation with me about how I would go forward."

Stanley put down his pen briefly, flexed his fingers, and asked,

"Elie, I am not clear on what happened. What did Vernon talk with you about? Who dreamed up the concept of faking your death?"

"Well it sure wasn't me. And to be fair to Daddy, I have no idea where his idea came from. I craved escaping for a while and figuring out my life. That February, I went to Hawaii with Ginger and her sisters, hoping that by going away I would get my head straight. Instead, we brought thirty people, and it was one big pajama party. Drinking and swimming and playing football. It was the same thing as Graceland with nicer weather. A total waste!"

"Why didn't you rent some private place and go away alone or with Ginger? She seemed to care about you."

"Oh, sure she did. She was a great kid. But that was part of the problem. She was a kid, and I was a kid. You know a forty-one-year- old kid. And anywhere we went, the press would follow. The photographers always snapping pictures of you when you least expected it. We had no real peace.

"Although I wanted to marry her, and I meant to, it was obvious that we were doomed as a couple. It was probably better for her anyway. I could never have given her all of myself in that environment. Not in the way I gave myself over to Shoshie and the kids. I needed someone who was older and wiser to help me figure this out. The Colonel was all business. Couldn't talk to him. As it turned out the older, wiser voice of reason was Daddy."

CHAPTER THIRTY-NINE

Elvis had been home for just a day or two when Vernon pulled him aside in the kitchen late one night. The house was quiet, and Vernon felt he could talk freely.

"That Tackett story, that was a hellacious thing. Wow."

"What are you talking about Daddy?"

"Tackett. You know. That whole story about Skalat."

"What?" Elvis looked up at his daddy as Vernon poured himself a coffee.

He sat across the table from Elvis. "The last time we sat here, you told me how you disappeared to the Fried's for a week. Son, no one knew where in the hell you went. It was craziness around here. When you told the Colonel you were in California with some girl, I didn't believe it for a moment. I had no idea where you might be. Anyway, you told me of your troubles and how the Fried's seemed to have helped. I went driving around Memphis one night. Just driving kind of randomly. No particular place to go, but I was turning over in my head how you wanted to run away. I struggled to figure out why and how.

"It was like the hand of G-d directing me, and I found myself at the Courts. I hadn't been there since we left. I hated the place. Lot of bad memories. Lots of troubles to put food on the table. You get that son, don't you?"

Elvis nodded. Vernon pulled a smoke from the pack in his shirt pocket and lit it. He sipped on the coffee and reached for the ashtray to hold his cigarette. "You see Elvis, seeing you in such pain hurts me, almost as much as it hurts you on some level."

Elvis looked at him quizzically, but Vernon continued. "I may not have been a great father…"

Elvis interrupted, "You did just fine Daddy." Vernon shook his head. "No, I was a real crappy father. Never quite got it right. Hell, your mother had to get a job in the cotton fields when you were a baby, just to keep our family hanging on. She would take you into the fields wrapped up in a bundle. She would carry you down the rows of cotton while she was picking. When you cried, she'd sit and feed you and then get up and return to picking. She was a tough lady and a good mother. I was not a good husband to her. Wish I could have been better. It got much easier after you started making all that money, but then she was gone. So young. Way too young." Vernon looked away and wiped his eyes with a handkerchief. Elvis also got teary.

They just sat at the table for a while.

"My son," Vernon said, "I know you hate this life. I do actually get it. There ain't enough money in the world to bring you happiness if what you do makes you sad. There is something I don't understand. You always loved your music. One would think that if you loved your music and were successful at it, then everything would be all right. But that's not true for you. It's also not true for many performers. I don't know why, but it sure seems true to me." Vernon reached for the smoldering cigarette in front of him. He tapped off some ashes, took two drags in quick succession, then stubbed it out. Sipping from his coffee, he spoke again. "It's been real tough for you, my boy. And I know you want out. At least I think so. Is that right?"

Elvis reached snagging Vernon's coffee cup and took a sip. "I don't know. I just desperately want to go somewhere by myself, where I'm a nobody to everyone, and just live like a regular Joe. Get a job. A nice simple life, a wife, some kids. And no one would be any wiser."

Vernon looked at him and joked, "maybe something like the

Witness Protection Program. You know, disappear into middle America, get a new name, a new life?"

They both grinned, and Elvis said, "Yeah, wouldn't that be great? Sure, wish I could figure out a way. That would be swell, Daddy. That would sure be swell."

Vernon pulled out another cigarette and lit it. He relaxed in his chair and blew the smoke towards the ceiling. He smiled deeply and took another drag, looking at the cigarette as he pulled it away from his lips. "Well, son, I believe I can make that happen."

"Are you crazy? No way. You couldn't do no such thing."

Vernon smiled ear to ear, "Want to bet on that?"

Elvis leaned back in his chair and looked into Vernon's eyes. "Seriously?"

Vernon just nodded, taking another drag from his smoke.

CHAPTER FORTY

Vernon left Graceland on the morning of July 6, 1977. In the trunk of his car was a large suitcase stuffed with cash. Vernon had always stashed cash away. He didn't trust banks. The Depression had taught him that the only money you could trust was the money you had hidden in a safe place. Banks really did fail periodically. He'd been there. He knew.

Not to say that the valise contained all of Vernon's money. Heck, no. He had a nice-sized bank account thanks to his son, and his stash of cash was spread out in a number of places. In truth, the valise in the trunk represented but a fraction of the cash he had amassed during Elvis' successful years.

He drove south of Memphis and picked up U.S. 78 by Olive Branch, after he had crossed into Mississippi. He cruised past Byhalia, Red Banks, and Holly Springs, heading through the Holly Springs National Forest. He zoomed past Hickory Flat and Myrtle before stopping in New Albany to fill his gas tank and buy cigarettes and snacks. He continued down past Blue Springs and Sherman until he reached Tupelo. He drove down North Broadway and parked in front of the county offices. He opened the trunk, lifted the valise out and carried it into the building.

When Vernon hit the road back to Graceland, he had two large manila envelopes with him. In one, he had an original birth certificate along with a new driver's license and Social Security card with a new number, all in the name of Elliot Polk. In the other envelope, he had similar new documents, only these were in the name of Elijah Pressler. This second envelope he would hold on to, until Elvis was settled into his new life. The first envelope would carry the documents Elvis would need to escape. He put them into the now empty valise and placed it in the trunk before he traveled home. He took an alternate route back to Memphis. He traveled west on U.S. 278, stopping at Oxford. He found a motel and grabbed an early dinner at Taylor Grocery, a rural mom-and-pop grocery store that also served blue- plate specials. He ate a hearty meal of fried catfish and hushpuppies with sweet tea and drove back to his room to sleep. In the morning, he traveled west to Batesville, and turned north onto Interstate 55, all the way back to Memphis.

Vernon was to make another trip into Mississippi before Elvis' departure. Elvis would never know the nature of this trip, even after he was safely ensconced in his new life. This was a secret Vernon would take to his grave.

On August 15, Vernon told his son that to go to the office of his dentist that night. Elvis was to complain loudly about a toothache and make a fuss about getting the dentist to take him right then, even though it was already nighttime. When he got there, a young woman drew three vials of blood from his arm. She placed them into a small ice chest, which she passed back to Elvis, telling him that he should hand it directly to Vernon when he got home. One of the last photographs of Elvis "alive" is of him driving into Graceland that night, returning from his dental appointment.

While this was all going on, Vernon drove south again into Mississippi. He drove to the capital city, Jackson. He had another valise filled with money in the trunk. He pulled up after dark at the University Medical Center. When he left, he had an empty valise and a cadaver in a body bag filled with ice, which he put into his trunk.

CHAPTER FORTY-ONE

"So Daddy's big elaborate plan made sure that he got some blood samples from me—I guess to help fool people about my death." Elie gave Stan a knowing look. "Meanwhile, he left to go somewhere, but he called from a pay phone later on to see if I actually went to the dentist."

"All this took place on the night of August 15th. I took a bunch of pills and slept most of the day," Elie said remembering the events. "When I woke around three-thirty in the afternoon, I sat with Vernon and he told me to start complaining to everyone in the house around nine about having a bad toothache. I was to raise a big ruckus and insist that the dentist take me immediately. I asked him why I was going there. He said to just shut up and do what I was being told to do. He handed me a little ice chest; the kind just big enough to hold a six pack to take to the park. Daddy said to give it to the dentist and then bring it home but only give it to him. I went back to sleep for a while. When Red woke me up at nine, I complained loudly about my tooth. I told him it hurt like hell and that I was going to get the dentist to see me that night. The dentist called and said that he could take me after eleven.

Stanley and Elie had moved to the porch as the sun was going down around them. The kids were wrapping up their playing in the street and would soon head into the house, leaving us alone.

"What was the deal about going to the dentist in the middle of the night?" Stan asked.

"Well, Daddy had a meticulous plan. He knew I would be kicking off the new tour on August 17. He had decided to help me escape but wouldn't tell me the plan. He required me to agree to do whatever he told me to do. There were going to be people who would help, and I was to follow their directions to the letter. Otherwise he would not help me. But if I did agree, he would get me to a new life. I couldn't ask any questions. I didn't understand exactly, but I had confidence in Daddy, so I agreed. He told me that after I went, we could never communicate again. That broke my heart, but I understood it was for the best. He also told me I can never get in touch with anyone from my life now. That included Priscilla and Lisa Marie. He knew that was going to be the toughest thing for me to do. But you know, I kept my word, even through today. And there were many times I almost broke it, but when I saw what Daddy had done to give me a new life, nothing could force me to change my vow. Even after his death.

"I didn't know why he said to go to the dentist in the middle of the night. But I did what he told me to do."

"So, what happened when you got to your dentist's office?" Stan asked.

Elie looked at him, "When I got there, there was a young woman. I think she was Filipino. She was a nurse of some kind, and she seated me and told me to roll up my sleeves. She gave me a shot in my right arm and had me lie down on the dentist's chair. I drifted off to sleep. Within a couple of hours, I woke up groggy. She handed me a cup of coffee. As I sat drinking the coffee, I saw a bandage on my left arm in the crease of my elbow. I asked her what that was from. She told me she had drawn three vials of blood. The blood was on ice in the cooler. When I felt better, I collected the cooler and drove home.

"I drove back to Graceland arriving, around one in the morning. It could have been a little earlier, a little later. I went to Daddy's room and gave him the cooler. He had just gotten in and was busy working on some papers. I was going to ask him why he needed my blood but thought better of it. I guess I really wanted to stay ignorant. What was going to happen was up to Daddy and the less I knew, the less likely I could screw it up.

"I went downstairs and sat with some of the boys and their girlfriends. I felt good. We talked about the upcoming tour. I told them that this tour was going to be different. I said I was excited about it and raring to go. Portland, Maine, was the next stop on August 17. I was ready."

"Elie, why would you say that to the boys? You knew Vernon was planning to get you out of there."

"Yeah, but I didn't know how or when. I just assumed that at some point on the tour, Daddy would arrange for me to 'disappear.' That sounded more logical to me."

"That's not what happened."

"Heck no, and in retrospect, it was much smarter for him to have me 'die' at Graceland. He could control it there. Besides, he knew everyone locally, so…"

Stan understood what Elie was saying. Vernon would need to control everything from the finding of the body to the autopsy and the burial in order for it to work. Vernon would have to get many valises of money and a lot of cooperation.

"I went to sleep around two thirty in the morning but didn't sleep well. I was edgy and bored. So about three thirty, I dressed and called Billy Smith, and asked him and his wife Jo to play racquetball with Ginger and me. I had this official DEA jogging suit that I had been given when I met President Nixon. I was wearing it that night. Kind of a strange irony. While we were playing, I swung at a ball and missed. I whacked myself really hard on the shin and raised a bump immediately, so we stopped while Jo went to the kitchen to get an ice pack." Elie laughed out loud for a second.

"What's so funny?" Stan asked.

Still chuckling, Elie said, "When the autopsy report came out, it never mentioned the bruise, and man, it was a large one. It turned blue despite all the ice I put on it, and it hurt like hell."

"So we sat around in the lounge area of the racquetball building. I sat at the piano, and we all sang songs until around six, when Ginger and I went up to my bedroom to read and watch television. Around eight, I told Ginger I was going into the bathroom lounge area to read. Now this where it will get interesting for you, Stanley."

"Why will I find it interesting?"

"Well that bathroom had its own back entrance. That entrance led downstairs."

Stan wore a puzzled look.

Elie said. "Stay with me on this. This is going to be one of the keys to my escape."

"Shortly after I went into the bathroom, Daddy came into the room through that rear entrance. He sat and explained that today was D- Day. I was going to 'die' today, and my new life was about to start. He asked me if I was ready to go."

CHAPTER FORTY-TWO

"A re you ready to go?"

Elvis looked stunned by the breadth of Vernon's plan. He couldn't imagine that people were going to help him pull it off. Vernon didn't tell him about the cadaver and ultimately never would. In fact, Vernon would take most of the details of the escape to his grave. Elvis would figure it out later. Vernon was a bottom-line man. Get his son safely out of Graceland, and the rest would come easy. At least, that's what he hoped for. The only one who could screw this up was his son himself.

Vernon got up from his chair and inspected his son's face. He tugged at Elvis' right eyelid and peered at it. It looked bloodshot. He also had a big blue bruise on his leg showing out from his bathrobe.

"How in the hell did you get that bruise?"

"I was playing racquetball with Ginger and the Smiths."

Vernon shook his head and wondered why his son had to go play racquetball in the middle of the night." Hopefully, nobody else would be curious about the mark except for Ginger and the Smiths. He worried about the autopsy results.

Elvis was very edgy and needed to sleep badly. Vernon told him to call Dr. Nichopolous and ask for some sleeping pills. The doctor was not there, but he spoke with the nurse and arranged for Elvis' aunt to pick them up. She prepared a few pills in a small envelope and told her husband, who had just gotten her to work, to take them outside so Elvis' aunt could pick them up.

At nine thirty, Elvis went downstairs. He received a special delivery letter, signed for it, and went to the kitchen for breakfast. His aunt arrived with the sleeping pills, but before she could give them to him, Vernon came in and snatched them away from her.

"You'll thank me for these later," he said to his son. At ten o'clock, Elvis went to the porch and brought in his newspaper. It would be the last confirmed sighting of him alive.

"When I walked into the kitchen with the paper, my father took me down into the basement. He sat me on a chair and wrapped a towel around my neck, like a barber does when you get a haircut. I started to ask him what he was doing, but he told me to shut up and trust him. Then he asked me again if I was ready to change my life? He said that he didn't intend to waste his time here, so if I weren't really ready to go through with it, I should get up, and he'd call the whole damn thing off."

CHAPTER FORTY-THREE

Vernon had arranged a big bath towel around Elvis's neck and shirt and like a barber and put electric clippers and a comb on the table. He got in front of his son and said, "Now listen, boy. Here's your chance." He thumped one finger into Elvis' chest. "It's the only chance you are going to get. I'm with you, and I'll help you. There are a lot of people who are going to help you along the way. None of them know what the other is doing except for a couple of us. If you follow directions, you will get a whole new life. If you fuck it up, a lot of people, including myself, will get into a whole heap of trouble. Do you understand?"

"I think so."

"Thinking so ain't good enough, Elvis! You're a big star. This ain't no lonely housewife disappearing or some husband running away from his responsibility and finding a nice cool beach in Mexico where he can spend his days drinking margaritas and bedding the local honeys. This is serious shit, boy! You are going to disappear.

"You are going to live as Elliot Polk for one year. And then when you are safe where I send you, you will get a whole other set of papers, and you will be that person for the rest of your life. If you have a good life, you'll get married, have a family and you'll die an old man. If you mess this up, you'll be..." He gestured at his son's robust belly, "this"! A mess, a total fucking mess. And it will be much worse than now. It will be anyone's guess how long you're going to live. And it's likely to just be the same old unhappiness, the same old nonsense.

"My boy, I didn't want to do this. But I saw your future, and you ain't going anywhere except down a bottomless pit. I see how messed up you are. I can't clean you up or make you happy. That's on you, and only you. I know that for sure. So, I am doing what you asked, and all you got to do is go for the ride. Never forget to follow the directions of everyone who is helping you. They will help you be happy. You don't know it now, but you will figure it out. You'll see. As this thing is happening, you are going to hear things about yourself on the TV or read them in the paper. You'll feel like telling someone that it ain't true. That the news is not being fair. You are going to realize that your daddy did some dreadful things for this escape plan to work. Forgive me for them and move the hell on. Forget Ginger, she is way too young for you. Forget Priscilla and Lisa Marie. I will make sure they are well taken care of.

"So, Elvis, are you ready to change your life? It ain't going to be easy being Joe Everyman, so be sure you want this."

Elvis looked at Vernon with tears streaming from his eyes. "Thank you, Daddy. I love you and will always love what you are doing for me. I'll miss you."

"Ah crap, now you're making me cry, boy." Vernon gave him a quick hug and then plugged in the electric clippers and ran them through Elvis's thick head of hair. Like when he was in the Army, Elvis was left nearly bald. Vernon ran the clippers through Elvis's eyebrows leaving them bare. He trimmed off all the hair on his face. Then he put a hot wet towel on his head, and when he removed it a few minutes later, he sprayed on shaving cream and shaved him totally bald with a razor. When that was done, he cleaned off the residue and placed a woolen stocking cap on his son's head. Elvis did not recognize himself in the mirror and that was the point. His father fished into his pocket and removed the pills that Elvis' aunt had brought home. He gave him three of them with a glass of water. Elvis drank them down.

Vernon helped him into a light jacket and swiftly moved him into the garage without being seen. By then the sleeping pills were starting to take effect and Elvis was drowsy. Vernon put him into a delivery van with "Memphis Meats" painted on the side. Inside the van was a gym pad and a pillow on the floor. Elvis lay down and went to sleep. When he was out cold, Vernon closed and locked the van and went back in the house. A young yeshiva student was waiting for him in the kitchen. This was the same young man who had hidden Elvis' car when he was staying with the Fried's. Silently, Vernon tossed the keys to the young man, who caught them and left the house.

Vernon heard the van drive out of Graceland but could not bring himself to watch it pass out of the gates.

CHAPTER FORTY-FOUR

"So, you don't remember leaving Graceland?"

Elie pursed his lips and shook his head at Stan. "I'm afraid not. I was out cold. I would stay out for hours. This guy drove me around Memphis all the rest of the day and into the night until I stirred a little. That's when he turned the truck around and took me to the Courts. He pulled up to the delivery dock and helped me out of the truck. It was nearing dusk and I had ridden around Memphis unconscious in the back of a meat truck while the whole planet had exploded with the news that Elvis Presley was dead.

"He helped me up the stairs and knocked on the Fried's door gently. They were waiting for me. Rabbi Fried told the young man to help me to the spare bedroom. He handed Rabbi Fried the envelopes with the remaining sleeping pills. I sat on the edge of the bed as he gave me some pills with a glass of water. Then the two of them got me undressed and put me to bed. I don't remember getting up for two days, although the Frieds assured me I had gotten up several times.

"When I finally woke up with real alertness, they led me into the kitchen and fed me. I told the Frieds I wanted to talk to Daddy on the phone. They looked at me and said no. Rabbi Fried showed me the newspaper and told me that Memphis was in an uproar. If I dialed Graceland, someone could trace it. I sat there, dejected, but knew he was right. I was on my journey."

CHAPTER FORTY-FIVE

For Rabbi Fried, this was his hardest decision about life and death since the war. The Ukrainians had destroyed his home. The work camps had nearly killed him and he had spent his life praying for the souls of all who had died and asking forgiveness for his choices that kept him alive while others died around him.

Thinking back to the night Vernon had come to their apartment. Vernon felt helpless about his son. He didn't really understand why Elvis was so messed up. So, it wasn't Vernon who had figured out what was necessary. Rather, Rabbi Fried guided him to use his wile and talents to plan for Elvis' escape from Graceland.

And the Rabbi felt terrible about it in every respect that could be imagined. He was to repeat a trick that he had to escape the Nazis. It had worked then, even though the Nazis were always wary about escape attempts. Substituting an already-dead body for his own had led to his successful escape. Now, he couldn't bear thinking about it.

The renowned Rabbi Abraham Aaron had escaped Buchenwald, and when he came to the United States, he met a young David Fried as a yeshiva student in Manhattan. They would walk to the water together over the hills of Washington Heights and discuss the Torah and life in general. Rabbi Aaron was a Rosh Yeshiva (one of the head rabbis) at the great Orthodox Seminary there and David Fried was a penniless student hoping to become a rabbi someday under Rabbi Aaron's tutelage. It was from Rabbi Aaron that David Fried learned to make peace with his wartime experiences. As the Rabbi was fond of saying to him, "Sometimes we faced decisions in the war that we should not have had to make. We must trust that G-d guided us to the right decision, even if it didn't seem the right decision in our own mind."

That statement remained crystal clear in Rabbi Fried's mind when he spoke with Vernon Presley. Vernon was an uneducated and somewhat rough-hewn individual. But he was not stupid. In fact, without having to have it spelled out to him in plain words, this seemingly parochial man had been able to devise a cunning plan. Vernon did not tell the rabbi how he was going to accomplish this plan, realizing that it would be unfair for him to even speculate about the particulars he was dreaming up. Vernon understood that the fewer people who knew of all the details, the better. What he needed to know, assuming Vernon could pull it off and get Elvis out of Graceland, was if the Rabbi could get him the rest of the way.

Miriam Fried answered instantly, "We will help you," she said, giving her husband "the look" as he showed reticence.

Vernon asked, "How would you do that? Where would you send him?"

Her husband was staring at the table, so she turned to their visitor. "We will get him where he needs to be. For the same reason, we don't want to know the details on how you are going to get him out of Graceland, we will not tell you how we will do this. This would be the best. It would protect you and your family. There is too much at stake and others will be involved for it all to work. So we will only tell you that we have been successful." Then she looked at Vernon seriously, "Or not! But we will tell you nothing else."

"Can you do it?" Vernon asked.

Miriam answered, "We survived the Nazis and the Ukrainians to get here. Do you think we did that without being cunning?" Vernon squinted skeptically. She gave him a hard stare, fiddling with a fork on the table in front of her. "We will take care of your boy. We will. I promise you that." Vernon tensed drifting off into his thoughts while he evaluated the earnestness of this old woman. Afterward, he nodded and let his gaze fall.

Rabbi Fried met Vernon's eyes. "Mr. Presley, you understand that if we do this, Elvis must do whatever we say, go wherever we send him, and trust the people we tell him to. He cannot be impulsive or do what he wants. He can never deviate. It will endanger everything. I am an old man. My wife and I have been through the wringer. Who can number our days in this world? You need to understand that we are performing a mitzva for your son. He is a Jew, Vernon, a full Jew under our ancient laws. We are, in a strange way, ransoming him from danger. Not in the way someone is kidnapped and threatened. Not like in the war, where we ransomed people from the Nazis. We are ransoming him from himself, from the damage he has done to himself. And not just the damage that he has done to his physical body. There is a beautiful soul within him. We call it a Neshama. And this beautiful Neshama is waiting to find its real potential. By helping him, we are ransoming that soul from…well…you know. In your own way, you will be doing the same. At least we hope so."

Vernon looked at them but said nothing. He understood. He shook the rabbi's hand and went home.

Miriam looked at her husband. She reached up to his face and touched his cheek.

He said, "Miriam, what have we done just now? Should we be doing this? Can we do this?"

She didn't respond. Nothing more needed to be said.

The next few days were spent on the phone and writing letters to Brooklyn.

CHAPTER FORTY-SIX

Elvis had awakened to the reality that his former life was now over. He read eagerly in the Memphis Commercial Appeal the details of his "death." In the three days since he left Graceland, he had learned enough to estimate the timeline of his disappearance. Memphis and the world were in shock, and his father was using that to his advantage.

From what he could gather from the radio, TV and the papers, Ginger had awakened from a long nap somewhere between two and two thirty in the afternoon. She called around, trying to find Elvis, and then remembered he had gone into the bathroom lounge earlier to read.

It was there that Ginger had discovered his body on the floor in front of the commode with reading material strewn on the floor besides him.

Elvis found it fascinating the amount of detail in the reports. The body was found in a "kneeling" position. His knees were almost touching his chin. He was sort of resting on his forearms, which were bent under him. His face was planted in the carpet. Ginger didn't move him at all. She had been frightened just by the sight of him. She yelled for help and ran out of the bathroom, jumping back into bed, crying. Artie, a friend, and employee came upstairs and spotted the body, but didn't move it. He ran down to find Vernon. Vernon sent everyone downstairs and called Dr. Nichopolous.

The Memphis Fire Department was called and soon an ambulance from Engine House 29 arrived at Graceland. It was obvious he had been dead for some time and rigor mortis had started to set in, the paramedics tried to stretch out the body and perform CPR. This was obviously unsuccessful, and they gave up pretty quickly. By two forty-eight in the afternoon, they were transporting the body to Baptist Memorial Hospital, which was about seven minutes away. Upon arrival He was declared DOA. At three o'clock, Vernon and the rest of the family were told he was dead. A half hour later, a press release announced it to the world.

By seven thirty that evening the medical examiner had performed an initial autopsy external viewing of the body. By eight, Dr. Nichopolous and the medical examiner for Shelby County, spoke at a press conference.

The next day, he would lie in state at Graceland, in the foyer by the front door. Elvis was astonished at the audacity. "I wonder how Daddy had pulled that off. Where did he get the body? Vernon must have gotten some makeup artist. That's a lot of people to fool."

In fact, it was amazing. Some 50,000 to 100,000 people paid their respects. Visitors were hustled past the body in quick order and the doors were closed at six thirty sharp.

A lifelong friend of Elvis described to reporters the mood inside Graceland. "Things are very quiet; they're just sitting around the coffin. Some are crying, most just sitting there subdued. Ginger seemed okay. Priscilla, not so well. She was taking it very hard."

On August 19, a brief funeral service was held in the Music Room in Graceland. The funeral was private. The mourners left Vernon alone with the coffin after the service was over. Vernon Presley led the procession with his car around three thirty in the afternoon. Behind Vernon's car was the white hearse that bore an un-draped coffin. The guests and family members left the grounds behind the hearse. Priscilla, holding onto Lisa Marie, was in the second car. They moved along to Forest Hill Midtown Cemetery.

The coffin was placed in a mausoleum, sealed and mortared in place, and covered with a marble slab.

Elvis marveled as he read the description of his burial, saying to himself, "So that's how Daddy did it."

CHAPTER FORTY-SEVEN

Despite the fact that Graceland was in a state of hysterical turmoil, Vernon was as calm and collected as he could be. Once the body was loaded into the ambulance, he jumped into the back with the body. He carried a briefcase with him, and he sat on the end of the gurney while the ambulance flew through the streets of Memphis to the hospital. Once there, Vernon jumped out of the ambulance and disappeared inside. Soon a doctor appeared in the emergency room. He was not a member of the ER team: he was one of the bigwigs in the hospital. He pushed aside the team of residents and wheeled the body directly into an operating room. He donned a gown, gloves, and a mask. He stripped the body of Elvis' robe and laid it on the table. Vernon slipped into the room.

"Vernon, give me some of those sheets over there in that rolling bin."

He strode over to the other side of the room, reached into a standing bin, and removed three folded sheets. They were warm to the touch. They had just been brought up from the laundry. He handed them to the doctor, who directed Vernon to roll the body onto one side. He slipped part of the sheet underneath and had Vernon roll the body over onto its other side. Once the sheet was secure under the body, they stretched it out and wrapped the body carefully, securing the sheet with tape around the head, the neck, the elbows, the waist, and around the knees. They taped the area around the ankles securely and then placed a second sheet on top. They moved the body to another gurney and called the medical examiner's office. Vernon handed the briefcase to the doctor before he left the room.

Vernon stayed with the body until the men from the ME's office arrived and he walked out to their ambulance with the body. He handed the attendants a manila envelope addressed to the medical examiner and marked "SPECIMENS - FRAGILE." In that envelope were the three vials of Elvis' blood drawn the night before. Also inside was a second envelope with two stacks of hundred-dollar bills. Vernon waved toward the ambulance as it drove away back into the hospital.

Shortly, he would be informed that his son had died from a massive heart attack.

Vernon returned to Graceland to try to get some sleep. He had just stretched out in his bed when the phone on the nightstand rang. He rolled over to pick it up. A voice on the other end, whispered in a European accent, "Your beautiful postcard arrived a few minutes ago. Thank you so much for sending it. We will treasure it always." Vernon hung up the phone, smiled, rolled back over, and fell deeply asleep.

In the morning, Vernon went into the garage and opened one of the standing bins. He reached inside and, with a bit of extra effort, he lifted a mannequin of his son out and laid it on the ground. It was a good likeness, he admitted. Soon, the medical examiner's truck would arrive to deliver Elvis's body to Graceland for preparation and viewing. The truck pulled into the garage but was empty. The attendants lifted the covered mannequin into the truck and delivered it to the mortuary. Under the "body", Vernon had placed another envelope. The mortician, finding the envelope, prepared the mannequin and placed it in the coffin that would be used for the viewing and for the burial. The mortuary delivered "Elvis" back to the mansion about an hour later. The coffin was placed by the front door and for the first time ever, Graceland was opened to the public.

People streamed by the coffin and were moved steadily along for hours. Vernon could not believe how many people came through the house. At six thirty in the evening, he closed the coffin. There were still thousands of people waiting to pay their respects, unfortunately, they would miss out.

CHAPTER FORTY-EIGHT

Elie went into the house for a few moments and returned with a stack of plastic bags. Contained inside, untouched for many years, were copies of the Memphis Commercial Appeal, The New York Times, USA Today, Time Magazine and Newsweek. He had taped them shut, so it was obvious they were an undisturbed keepsake. Elie showed Stanley these periodicals which all chronicled the day he "died."

"I've had these hidden away in the basement for years. I wasn't sure if I would ever want to read them again." He gestured to the stack. "Stan, you take them. They will probably help you more than me. I can only tell you the story. Read for yourself how they all got the story wrong. I can't blame them. They had no inkling that any of this was going on. I used to look at them occasionally and laugh about how everyone just believed my death. I used to get afraid when the people who claimed it was a hoax would present something, usually on the internet, which "proved" I was alive."

"Were any of them right?"

"They all were right! I am alive! They just had the details wrong. Their misconceptions were so comical. It was crazy to read their theories. They had no idea, I tell you. But once in a while, their craziness got a little too close. Then I would shut off the computer or the radio or whatever. I couldn't stand to know what they were saying. No one, and I mean no one, ever figured out how Daddy pulled it off. Even I have no real idea how he did it, and that was the way he wanted it. Not Priscilla, not Lisa Marie, not the boys, not even Ginger knew. Daddy had set the body in such a way that Ginger never saw the face. Nobody ever guessed what happened. If they suspected something, they never mentioned it publicly. I suspect that the gravity of what he had done rested heavily on Daddy. He died less than two years later, on June 26, 1979. Had a heart attack and that was that. Heck, his mom, my Grandma Minnie Mae, outlived him. She died on May 8, 1980, at eighty-nine. Daddy was only sixty-three when he passed. Holding in this big secret must have run the gas out of his tank. That and the smoking and of course, the drinking."

"Elie, I've got to ask this. Vernon pulls off this big hoax and now you are sitting half drugged out, with a shaved head and eyebrows in Rabbi Fried's apartment in the Courts. What happened after that to get you to be here in Brooklyn?"

"Fair question."

"Damned straight it is."

Elie and Stan both laughed.

"And I'll tell you that tomorrow. It's late and I'm tired. I'm going to go to sleep. You will have to sit on that for a spell. Don't forget the newspapers."

He got up and went inside. Stan collected the papers and went into his house as well.

CHAPTER FORTY-NINE

"I stayed with the Frieds for two months." Elie chuckled and added, "Or rather, they watched over me for two months. They fed me and nourished me, and probably the most important thing they did was wean me off all of the drugs." His face grew serious. "That was hard, but it was something I had to do."

"How did that go? Did you get the shakes or other physical reactions?" Stan had seen some good athletes taken out by drugs over the years, and he knew how bad it could get.

He reached for another sip of morning coffee in the welcome shade of Elie's front porch.

"I shook a lot at first. Nausea, bad headaches. They wouldn't let me have anything for the pain other than an occasional aspirin. Miriam fed me soup for the first week. Soup and tea. That's all I remember from the first week. Soup and tea! Then came the Sabbath, and they brought me into the dining room for the traditional meal. I ate and ate. More soup, fish, chicken. They didn't give me wine, only grape juice for the kiddush. She baked yummy challah and I wolfed it all down. Rabbi Fried told me to eat slower or I would get sick, but I didn't listen. Later that night, I paid the price."

"How so?"

"Threw up and had bad stomach cramps. I should have listened, but my head was still so into indulging my body that I couldn't resist all the tasty food. By lunch the next day, I was eating normal portions and felt a whole lot better. No repeat performances, one might say."

"But what did you do while you were staying with them? What did you do with your time? Didn't you go stir-crazy?

"Of course. Rabbi Fried knew it would be hard for me to just stay in their cramped apartment, especially in the Memphis heat. Every night when it got cooler, he and I would traipse around the neighborhood. I wore a black suit with a white shirt. I had tzitzit hanging out, like a Yeshiva student. In fact, we often walked to the yeshiva. We would sit at one of the tables, the rabbi would take out one of the books and we would study together. He said that now that I was certain that I was a Jew, I should live like one. He told me that it would be a 'marathon, not a sprint' and I would be challenged throughout my life. He said that he hoped I would be an observant Jew ultimately. He used the expression 'a Shomer Shabbos Jew.' He was speaking of someone who kept the commandments and observed the Sabbath.

"I just was following along, trying not to be noticed. Sort of keeping my head down and the men in the yeshiva never took notice of me. I looked like them, and I was learning with the rabbi. He told me not to shave and just let my beard grow out as much as possible. It itched like crazy for a couple of weeks, but then it stopped and I was fine. What I found interesting about the process was that my beard had begun turning gray. Not like it is today, all white, just enough gray to show my age. My hair started to slowly grow in, but that took a long time. He took me for a haircut after about a month. There wasn't much to cut, but at least it was trimmed and neat. I started to grow side curls, but they took forever to become like these." He fingered one, curling it around his index finger. "I tried not to mess up the kosher kitchen, but I did mix up some of the silverware at first. Before long. I was comfortable with where things went, what to do, and what not to do.

"I got into a rhythm that became familiar and nice. I learned the blessings and how to get up in the morning, pray and be at one with G-d and with myself.

"After six weeks, Rabbi Fried came into my room, and handed me two velvet bags. I opened the larger bag and found a white and black Talis (Prayer Shawl). In the second bag were Tefillin (Phylacteries). You know what those are, right?"

Stan nodded." Actually, I still have mine from my bar mitzvah."

"When was the last time you put them on?"

"At my bar mitzvah." Stan smirked.

Elie smiled back. "You should put them on. At least once in a while."

"I wouldn't even know how to."

"I can show you. It's really not hard."

"Someday, maybe."

"Why not right now? Go get them - we'll put them on you."

Stan shrank away from doing that. "It's okay, Elie. Some other time."

"What are you waiting for Stanley? Go get them. We will do it now."

Stanley seeing that there was no way out, got up and said, "Well, if you insist."

"I do insist. You will be surprised, Stanley. It will do you some good."

Stan shrugged and went into the house. He returned shortly with a small Talis bag and his Tefillin. Elie went into the house for a small prayer book.

Stan said the blessing for donning the Talis and then watched as Elie took out the Tefillin. First, Elie placed the hand Tefillin on his arm and told Stanley to repeat the blessing after him. Elie tightened the box in place and wrapped the strap around Stan's arm seven times. Then he placed the head Tefillin on Stan as they said the blessing for it as well. In the last step, he wrapped the strap from the arm onto Stan's fingers. Elie opened up the prayer book to the Shema, and together they read the prayer. As they were doing this,

Stanley started to cry. He started to tremble, and his insides hurt. His tears flowed without restraint. When the prayer was over, Stanley sat back down and tried to gather himself.

"Are you all right, Stanley?"

Stan dabbed at his eyes with the edge of the Talis and nodded.

"Stanley, you have nothing to fear. You are experiencing the power of Tefillin, as I did when Rabbi Fried taught me to wear mine. It is an overpowering thing. It was for me then, and sometimes even now I find it overpowering. It's the pintele yid in you coming out. Welcome back, my friend."

CHAPTER FIFTY

And just as Isaac said, the phone call came. It was Rabbi Fried, who was mulling over a problem. The problem was Elvis.

Rabbi Abraham Aaron was now well into his late eighties. While he felt like his bones creaked when he moved, his mind remained agile and very quick. Escaping Buchenwald had been no easy task. Like most escapees, he did not dwell on the details nor the choices he had to make at the time. Sometimes, in moments of quiet contemplation, he would remember and shudder. Those were hard memories to relive. But he always remembered that without G-d's guidance, he would never have gotten to the here and now. He would calm himself and return to his Torah.

Isaac had appeared at various stages in his life. The first time was when he was a boy of six or seven. He did not believe that this man who had appeared to him was real. He told his father about the visitation. His father, Reb Moses, was an exceeding spiritual man. He asked his rabbi about what his son had encountered. The Rabbi questioned the boy for some time in his study. When he sent the boy home, he called for the father and told him that his son would someday be a great rabbi. He added that his son had been given a very unique gift. There would be times when his son would be guided by the great Patriarch, Isaac.

Abraham grew up to be that great rabbi. He survived the war and the resettlement camps, he moved to New York. There he taught in the great yeshiva in Washington Heights for many years. He ultimately settled in Brooklyn and had a large following of people who came to him for advice and comfort.

When his old student Rabbi Fried called from Memphis, Rabbi Aaron was not surprised. They discussed the problem in great detail. Rabbi Aaron understood the world and had always stayed aware of the happenings around him. To Rabbi Fried's surprise, he knew who Elvis Presley was said he would help. He realized this was the person Isaac had spoken of, and he knew why Isaac had asked him to solve this problem. And he would.

He instructed Rabbi Fried and hung up the phone. He mused to himself about whether this Elvis was up to the task. He got up from his table and poured himself a cup of tea. As he sat and contemplated, he was aware that if Isaac had visited him about this, it was out of his control. It would be all in the end.

CHAPTER FIFTY-ONE

Vernon had done everything he could to get Elvis out of Graceland. Now that his son was safely ensconced in the Frieds' apartment, Vernon worked hard to keep the Elvis enterprise alive. But he did this while wondering when his son would be moved out of Memphis proper. His biggest fear was that Elvis might have a change of heart and pop up one day at Graceland. He had not spoken with the Frieds in six weeks, and finally he couldn't stand it.

He drove onto a side road and found a phone booth. He pushed some dimes into the slot and dialed Rabbi Fried. Miriam answered the kitchen phone and said Elvis was doing fine and that in a couple more weeks they would send him to another safe house. Vernon was tempted to ask to talk with his son, and Miriam sensed that. She considered handing the phone to Elvis, but before she could, Vernon hung up. She realized that her impulse would have been a huge mistake and reproved herself about it.

She did not tell her husband about the conversation with Vernon, figuring it would unnerve him. Vernon did not call back, and he stayed at Graceland.

In the meantime, Elvis was getting healthier by the day. He worked hard at his religious studies and was reading Hebrew pretty well. He did not really understand what he was reading, but his pronunciation was good, and he knew how to pray the three daily services. On the Sabbath, he knew how to make Kiddush, break bread, and say the Grace after Meals. He listened intently when the rabbi explained something he did not understand. Elvis felt comfortable with the arrangement so far and kept his end of the bargain to not leave by himself.

When Elvis looked in the mirror, he saw a decent growth of beard and his shaved head was sporting a short crop of hair. He also saw something different in himself. It was a peace he had not known in a long time and he was satisfied.

Every evening, after dinner and their neighborhood stroll, the rabbi would come home and go into his study, close the door and speak on the phone with Rabbi Aaron in Brooklyn. Soon the next phase of Elvis' escape was to come to fruition.

One Wednesday night Rabbi Fried came into Elvis' bedroom. "Elie, you have been with us for about two months. You've spent Rosh Hashana and Yom Kippur with us and Sukkoth as well. You've done well. But your journey to a new life must go on now."

Elvis blinked at him. "I've loved being here with you and Miriam. Where am I going from here?"

"I can't tell you. You'll find out when you get there. It is only a waystation to your final destination and your new life."

"How long will I be there?"

"I'm unsure, and it will be out of my hands. I got you this far and now other people will take you further. There will be challenges along the way, but if you remember what I've taught you and practice it, you will be just fine. But it's too hard for Mrs. Fried and me to keep your presence here a secret. People will start to question. Surely, they will find you out. It's best that you go now. I hope I've taught you well enough that you can survive temptation and go back out into the world."

"I won't fail you, Rabbi. I promise."

"I appreciate your saying that. I hope so, for your sake. The world will be most unkind if you are found out. For me, I am an old man, but for you it could be very tough. Stay strong."

The rabbi brought in the big valise that Vernon had sent along with Elvis in the van when he first left Graceland. Elvis packed his belongings and came into the kitchen to say goodbye to Miriam and to Rabbi Fried. Around ten, two young men from the yeshiva knocked on the apartment door. Elvis went with them to a big Chevy station wagon and got into the back seat. The three of them drove north.

They drove for twelve hours through the night and into the early morning. They dropped Elvis off by a modest house in West Bloomfield, a suburb of Detroit, Michigan. He was brought into the house by a young Orthodox Jewish couple named the Brenners. They introduced themselves as Chaim and Chana. They called him Elie. They didn't know his real identity, only that Rabbi Aaron had asked them to house him for a couple of weeks, and they were willing to do so.

They had two children. One was a boy around a year and a half. The other was a newborn boy about two months old. They gave Elvis a room upstairs near the nursery. He unpacked his things and came downstairs. They fed him lunch and Chaim said it was time for him to go to the yeshiva. "Would you like to go with me, Elie?"

Elvis was exhausted from riding the whole night and said, "If you don't mind, I've been up all night. I think I would like to get some sleep." Chaim nodded and left the house. Elvis went upstairs to rest and quickly fell asleep.

For the next two weeks, he integrated himself with this young family. He got up early and went to synagogue with Chaim. He spent most of the day in the yeshiva learning, came home and ate with the family and played with the kids. Shabbos came, and he joined fully with them. Rabbi Fried had taught him well, and no one was the wiser that he grew up completely isolated from the culture.

During his second week with the Brenners, he developed cabin fever. One afternoon, he took the bus into Detroit to get away for the day. As the bus got into Dearborn, he jumped off and looked around. He had been to Detroit before and this looked familiar to him. He was also starving but had forgotten to pack some food. He was about to fail his first real challenge as a Jew. He walked into a local McDonalds and ordered a couple of Big Macs, fries, a Coke and an apple pie. He sat down and dug in.

The food was delicious, and he drained the last of the coke, very satisfied. When he left the restaurant, he wandered for a while and then started to feel bad. His belly hurt and he threw up in the street. He didn't know whether he felt bad for deliberately eating non-kosher food or because he felt guilty for breaking his promise to Rabbi Fried. Either way, it didn't matter. He got on a bus back to West Bloomfield and never ate non-kosher food again.

Right after his second Sabbath, he was visited by the two young men who had brought him to Michigan. They told him it was time to travel again. He packed his bags, said goodbye to the Brenners, and got back into the station wagon that had brought him this far. They drove away to the next leg of his journey.

CHAPTER FIFTY-TWO

The three men drove east through the night. They passed Cleveland, Ohio. Then on to Pittsburgh. From there, they traveled across Pennsylvania, passing through Philadelphia before finally arriving at the Town of Lakewood, New Jersey, mid-morning. There in Lakewood was the Great Yeshiva. He and his possessions were dropped off on the sidewalk in front of that building. He seemed a little confused about what to do next. Some young men saw his predicament and helped him by grabbing his bags and escorting him to the office.

When he introduced himself in the office, to his surprise, he was expected. He received the key to a dorm room that he would have to himself. Looking around, he saw that it was a neat little room with two beds and desks with two closets for clothing. There was a sink for washing. Some sheets and pillowcases were folded on the foot of the bed. He unpacked and, being exhausted from the long trip and tension promptly fell asleep in his clothes.

Elie awoke in time for dinner. He walked downstairs to the dining room and saw a cavernous room packed full of young men and older boys. He gingerly wove his way to the serving line. The fellow running the line said, "You're new here?" Elie nodded. "No problem," he said. "Grab a plate and serve yourself." He surveyed the line and took a piece of chicken, some potato kugel, bread, and juice. He went to wash and sat down to eat. After he ate, he searched for the study hall. To his amazement, there had to be at least a thousand men in there. The din was deafening. All these men sitting in small groups learning the Torah. They were oblivious to the noise. He wondered if he would ever get to the point where he would not notice all the goings-on around him. He wandered through the whole room dazed. Finally, Elie took an empty seat waiting for the evening service to begin. The room quieted when they heard a bang on the lectern, the praying commenced. When it was over, a number of the men left, but a respectable number stayed and continued to learn. He buried his head in his prayer book, unsure what else to do.

CHAPTER FIFTY-THREE

"So, I end up in the Great Yeshiva in Lakewood," Elie said. "There are those who bragged it was the largest yeshiva in the world. Some of the men had also studied in the Mir Yeshiva in Jerusalem. They would argue that Mir was bigger. I couldn't say, I've never seen the Mir. All I know was that this was one huge school. I was so lost that first night. Of course, I knew nobody, and I wasn't sure what to do. But the next day that would change.

"I came down in the morning to pray. The room was full of men dressed in their talises and tefillin. They swayed and bowed in a repetitive way I had seen before but never really understood. I tried to pray but was distracted by everything around me. After we were done, people moved into the dining hall for breakfast. I grabbed some bread and eggs and sat down to eat. People sat alongside me, greeting me quickly and gobbled their meals. Really, it was like watching machines working. They would finish and quickly pray the Grace after Meals. Then they were out of there. All around me, it was the same! Maybe a handful of people lingered over their food. I remember watching in disbelief. I turned to my food and ate at my own pace. I got up and poured a cup of coffee and sat back down. I became aware of a tall man standing next to me. He wore one of those long coats that rabbis wear. He had on a large black hat that he removed as he sat down next to me at the table.

'Elijah?' he said as he reached out to shake my hand. I smiled and answered, 'Yes, that's me. Most people call me Elie.'

'Elie it is! Welcome, I am Rabbi Menachem Zweig. I am one of the roshei yeshivas here in Lakewood. Rabbi Aaron in Brooklyn and I have had several conversations about you.'

"I asked him," 'What have you heard about me, sir?'

'I know what I know. It's only important that you are earnest about living this new life. I run the program here for baalei teshuva (people becoming religious). I am here to help you achieve as much as you can while you stay here.'

'Do you know how long that will be?'

"He shook his head. 'I am not sure. It's close to Chanukah time, so, you will stay at least until before Passover. It might be longer. That is partially up to you.'

'Do you know where I will ultimately end up?'

'That will be up to Rabbi Aaron.' I asked. 'I'm sure it will be in due time.'

'Who is this Rabbi Aaron? I've heard his named used in hushed tones. Will I meet him someday?'

"Rabbi Zweig's laugh was gentle, 'Almost certainly. He is very old, but vigorous. He will certainly want to meet you, and he will help you in many ways. For now, Elie, let's get you set up. The first order of the day is to go shopping for clothes. Are you done eating?'

"I nodded and told him I had to pray the Grace after Meals. He pointed to the lobby. 'When you're done, meet me there.'

"We went to a men's store and he outfitted me with four black suits, six white shirts, two black ties, two black skullcaps and a black fedora hat. I also got two pairs of black shoes and a bunch of black socks. I didn't need underwear, but I was also given three pairs of tzitzit.

'Because you are older, you will learn with the married men in the Kollel.' He told me. 'There is a small stipend to help you with incidentals. Now you will be able to fit right in. Keep growing your beard. It is a good sign and will help you.'

"I didn't understand that then," Elie said to Stan. "I do now!"

"How so?"

"Oh, my friend, a long beard is a sign for prosperity, and I don't mean just financial. Plenty of wonderful things have happened in my life. I say to myself that it is, in part, because I grew this long beard."

"Elie, you realize that's ridiculous."

"To you, it would seem so. To me everything that has happened is the work of G-d. I sit here today because G-d willed it. I just followed the plan."

"But Elie, what about the cancer?"

"That's also G-d's plan. I can't fight that. I live as long as he allows me to. No doctor can change that. No doctor is G-d. All a doctor can do is carry out the will of G-d. If most doctors understood that, we would have better doctors. Don't you think?"

Stan didn't answer right away. "Well, I guess."

Elie laughed, "Well I don't. That's the difference between us. But it's alright. Someday, you too will understand."

Stan shook his head in wonderment.

"Anyway," Elie said, "for the next six months, I stayed in the yeshiva in Lakewood. I sat every morning and afternoon in the study hall. My Hebrew improved, and I learned from all these amazing texts, like the Talmud and the Code of Jewish Law. I fit in fine, lived quietly, and made friends among the older Kollel students. I was invited to their homes for the Sabbath and the holidays. When Purim came, I got a little tipsy, but not so much that I lost my inhibitions. Rabbi Zweig saw me every day and ensured that if I needed anything, I was able to get it. I would go out in town some nights to stretch my legs. It was a bitterly cold winter that year. You remember the Blizzards of 1977 to 1978? I was walking around outside. The temperature dropped thirty- one degrees over the course of four hours. Man was it cold! And we were all snowed in. But life inside the yeshiva didn't change much during the cleanup, which took days. It was even worse in Buffalo. They were trapped inside for weeks."

"I remember," Stanley said. "I was trapped inside. Thought I was going to go stark raving mad trapped in the apartment."

"Soon, however, it started to warm up and life returned to some sense of normal. One Sabbath, we had a scholar-in-residence, the great Rabbi Abraham Aaron from Brooklyn. This was about two weeks before Passover. He came into the study hall and lectured for two hours after the morning service. Riveting stuff. I didn't want to leave. He spoke about the meaning of the Exodus from Egypt and how it impacts us to this day. Afterward I went up to the front and introduced myself. He was a small man, kind of wiry. Black three-piece suit and the big hat some of the rabbi's wear, with the upturned brim. He shook my hand swiftly and scrutinized my face. Then he left the room without another word to me.

"I must tell you that I was kind of shocked. I mean, this was the person to whom I had entrusted my entire existence, and he barely acknowledged me. My ego reared up, and I had an ugly thought enter my head. Doesn't he recognize me? I am Elvis Presley! The great Elvis Presley!

"I was so pissed off that I stomped out of the study hall and went up to my room. Rabbi Zweig had watched my reaction from the side of the room. He intercepted me as I was about to go up the stairs.

'Elie, don't get mad.'

'Why not?'

"Rabbi Zweig sighed. He had so little information about the man he had mentored for months. He had often wondered about his protégé and what his deal was. He told me later that Rabbi Aaron had only instructed him to mentor me, see to my needs and ensure that I grew in learning and practice.

"He looked up at me from the bottom of the stairway. 'Listen, I don't have your whole story, Elie. I don't know who you were before you came to Lakewood, but I think it would be safe to say Rabbi Aaron was not going to acknowledge you in front of everyone. Believe me, he knows you are here, and he will be talking to you soon. Don't get excited."

"I nodded and climbed up the stairs."

CHAPTER FIFTY-FOUR

braham looked up at the man who had extended his hand. With a fleeting look, he tried to size him up. He was taller than the old rabbi thought he would be. As he left the study hall, he mused, "So, this is Elvis Presley?" On some level, Rabbi Aaron was surprised that Elie was even still there. But he understood that was the skeptic in him. He did not fail to recognize the hand of G-d in the fact that Elvis Presley stood in front of him.

He was met by Rabbi Zweig as they exited the building. He was walking nearby to have lunch with friends. Rabbi Zweig accompanied him.

"Is he ready?" Abraham asked in a quiet, serious voice.

"I think so."

"Any problems with him?"

"None. Actually, he has melted into the yeshiva without anyone taking particular notice. Elie has a study partner, and a few friends or acquaintances. Otherwise, he is just another Kollel guy."

"I want to meet with him after Shabbos."

"He wants to meet you. He seemed disappointed that you scarcely acknowledged him."

"He will get over it."

"I will arrange for you two to meet. Would you like it to be at the Yeshiva or someplace else?"

"Not the yeshiva. Everyone would know about it soon enough.

Too many questions. No, not there." He pondered as they walked. "Bring him home with you after Maariv (the evening service). I will visit you there, and we will talk."

"Okay," Rabbi Zweig answered. Then stopping in his tracks, he turned to Rabbi Aaron and asked, "Rabbi, who is this man? I have tended to him for nearly five months. He is a wonderful person. I have had him in my home for Sabbath meals, and he is so polite and so nice. You asked me to take this man on, and he's been a pleasure. But I have to wonder who he is and why you sent him to me? Really, what is his purpose being here?"

Abraham patted his colleague's shoulder. He smiled and said, "Menachem," and then he shook his head no. He seemed about to say something but didn't. He simply turned Rabbi Zweig around, and they continued walking without saying another word.

When Abraham arrived at his host's home, he said goodbye to Rabbi Zweig and went inside.

Rabbi Zweig continued on, he kept wondering how Elie had been with him for months without revealing his identity or why he was so important to Rabbi Abraham Aaron.

CHAPTER FIFTY-FIVE

"After the Sabbath was over, Rabbi Zweig brought me to his home for what I thought was going to be a light dinner," Elie said. "When we arrived, Mrs. Zweig offered me a seat in the dining room, and her husband went into his study briefly. He emerged and the family gathered to make Havdalah, (a set of prayers formally closing out the Sabbath). After that, we all sat and ate. Rabbi Zweig periodically checked his watch and then rejoined the conversation at the table.

"Around an hour after we had come home, the doorbell rang. Rabbi Zweig left the table to answer the door, and in came Rabbi Aaron. He removed his coat and hat and joined us all at the table. He looked at me briefly, waved to Mrs. Zweig, and put some food on his plate. He got up to wash and broke bread, and he started talking with Rabbi Zweig about a curious case he was learning in the Talmud.

"Soon, the meal was over. We recited the Grace after Meals and I was invited to join the two rabbis in the Zweig study. Rabbi Aaron settled into a chair and invited me to do the same. Rabbi Zweig left the study and closed the door behind him.

"Rabbi Aaron stared at me for what seemed like forever. It was just a few seconds. He had piercing blue eyes and an impressive white beard. For such a small man, he had a huge presence. Dressed immaculately in a black three-piece suit with a pocket-watch chain on his vest, he adjusted his skullcap's position back and leaned forward in his chair. I was drawn to his shoes and the way he had his right foot turned in at the ankle, in what looked like an impossible and very painful angle. But he was indifferent to it as if it had always been his way to sit.

'Elvis Presley?'

'Yes sir. That is me.'

"He nodded. 'I am sorry if you felt slighted by my greeting in the study hall. I did not want to draw any unnecessary attention to you in front of all those men.'

'I understand, sir. It's all right. Thank you.'

'Are you well, Elvis?' I nodded back at him. "It has to have been disorienting for you up until now.' He stopped and pinched at the inside corners of his eyes. 'You've done an excellent job so far staying…let us say, under the radar.' He smiled and leaned back into the chair, absently tapping his fingers against his mouth. 'Elvis, is this what you really wanted?'

'I don't understand, sir.'

'Are you sure this is right for you?' He hunched forward as if to whisper.

'What I mean is that you gave up everything in your life. Everything. Your family, your father, even your little girl. You gave up your friends, your money, your fame. You have let us take you far from your roots.'

"I started to protest, but he held up a hand. I sat back saying nothing."

'Elvis, let's talk about this. I have helped you to get to this place and did it willingly because of circumstances I can never explain to you. You are obviously a good man who has gone through your fair share of troubles. But the reality of all this is that you sit here having faked your own death.'

"When he said that, I wanted to crawl into a hole.

"Rabbi Aaron continued, 'People who love you took extraordinary risks to get you here. So, I have to ask you, was your life so bad before, that you felt compelled to seek out such a drastic change?'

"I answered him with one word. 'Yes.'

"He paused and closed his eyes in thought. Then his eyes snapped open, and he asked, 'Why?'

"I focused on the question. At first, escaping my life was about relieving the stress. At that point, Stanley, I was pretty calm. My life had a routine, limited as it might be, but I felt comfortable that every day was essentially the same. When it occurred to me though, I sometimes missed the road trips and making movies with stunning women and all of that attention.

'Rabbi, I will not pretend to you. Sometimes I do miss it all.'

'Not surprising. You had an incredible life. Just no self-control!"

"I smiled. He had a point 'That's definitely the truth, sir.'

'You have been off the drugs for many months. Do you ever feel the urge to get high?'

'The truth is that I haven't felt the need since I left Memphis. No, that's not true. I forgot about all that once I came here to Lakewood.'

'Do you like it here?'

'Most of the time. Sometimes I'm lonely. I sometimes thought about going into New York, but I was afraid someone would recognize me.'

'Why would people recognize you? And even if they got a fleeting glance, I guarantee you Elvis, most everybody accepts that you're dead.'

'But I'm not.'

"Rabbi Aaron then laughed heartily and said, 'No, you most certainly are not dead. More important, though, if you had to make a choice, which life would you want?'

"I sat there without answering him and he just kept watching me."

Stan asked, "What was that like?"

"He seemed to be immersed in his own inner world. I tried to answer him, but the question shook me."

"How so, Elie?"

"Since the beginning, I was told I had to follow the directions of people that I did not necessarily know and trust that they would lead me to a proverbial 'Promised Land.' I never considered whether I had free choice. Now this rabbi, who was in charge of getting me to a new life, was point-blank asking me if this is what I truly wanted. For the first time, I faced a true choice."

"Why did Rabbi Aaron say nothing?"

"I have no idea, even now. But this was my moment of truth. I originally believed that my moment of truth was when Daddy got me out of Graceland. But I was sick then and couldn't think clearly. I was all emotions, running away from everything and not wanting to be recognized. I was so tired of being a goldfish in a giant fish tank. Does that make sense, Stanley?"

"Certainly. You were also exhausted and strung out on drugs."

"And I was afraid."

"You were that as well." "I have the same question that Rabbi Aaron was asking you back then. Only I am asking it in a different way. What exactly were you afraid of?"

"I'm not so sure now, and I have had decades to consider it. I guess that if I had returned to my music career, at some point, I would have eventually gone back to feeling choked by the whole entourage thing. People telling me where to go, what to do."

"And the life you ultimately chose, has this been free of being told where to go and what to do?"

Elie thought about it. "It's different. Of course, life cannot be lived with total freedom. But this has been different. For one, Shoshana has loved me in a way no other woman besides Mama has ever done. She loves me because I am a big doofus." Elie's eyes twinkled, but then his face sobered. "Everyone else in my life loved me because I was Elvis Presley. Even Priscilla as a young teenager was dealing with me as a famous person, even if I was so immature. Everything was in the context of all that money, all that fame. Even in the Army, it never let up. I was always under someone's thumb.

That's why my whole relationship with Priscilla was so ridiculous. I was a grown man, but psychologically I was younger than her, even when she was a young teen. It was free and easy because I was such a baby. No one called me on that but Linda Thompson. She really cared for me, but I was a human train wreck. A grown man tornado, filled with impulsive behavior, drinking, drugs, and selfishness. With Shoshana, I never did that. To answer your question Stanley, I'm not sure what I was so afraid of, but it was a powerful fear that drove me."

"Why did you never act out with Shoshana?" Stan asked.

"She would never put up with that."

"Really?"

"Yeah, when we got married, all she knew was that I was a baal teshuva. In a sense, she taught me everything about being a responsible man. Look at my family, Stanley. All these kids and grandchildren. With Shoshie, all the anger evaporated from my life. It has been a wonderful marriage for me. I am so blessed that I met her."

"How did you meet?"

"She is Rabbi Aaron's daughter."

Stanley nearly fell out of his chair. "Really? You've got to be kidding me. Wow! That must be some story."

"Actually, it's a rather simple story. And it goes back to what I was saying about my talking with the rabbi the first time."

"Yeah, let's get back to that. So, when you didn't answer him right away, what happened?"

"Well, time ticked past with the two of us sitting there, saying nothing."

"How long do you think?"

"It seemed like forever. But during that time, I imagined what returning to that life would be like. I felt something I had not felt in months: My chest started to hurt, and I couldn't catch my breath. My thoughts ran wild. I envisioned going onstage again in one of those big concert locales. It paralyzed me. Thoughts about dealing with Colonel Parker nauseated me. I started sweating buckets. I reached into my pocket for a handkerchief to wipe my face. All that time, Rabbi Aaron just sat there, looking at me and not saying a word."

"Did he realize you were having a panic attack?"

"I think he could tell, but it was like I was being tested or something."

"Were you?"

Elie shrugged. "At the time, I didn't know. Later on, Rabbi Aaron admitted to me that, in a sense, he was testing me."

"Testing you for what reason?"

"To see if this was really what I wanted."

"Why?"

"He had invested a lot of effort to get me to that point. He told me he was confirming that this was the life for me. He wanted to ensure I wouldn't change my mind after he executed the final stage of the plan. So, he watched me gauging my reactions to his question."

"Very interesting, Elie. I can see that."

"So could I. He was an elderly man. He had lost his entire family in the war. He came to the United States, remarried, had more children, started a new life."

"Was he married in Europe?"

"Yes, he lost his wife and six children in the camps. Two sons and four daughters."

"Wow, six kids. Must have destroyed him."

"At the time, yes, but he found a way to escape and came to this country."

"Escape? Where in Europe did he escape from?"

"He escaped from Buchenwald."

Stan whistled "That must be a heck of a story."

"I'm sure it was. He never spoke about it. I know none of the details."

"Still it must have been hell."

"I imagine it was."

"Getting back to the story: Finally, I just looked at him and shrugged."

"What did he do?"

"He got up and left the room."

"No!" Stan exclaimed.

"Actually, yes. He got up and went into the kitchen."

"What did you do then?"

"I was paralyzed. I didn't know what was going other than think I had just screwed it all up and was done for."

"Well, obviously not. You ended up marrying his daughter."

"Uh-huh. I got the courage to get out of the chair and leave the room myself. I drifted into the kitchen, where Rabbis Zweig and Aaron were sitting, drinking tea and noshing on chocolate cookies. Rabbi Aaron said, 'Elie, sit down and have some tea.' I was dumbfounded but sat with them. Mrs. Zweig poured me a tea and then went into the living room. The two men didn't speak as I sipped tea. Rabbi Aaron pushed the plate of cookies towards me and motioned that I could have some.

"Rabbi Zweig excused himself and put his teacup in the sink. He joined his wife in the living room.

"Rabbi Aaron eventually spoke. 'I asked you a tough question, Elvis. But I didn't expect you to answer it in the blink of an eye. You have choices even if you don't think you do. If you resume your life as a musician, you can control your life! That is something you had to learn for yourself.' He paused to assess me. 'I see you don't believe that.'

'No sir, I am not so sure. That would be so hard.'

'Or it could be very easy. It depends upon you, Elvis. If you have been able l to trust total strangers over these past few months, then you can learn to trust yourself as well. If there is anything that you can take from all this, it is that you have that power. If you didn't, then nothing we have done for you would have made a difference. You would have relapsed, and then you would have absolutely nothing.'

"So I asked, 'Rabbi, why did you do this for me? After all...'

"Rabbi Aaron got up from his chair and stood facing me. He placed one arm on my shoulder. 'I did it because I was commanded to.'

"I didn't get it.

'Elvis, you are here now because this is where you should be. That is why. Think of it as a heavenly decree. That is why I am asking you: is this what you really want?'

'What other choice do I have?'

'Oh, come now. You could announce to the world tomorrow that you are alive. You would instantly return to fame. You could give interviews of how you managed to pull it off, and after all the uproar fades away, everyone will think it's a terrific story. You would be back singing in short order. Don't you realize that?'

"I sat there dazed. It had never occurred to me that despite it all, I had the option to return to my old life. A few envelopes of money would probably silence all the law guys and the outrage would die down rather quickly. I wondered, "How did this old rabbi have this all figured out?'

"I sat in a state of amazement at this old man who obviously was much more worldly than I expected him to be. He left the kitchen and returned with a brown manila envelope. He handed it to me and said, 'These are from your father.'

"I tore into the envelope furiously. I don't know what I expected from Daddy in that envelope. Maybe a letter, some pictures, anything like that. Instead I pulled out a birth certificate from Tupelo, a new passport, a new driver's license from Mississippi and a new Social Security card. All of these papers came with the name 'Elijah Pressler.' I looked at it all in awe. Then a voice broke through my fog. It was Rabbi Aaron.

'Go back to the yeshiva and pack all of your belongings. You are coming to Brooklyn to live with me for a while. There we will help you set up your new life. It will be good, Elie. It will be a blessing for you.' He smiled warmly, 'You see, I didn't call you Elvis. And I won't ever again call you that. You are Elijah, and your past is the past. Welcome to your new life.'

CHAPTER FIFTY-SIX

"Brooklyn was different from anything I had expected it to be," Elie said. "Without me actually vocalizing it, Rabbi Aaron had instinctively understood that I did not want to return to Graceland and my old life. I never said it outright, but it didn't matter. For in the end, I chose this life. And it was a choice I made on my own. Sure, you could say that Rabbi Aaron had stacked the deck, and I was somehow 'brainwashed.' But it would not be true. This new life was my destiny. I felt connected to G-d and to my heritage. And Stanley, I just really wanted this."

"Elie, you sound as if you were so certain then. I wonder, though, how could you be sure? You had been living for months either in someone's small apartment or buried away in a large yeshiva far from your home in Memphis. For an extended period of time, that's all you knew. That's all you had. They fed you; they clothed you. They kept you close to the vest."

Elie was shaking his head, but Stan said, "Elie, have you ever heard about Stockholm syndrome?"

"I know. It might seem that way, but it wasn't. Believe me, I'm no Patty Hearst."

"Well, of course not. But you were closely watched and steered."

Elie shook his head. "Probably so in some ways, but the intent was different. They had to watch me and steer me. I was one of the biggest personalities in the world. And Stanley, I was sick of the entertainment business. That was a far bigger 'Stockholm syndrome' for me. Graceland, with all the people and the Colonel controlling my entire life - that was way more confining and difficult for me than what I was going through when Rabbi Aaron packed me into his car and we drove to Brooklyn."

"Where did he live?"

"Right around the corner, so to speak. East Tenth Street between Avenues N and O."

"And so, it turns out that you ended up relatively close to his home when you and Shoshana bought this house."

"Honestly, it was not by design. We were looking at a house in Boro Park on Fifty-Seventh Street between Twelfth and Thirteenth Avenues. We had put a binding payment on the house. Then a young couple made a much higher offer. I think their parents financed the purchase. So suddenly Shoshie and I had to find another house, as our apartment in Boro Park was getting too small for us with the kids and all. Someone in Rabbi Aaron's synagogue was selling their deceased parents' house to close out the estate. It happened to be this house. Shoshie and I looked at it. She liked it. The house is smaller than the Boro Park house would have been, but not by much. It was close to her parents. The neighborhood was changing into a more Orthodox one. So, in the end, we bought this house. On the whole, it has been good, very good. Just right for us. We raised an entire family here and the grandkids come and stay for visits. Wish we had more room, but things could be worse." He laughed gently for a moment, pointing at the house with an expansive swing of his arms. "My Graceland 2!" He chuckled again.

"Where did you stay when you first got to Brooklyn?"

"With the Aarons. They had converted the basement into a tidy apartment. It had its own entrance and was separated from the rest of the house by a locked door on the side of the house. I would go straight into the apartment after my day. If I needed something from the Aarons or was invited for a meal, I knocked on the inside door at the top of the basement stairs and did not have to go outside to come into their home. Mrs. Aaron would simply unlock the door for me. This way, I had my privacy, and yet they were there for me if I needed them for anything."

"How did you meet Shoshana? I assume she was living in the house."

"Actually not. Believe it not, she went to law school and was a practicing attorney for a firm in midtown Manhattan. She had her own place on the Upper East Side, a studio apartment near the Park East Synagogue. She would come home for most Sabbaths and for the holidays, but during the week she stayed in the city. She worked crazy hours anyway, so it was more convenient for her to live in the city."

"Did she practice law after you were married?"

"For a short while." Elie barked out a short laugh. "How we got together was a completely different story."

"Now you've opened Pandora's box. What went on between the two of you?"

"It's a long story."

"Ah, come on now. Spill it."

"Tomorrow's another day. See you then." Elie grinned as he got up and went into the house. Stan wondered how those two got together right under the Aarons' noses. Or maybe that was G-d's plan after all.

CHAPTER FIFTY-SEVEN

The drive from Lakewood to Brooklyn takes a little less than two hours if there is no traffic. They left about eleven o'clock Saturday night and arrived by Rabbi Aaron's home around one o'clock in the morning. Elie slid out of the car, helped the rabbi with the bags, and followed him into the house. It was dark and quiet inside with his family sleeping upstairs. They left the bags in the vestibule, and Elie followed Rabbi Aaron into the kitchen. The old man flipped on a light switch, and the kitchen was bathed in the white light of a circular fluorescent bulb on the ceiling. After hours in the darkness, the bright light startled Elie. The rabbi filled a teapot with water and put it on the stove to boil. He scanned the contents of the refrigerator and shuffled things around until he found what he was looking for. He placed a round chocolate cake on the kitchen table and pulled out two plates, a knife and two forks. When the water boiled, he said over his shoulder, "Coffee or tea?" Elie yawned louder than he intended. "Coffee." The rabbi stirred in a spoonful of instant coffee into both cups. "Sugar?" Elie nodded. "Milk?" Elie nodded again.

Once the coffees were prepared, they sat at the table. Elie cut two slices of cake, and they didn't talk while they drank their coffees and ate the cake. Once they finished, they cleared the table and put everything away.

Rabbi Aaron opened a door adjacent to the kitchen. He turned on the light and motioned to Elie to get his belongings and follow him downstairs. The rabbi turned on the basement light, and Elie saw his new home for the first time. It was a small basement apartment. Some chairs, a small couch, and a bed off to one side. There was a kitchenette unit and a bathroom with a shower in the back. Elie was shown where there were towels and bed linens. The rabbi, satisfied that his guest had what he needed, bade him good night and went upstairs. Elie heard the door lock and sat alone in his new surroundings. The room was clean and neat, but he was too tired to make the bed. He removed his shoes and laid his head on the pillow. He pulled a blanket around himself and soon was fast asleep.

CHAPTER FIFTY-EIGHT

"Y ou look perplexed, Abraham."

Rabbi Aaron looked up from his seat in the kitchen, where he had returned after setting Elie up in the basement. He saw Isaac sitting across the table. Abraham scratched the back of his scalp and pushed his skullcap into position.

"Well?"

"I am perplexed, actually."

"About what? You accomplished what I asked you to do."

"It seems deceitful."

"How so?"

"We faked a death!"

"Did we?"

"Of course, we did. I hoped that was past me. I guess not. Shame on me. It has brought up so many memories, so much pain. I'm an old man. I had put it all to bed a very long time ago."

"You think so? Abraham, you never put that to bed. Maybe you are looking at it wrong."

"Looking at it wrong? I conspired to fake a death, not once, but twice! The first time to save my own life. I can live with that, as hard as it has been for me. The Nazis would have ultimately killed me, and, besides, they murdered my family. All I had was myself and nothing to lose. Now, I've done it for a second time. There was no danger of Nazis killing him or working him to death. There was no imminent danger. I faked the death of a perfectly healthy man. Tell me Isaac, how can that possibly be right?" Pointing his old bony finger at Isaac, he demanded, "Why did you ask me to do that?" Then pointing the same finger at his own chest, "And why did I agree?" He pounded his chest with his fist.

Isaac rose from the table and went to the sink. He leaned his back against the counter as he stroked his beard and pondered.

"Maybe you're right."

Abraham's eyes opened widely. "Maybe, I'm right?"

"Yes," Isaac said. Maybe G-d asked too much of you this time, more than you could tolerate. Possibly more than you should have been asked to do. Could be. Yes, could be!"

Abraham sat there in tears. "How can you say that? I have always given my life to perform whatever G-d asked me to do." He said this while shaking his head.

"Then why is this so troubling?"

"I don't know. For once, I am without answers."

Isaac stroked his beard and looked thoughtful. Abraham got up and turned the fire on under the teapot. He stood facing the pot until the kettle whistled. He reached into the cupboard and removed a new cup and a teabag. He poured the water and dropped in the teabag. He watched as the water started to turn orange, saying nothing. He took the cup to the table, poured some sugar in, and mixed it with his finger.

"Isn't that hot?" Isaac said.

Abraham shrugged. "I barely noticed."

"Why is that?"

"I lost most of feeling in this hand in the freezing cold at Buchenwald."

"Never came back?"

"Nah. My feet, they are always cold, but my hands lost most of their sensitivity to heat or cold."

Isaac said, "Your feet, you need. Your whole weight rests on them. The feet must be able to feel so you can negotiate your surroundings.

Everything you are rests on them. Your hands…eh…they are how you express yourself. Normally, they are the most sensitive of your limbs. If they've lost sensitivity, it is because something in you has lost sensitivity. It may be a deliberate thing that your mind has done. On the other side, it may just reflect that you do not want to 'handle'" your pain about something. And it shows up in your ability to stick your finger in boiling hot water, and well…"

Abraham scowled. "I've done everything you asked me to do."

"I didn't tell you how to do it."

"Yes, you did! You told me to use the skills I learned at Buchenwald."

"And you did. And you have rescued a man in the same you rescued yourself."

"How can you compare the two? I was facing certain death. It's not the same."

"What makes you think that Elvis was not facing certain death? You don't know what the Heavenly Court had in mind."

Abraham swallowed his protests as Isaac continued, "Even the most righteous amongst us, in this plane of existence, do not know what our Maker intends. Perhaps Elvis' self-struggle might have been his way of understanding that his life had a different purpose. You do not know what his interaction with you is about but let me tell you that it is not coincidental or random.

"Abraham, you may be an old man, and you have lived two distinct lives: that which was before the war and that which came afterward. Through all of that, one thing has held true for you: it is that G-d had a purpose for all the suffering as well as for all the subsequent success and joys. You have seen a whole new family grow around you and have lived the lives of many persons. Yet still you wonder why old pains feel the same. But it is not the same world, and the pain is not the same. You judge yourself far too harshly. Elvis came into your life for a reason. Look around you and determine why."

Abraham closed his eyes to absorb those words and then opened his mouth to say something to Isaac, but he was gone. All he had was a cup of tea, a man he hardly knew sleeping in his basement, and his family sleeping above him in their beds. His mind wandered to his former home in Europe. He started to cry to his long-dead wife, "Oh, Chava! What do I do?" In his mind's eye, he saw her clearly, giving him her knowing look and her sweet smile. He wiped his eyes with his shirtsleeve. Then he put the cup in the sink, rinsed it out, and climbed the stairs, seemingly renewing his new life. He quietly undressed, slipping into his bed, next to his wife, Devora.

CHAPTER FIFTY-NINE

Elie knocked on the interior door that led from his basement apartment into the main part of the Aarons' house. It was late Friday afternoon and he was going to synagogue with the rabbi. He knocked again, lightly, and soon a young woman in a long black dress opened the door She had a pale complexion and was very slim, almost skinny. What stood out to Elie the most was her bright red hair. She had big blue eyes, although her large square glasses hid her eyes. She wore an apron, as she was helping with the cooking.

"You must be Elie. The one staying in the basement." She said it in a matter-of-fact way and returned to what she was doing. Elie stood there at the entrance to the kitchen doubtful about what to say or do with himself.

"I'll go into the living room and wait for the rabbi to come down," he said to her as he passed by her on his way out of the kitchen.

"You do that! He will be down soon," she said without glancing at him. Elie stood there uncertain of what to say, and then he just shrugged and went into the living room and sat on a sofa.

Rabbi Aaron and his wife, Devora soon came down the stairs and greeted him. The rabbi went to the front closet, donned his coat and hat, and motioned to Elie to follow him. As they left, Rabbi Aaron asked him if he had met his daughter, Shoshana.

Elie had been living in the Aaron's basement for about three weeks and had gotten used to the rhythm and routine of the house. This was his third Sabbath with them but their daughter had been away those first two Sabbaths. This was the first time he had met her.

"Yes, she let me into the house."

"Good. She is usually home every Sabbath but was away on vacation for the last two weeks. She lives in Manhattan on weekdays because it's close to her work."

"What does she do?" Elie asked.

Rabbi Aaron shrugged as if in amazement and half chuckled. "She's a lawyer with a prestigious firm in Manhattan. Works very hard."

"You don't seem pleased."

"Actually, I am quite proud of her. She is excellent at what she does. I just never saw her growing up to be a lawyer as a little girl. She was always so quiet. Always with a book, reading for hours at a time. Devora and I have hoped she would be married by now, but she has her own ideas and has fought any idea of a matchmaker."

They walked together toward the synagogue. It was a cool spring evening. Passover was coming and the winter weather had stopped blowing cold.

"Rabbi, would you prefer her being married, or for her to be a successful lawyer?"

"I want both for her. Elie, it is not good for a person to be alone. It is not about the loneliness, although that can be powerful. After the war, with my Chava gone…" He stood still to fish in his jacket pocket for a handkerchief. He opened it slowly and touched it to his eyes and then carefully refolded it, clenching it in his right hand as he resumed walking. Elie followed alongside. "I mean that being alone brings out the selfishness in a person, even if they do not intend it to be. Reliance on oneself is important, but not at the cost of having shared experiences. Being together, children, grandchildren. You know what I mean."

Elie nodded as they reached the synagogue. Rabbi Aaron added as they entered, "She's a tough girl. Life has made her that way. That's why she is good at what she does. She tells me that she loves her work. But work is not a life; Work is work. I hope that someday she finds someone to share her life with." He hung up his coat and worked his way to the front of the synagogue, greeting his congregants as he worked his way forward. Elie hung back and took a seat in the back pew. The Sabbath service began.

CHAPTER SIXTY

Shoshana had seen many young men stay in the basement over the years. She guessed that her parents were trying to set her up for marriage. This was, of course, the truth.

She had other ideas. She enrolled in Brooklyn College after high school rather than going to seminary or to Israel for a year or two. Her parents were opposed at first but seeing that she had her mind set on the matter, they ultimately relented. Their only insistence was that she had to live at home. To that she agreed, and every morning, no matter the weather, she boarded the train at Kings Highway and East Sixteenth Street and went off to school. Even in the heat of the summer and through the blowing snows of winter, she rode the subway to school.

She graduated after three years and her parents were relieved and proud. But then she informed them that she had applied to law school and was accepted to Columbia Law School in Manhattan. So, for the next three years, she still rode the subway into Manhattan early in the morning for school and then late into the night to get home.

She came to like Manhattan. Some of her favorite things were walking downtown to the theater and traveling uptown to the concerts in Lincoln Center. On days when her schedule allowed, she would sit out in Central Park, take in the sun, and people. Shoshana especially loved to browse at FAO Schwartz, the greatest toy store in

New York. She watched children with their parents and felt the first tugs of the desire to be a mother someday. But that did not deter her from her mission to become a lawyer. She studied hard and acquired a voice and persuasiveness she hadn't known was within her.

She graduated near the top of her class and was offered a clerkship with a federal judge. She was also offered a job at a prestigious law firm in Manhattan. The pay was very generous and would allow her to help her parents who had mortgaged their house in Brooklyn to send her to law school. So she refused the clerkship and took the job with the law firm. Her heart was set on staying in Manhattan and she found a small one-bedroom apartment in a Pre-War building on East Sixty- Sixth Street, a short walk to the Park East Synagogue in a neighborhood with Orthodox Jews and kosher restaurants nearby. It was a relatively short subway ride to her office near Wall Street. She decorated the apartment comfortably and began her life as a young lawyer in New York. She tried to come back to her parents' home in Brooklyn every Sabbath. This did not always work out because of her workload, but she returned home most weekends to her family.

When Elie knocked on the inner door in the Aaron's house, he appeared unsure when she let him into the kitchen. She looked him up and down when first greeting him and then turned back to her work in the kitchen.

Elie nervously went into the living room to wait for Rabbi Aaron. Soon after, the two left to go to the synagogue. Devora Aaron came into the kitchen and began her final preparations for the Sabbath. Shoshana and her mother lit the Sabbath candles and finished the table.

As was the Aaron's custom, there were several guests who dined with them on Shabbos. Rabbi Aaron was always inviting people from the synagogue back to join him for the Sabbath meals. Most were young men from the yeshiva or older men who were widowed and alone. Between the family and guests there were often a dozen or more people eating with them.

Elie, now accustomed to the happenings of a Sabbath meal,

readily joined in the eating, singing and conversation. Periodically he looked down the length of the table where Shoshana was sitting, but she was too involved in conversation with the women sitting near her to pay attention to Elie's gaze. His innate shyness seemed to zip his lips when he tried to engage her in conversation. He found that surprising as he had been with so many gorgeous women in his previous life, and back then Shoshana would never have gotten a passing glance from him.

Soon the meal was over, and the guests got up and left. Elie helped to clear the table, and then said his good nights and went down to his apartment in the basement.

He was not yet sleepy, so he sat in an old armchair the Aaron's had placed in the basement. He stretched out his legs and leaned his neck against the chair's top cushion. He opened a book to read and soon drifted off to sleep in the chair.

He woke up about two in the morning but couldn't keep his eyes closed anymore. No longer tired, he got up and went to his sink and ran a glass of water. He sat at the small round kitchen table, intending to read his book.

But something was strangely off. He read a few pages, but that odd sensation did not escape him. He looked up from his book was startled when he saw an old man sitting in the chair opposite him.

"Sorry to have made you jump."

"Who the heck are you?"

"What's a heck?"

"Huh?"

"What's a heck? You asked me who the heck I am. I want to know what's a heck."

"It's just an expression. You caught me by surprise. But who are you and how did you get in here?"

The old man was dressed in a black robe and sandals. His white hair and beard were long and flowing. He had piercing eyes that seemed to penetrate Elie's soul.

"My name was originally Jacob, but it was changed later to Israel."

"Why?"

"G-d willed it so!"

Elie looked so confused.

"Elvis, my father's name is Isaac. His father's name is Abraham. Does that clarify things?"

Elie's jaw dropped. Then he stood up and stared at the man.

"You have nothing to say? You look shocked."

"I am! Are you real, or am I having some sort of a dream?"

"You're not dreaming. I am very real. Touch my arm. You will see that I am truly here."

Elie reached out to the man's arm. It felt solid.

"How can this be? You are dead!"

"Elvis, the world thinks you are dead. How is this any different?"

"But you've been dead for thousands of years. You are buried in a cave in Israel."

"Elvis, time is a human concept. In your learning have you heard the expression that Yaakov Avinu Lo Mais (Jacob the Patriarch) did not die?"

Elie nodded. Jacob said, "Well, it's true! Physically, I passed away, but spiritually?" Jacob shrugged.

Elie slumped into his chair. He squeezed his eyes shut certain he was dreaming. When he opened his eyes again the man was still there.

"Convinced yet?"

"No, I've got to be dreaming."

"Aren't we all dreaming?"

"What?"

"You heard me. Aren't we all dreaming? Is it possible that this life is really a dream?"

That shook Elie, but Jacob quickly calmed him.

"Your life is very real, Elvis, but you are separated from what is the true existence of G-d. Anything is possible, if you believe."

"Why are you here?"

"And why are you?"

"I don't understand!"

"What are you doing here, Elvis Presley? Everything you had was larger than life. Yet, you walked away from all of that, and now you are living in the basement of an old rabbi's house in Brooklyn. It is far from where you grew up, far from whatever you previously knew. Yet here you are. Quite miraculous, you might say. What brought you here, Elvis?"

"Well, you see, my life was a mess, and Rabbi Fried took me in, and with Rabbi Aaron…"

"No! No, no, no, Elvis. I understand how you physically got here. That's not what I am asking. You asked me why I am here now. I asked you, in exchange, why you are here. So, Elvis, why are you here?"

"Don't call me Elvis. My name is Elie…" He stopped talking for a moment to ponder Jacob's question. "Jacob, why am I here?" he asked quietly. He put his head on the table.

They were both silent. Jacob watched the man wrestle with his demons. Elie was rubbing his neck and crying.

"I don't know all the reasons you are here, Elie. You see I called you Elie, because you have stopped being Elvis. I don't know *all* the reasons your journey brought you to this place at this time. But I do know one of the reasons."

Elie froze. "So, what's the reason?"

"One of the reasons you are here is…" Jacob sighed for a second and gestured to the second floor, eyes looking up towards the ceiling. "She is sleeping upstairs right now."

"Shoshana?"

Jacob nodded.

"I don't understand. She hardly notices my existence."

"Things are like that sometimes. Trust me when I tell you that it is decreed from above."

Elie closed his eyes, organizing his thoughts. He had a bunch of questions on the tip of his tongue, but when he reopened his eyes, Jacob was gone. Elie was not sure if he had dreamed it all up. He quickly got undressed and went to his bed. And for the first time in years, restful sleep came quickly.

CHAPTER SIXTY-ONE

Shoshana woke up in a state of fright. Had someone touched her? But as her eyes scanned the dark bedroom, she saw that it was empty except for her. She calmed herself down and fell back to sleep.

She slept fitfully for a couple of hours, then fumbled for. the clock radio by her bed and saw that it was almost 4:00 in the morning. She rolled over to her other side but could not sleep. She got up, put on her robe and slippers, and went downstairs to the kitchen. She poured hot water from the urn set up for the Sabbath and made a cup of tea. She sat down at the table and flipped through magazines while she sipped her tea.

It had been an exhausting week at work. She had worked well into the night almost daily that week, preparing her cases for trial or settlement. She was glad that she was a person the firm could rely on for large billing hours. She hoped this would put her on the partner track someday.

Now she was just tired and unable to sleep. She closed her eyes as she yawned. When her eyes reopened, she saw at a truly radiant woman sitting opposite her. She closed her eyes again. It must be just a dream! But as her eyes reopened, she saw that the woman remained sitting in front of her, smiling. She closed her eyes a third time, but the result was the same as she reopened them.

"You don't trust your eyes, Shoshana?" the woman said.

Shoshana held her gaze. "I'm not sure. Who are you?"

"My name is Rachel."

Shoshana furrowed her brow, "Rachel who?"

"Rachel."

"I got that the first time. What is your last name?"

"Last name? What is that?"

Shoshana spoke in an irritated tone, "Your last name. You know, your family name. Surname?"

Rachel looked confused. "I am not sure what you mean. I am Rachel, daughter of Laban, sister of Leah, wife of Jacob."

Shoshana sat up straight in her chair. Part of her thought this was a hoax or a seriously ill young woman who had wandered into her house in some way.

"Rachel. Are you feeling all right?" she said to the woman while walking to the other side of the table to see if perhaps, the woman needed her help.

"I'm fine. Thank you. Are you okay Shoshana? You seem so tired."

"Where are you from, Rachel? And how do you know my name?"

Rachel just sat there with a calm, kind expression. Shoshana became concerned that the young woman had mental problems. She should go upstairs and wake her mother. Before she could, Rachel said to her, "Don't wake your mother. I am not crazed or otherwise mentally ill. I will not harm you."

"Then what are you doing here?"

"Shoshana, you are not getting any younger. You work so hard, but your life is…incomplete."

Shoshana asked sharply, "How do you know anything about me?"

"I've known about you for some time. My father-in-law speaks with your father from time to time."

"What?" Shoshana replied. Her expression was incredulous. "Your father-in-law? Who is he?"

"Isaac. Who did you think I was talking about?"

"Either this is the craziest thing, or I am still asleep."

"Do you feel as if you are asleep?"

"No, actually, I don't. I feel awake but very confused. What do you want?"

"It's not what I wish that brings me here. It's what you want, even if you are not aware of it."

"And what do I want?" Shoshana asked with an edge to her voice, implying that this stranger Rachel could not possibly guess what she wanted. She crossed her arms across her chest.

Rachel watched as Shoshana returned to her chair and sat.

"So, what is it exactly that I want?" Shoshana demanded again.

Rachel 's smile lit up her face. Her teeth were bright white and straight. She wore a long dress with her hair wrapped up in a kerchief. Her eyes were clear, but the corners of her eyes showed the faint lines of someone who has cried often.

Shoshana stared wordlessly at her, still not believing that was taking place.

"There is a man sleeping in the basement right now."

"Yes, but there's nothing unusual about that. We often have guests. They stay down there."

"This is no ordinary guest."

"What? I don't understand."

"He is your intended and I was sent to tell you that."

Shoshana snorted. "Are you kidding me? Him?"

"Trust me when I tell you he is a person of importance."

"What are you talking about? I met him for the first-time last night. We barely spoke. He is not a man of importance. He is just an older bachelor that my father is helping. Believe me, this has happened before! I've seen this happen many times over the years."

Shoshana was getting tired of the whole conversation and was ready for the woman to leave. "Who are you? Really. Are you some matchmaker? My parents promised they wouldn't go behind my back to set me up."

Rachel, as calm as ever, looked towards the basement stairs. Shoshana followed the direction of her movement, and then they locked gazes. "Shoshana, would an ordinary matchmaker be sitting in this kitchen at four thirty in the morning, talking with you about some man sleeping in your basement?"

There was quiet. The answer was self-evident. Shoshana had to admit to herself the truth to herself, but she protested. Looking across the table at Rachel.

"He is much older than me."

"Maybe so, nonetheless…"

"Nonetheless what?"

Rachel raised her hands and shrugged. "He's a complicated man, but a good man. This one has a great heart and a huge capacity to love. He will take loving care of you, but he will need your care too. You may resent that at first, but you will find the innate greatness in him. I assure you that he will try very hard for you."

Shoshana shook her head. "Thank you, but I don't think so. I have a life of my own. My work is exciting, and I adore living in Manhattan. Someday, if G-d wills it, I will find a sophisticated, urbane Jewish gentleman, and we will live in the city, and raise a family. I know it."

Rachel pondered that. "You have it all planned out?"

"As a matter of fact, I've had it mapped out for years."

"Why hasn't it worked out?"

"Who says it hasn't?"

"Well, has it?"

Shoshana sat there, reflecting on the question. When she was concentrating, she had a habit of nibbling at her lower lip. She was doing it now.

Rachel waved an arm at her. "We have all had plans. Jacob and I, we waited seven long years. And in the end, my sister Leah! Then Leah had children and I couldn't for a long time. Nothing goes as we plan it because despite our best efforts, we don't control the world."

"So, you are telling me…what?"

"I'm telling you nothing I haven't already said."

Shoshana got up and rinsed out her teacup in the sink. When she turned around, Rachel was gone.

She looked in the dining room and the living room, but they were quiet. She went back into the kitchen. She opened the door to the basement stairs and listened, but there wasn't a peep. Tiptoeing down the stairs, she looked at the bed and saw Elie sleeping soundly and returned to the kitchen. She closed and locked the door and climbed the front stairs to her room. She removed her robe and slipped into bed. As her head lay on the pillow, she realized that she was crying softly. Her mixed emotions were overflowing into tears. Rolling over, she drifted into sleep.

CHAPTER SIXTY-ONE

They were married six months later. Rabbi Aaron shed tears when he read the blessings that united the couple. Elie looked so happy and Shoshana was radiant in her white gown and red hair. As she approached the Chuppah she saw that Elie was smiling broadly.

She walked around him seven times with her mother carefully lifting the long train to her gown. The couple stood together and he placed the ring on her finger saying in Hebrew, "With this ring, you are consecrated to me, according to the law of Moses and Israel." Various rabbis and family members from the Aaron's side said the seven blessings and the couple drank the wine. Then a glass cup was wrapped in a napkin. Elie stepped on it, and the crowd yelled "Mazel Tov!" and they were married.

They moved into an apartment in Boro Park in Brooklyn. After a short time, Elie was recognized for his singing, and a local cantor began teaching him the services. He was then asked to be a cantor for the High Holidays, and with trepidation and encouragement from Shoshana, he soon mastered the service and was hired by a synagogue in Florida to lead their services. Shoshana and Elie traveled South and stayed through the holidays while he led the services. Later on, he would become a full-time cantor in a synagogue in Flatbush, where they ultimately would move.

Shortly after they were married, Shoshana became pregnant,

and there was such joy when they were blessed with a little girl. They named her Bathsheba, and Elie loved them both with all his being. He had never known such love since his mother had died.

After the birth of their son, Moses Jacob, it was obvious to Elie that they needed more room. They looked at many houses in Boro Park in Brooklyn and finally made an offer on one they liked. But it fell through, and, as luck would have it, a house became available from someone in Rabbi Aaron's synagogue. The house was located at 1652 East Seventh Street between Avenues O & P in Flatbush. This house appealed to them too, and they bought it. Shoshana was glad because she wanted to be near her parents. Her father was by then in his nineties, although still vigorous, so it worked out well for them.

Over the next few years, they had three more children: a little girl named Rachel and twin boys. The older twin was named Abraham in memory of Shoshana's father who had passed away, the year before. The other twin was named Sholom, for he symbolized the peace that Shoshana and Elie felt as a family. With Rabbi Aaron's passing, a great sadness descended upon his wife, descendants, and other relatives. He was responsible for everything Elie now had in his life. For Shoshana, it was a terrible loss. There was great mourning in the community, as the simple man was greatly beloved by all who knew him. It would take a while for them all to recover.

CHAPTER SIXTY-THREE

Stanley sat in a chair close to Elie's bed in Coney Island Hospital. "So, in the end you never told her you were sick?" Stanley pressed his lips together disapprovingly at Elie who looked back at him in his hospital gown with tubes and I.V.'s hung from his bed and his arms.

Elie shrugged and shook his head.

"Must have been a hell of a shock to her."

Elie shifted his gaze away from Stanley.

Changing the subject, he said, "Do you think her father ever told her about who you were?"

"No, I doubt it. I can't imagine he ever told her. He wanted her to have a quiet Jewish life. If she knew who I was, she would never have married me. Rabbi Aaron once told me that I should never tell anyone, and with the exception of you, I have never told a soul."

There was quiet between the two men. Then Elie said, "The doctor is pushing me to do chemotherapy. I don't want to."

"Why not? What have you got to lose?"

"Stanley, I've heard it's like torture. I don't want to do it. It will make me very sick."

"Like you're not sick anyway? Look at yourself! You're in the hospital. If chemo gave you a few more months, wouldn't it be worth it? For your wife, your kids?"

"Yes, but it will make me really sick. The doctors told me what to expect. The big pain in my belly is already hard enough to endure. How would chemo help my family?"

"Idiot, they would have you!"

"But at what cost? They will remember their father as a sick old man. They would be miserable."

"You don't know that."

Elie scrunched up his face. "It would be no good."

Stanley flung his hands up in exasperation and rose from his chair.

"Now you are being a martyr! And a selfish one at that."

He lowered his voice when a nurse entered the room. She came in and took his vital signs, shooing Stan into the hallway. As he stood outside, leaning against the wall, Shoshana came into view around the corner. Moving towards him, she recognized Stanley and looked at him with a question in her eyes.

"What are you doing here, Stanley?"

"Came by to see my friend." Stanley looked down at his shoes.

"Did you know he was sick?"

Stan said nothing and wouldn't meet her gaze.

More firmly, she said, "Why didn't he tell me?"

"He was trying to protect you. He didn't want you to worry."

"But he told you?"

Stan looked up and shrugged.

She gave him a look of disgust, shaking her head.

"Is there anything else he hasn't told me? You seem to be so close that he felt he could tell you he was sick, but not his wife." A bitter tone crept into her voice. "No, he couldn't seem to do that! Couldn't tell his wife he was dying, but the neighbor…" With that, she broke down into tears. Stanley reached for her, but she pulled back.

"Shoshana, I told him he should tell you. But maybe for him, telling you would mean he had to acknowledge to himself that he was so sick."

She wiped her tears with a tissue and lightly bit her lower lip composing herself.

Her voice was calm again when she spoke. "I am not angry with you, Stanley. You kept him going these past few months. Whatever you talked about revived him. He seemed to have lost that for several months before you moved in."

She touched his arm. "You are a good man, Stanley. I'm sure you tried to convince him to tell me." She t shrugged and entered Elie's room. She closed the door behind her with a resounding bang.

CHAPTER SIXTY-FOUR

Stanley walked away from the hospital and to the subway. Rather than return to his house, he went back to the office watching the sun set through the window of the subway car. The train descended into the tunnel between Brooklyn and Manhattan.

He came into the newsroom and sat at his desk. It was mostly quiet. There weren't many people working on stories overnight. He tried working on a feature story for the weekend edition but couldn't concentrate and soon gave up. He was in turmoil and got up and walked to a bar around the corner. Ordering a beer and a hamburger, Stan sat by himself at the bar.

He pondered how Elie lived with Shoshana for so long and never hinted at what his life was before they met. How Elie must have ached to share that with her in their most intimate moments. But he had felt duty bound not to. That was unusual restraint from a man not known for that quality in his younger days.

Soon, it would all be over. They would be burying a man who once had the entire world in the palm of his hand. And he would be buried as a simple old Jew, in a grave belying his previous greatness, and wealth beyond imagination.

It was remarkable that Elie had given it all up. Stanley knew that, given the same circumstances, he would not have made the same choice. Hell, he would have ridden that wave of success to the bitter end. Anyone else would probably have done the same as well. Stanley thought of all those women.

Elie, who could have had almost any woman, chose to live out half his life with a pale, plain, skinny woman who always was besieged with the tumult of a large boisterous family in her house.

He wondered why. What did Elie see in her? What did he know inherently? What did the two of them have to talk about? Stan didn't see any commonality between them. But what did he know? He had messed up his own relationships.

Stan chomped on his burger and took a long draw on his beer. Trying to figure out Elvis Presley was the most perplexing puzzle he had encountered. But fate had brought him together with the biggest story of his life. Now he was not sure that he even felt like spilling the beans. Maybe Elie should be allowed to peacefully enjoy the life he had chosen so many years ago.

But Stan had promised. He gave his word to Elie that he would tell the story and share the money with Shoshana and the children. It was a quandary. He had been shaken by the question she had posed in the hospital: "Is there anything else he hasn't told me?" If his illness was a shock to her, learning of his previous life would be a catastrophe.

Furthermore, it felt wrong to be the one who told her of the Elvis portion of his life. That was for Elie to do. But he couldn't figure out how to convince him.

Finishing his meal, he paid his bill and headed for the subway to Brooklyn. His steps were slow and heavy as he went down to the train. When the train pulled into the station, Stan stepped on and found a seat. He closed his eyes and stretched his neck back, trying to escape all of his thoughts.

"Is there anything else he hasn't told me?" That question kept playing on a loop in his brain all the way to Brooklyn. In the end, Stan got no respite from his thoughts.

CHAPTER SIXTY-FIVE

Stan went to the hospital directly after work. Elie was wavering on whether to start chemotherapy. Shoshana had been with him all day and when Stan came in, she looked relieved.

"Stanley, I'm glad you are here. I've been here all day. I am dying for a cup of coffee and to take a short walk outside for some fresh air. Can you stay with him while I go out for a while?"

"Of course. No rush. I'll sit with him for a bit."

"Maybe you can talk some sense into that fat head of his." Shoshana collected her bag and coat and turning to Elie, she said,

"Be back in a little while." Elie nodded and closed his eyes. Shoshana waved at Stan and left the room.

"Well buddy, how you doing?" Stanley said, as he sat in the chair by the bed. As he descended into the chair, he tapped Elie's knees, which were under the blanket.

Elie laugh was brief. He looked terrible, Stanley thought. His friend had dark undereye circles. He sat propped up with a pillow spilling out from behind his head. His skullcap was askew and Stanley adjusted it more squarely onto his head.

"Having fun?"

Elie grimaced. "Tons. I am a human pin cushion."

Stanley looked around. Elie was hooked up to a bunch of equipment monitoring everything. There seemed to be a million tubes and wires attached to him. He was in a sorry state.

"What did your wife mean by telling me to talk some sense into you?"

"She wants me to start the chemo."

"So, do I, my friend. You're giving up too easily."

"What if this is my time? Maybe G-d is calling me home?"

"Listen to yourself. You sound like an idiot. You may be sick now, and the chemo may make you feel even sicker. But if it works, you could have…"

"More time?"

"Yes."

"How much? Perhaps a few months. Is it worth it? This will bankrupt my family, and it is destroying the kids. They come here and cry." He teared up. "What do I tell them?"

Stan shook his head. "You tell them to be strong for you so you can be strong for them."

Elie shrugged, wiping his eyes with a tissue. He picked up the TV remote control and muted the news. "What rubbish on the television. I used to be addicted to watching it at Graceland. I haven't watched it in years. I see that it has gotten much worse. Such garbage. I'm glad my children don't watch."

"At least you can't shoot at it in here." They both cracked up.

Elie joked, "If I had a gun now, I definitely would shoot it out." Stanley rolled his eyes, and Elie chuckled. A young girl brought in a hospital tray and set it on the rolling table in front of him.

"Well at least they feed you here." Stan said, his tone light. He reached to open the cover for Elie. "Looks pretty good." On the tray was a small piece of fish, a scoop of mashed potatoes and green beans. There was also a bowl of Jell-O and some hot tea. Stanley opened the package with plastic utensils and placed the teabag into the hot water. He stuffed a napkin under Elie's chin. Mixing sugar into the tea, he saw that his friend had no interest in eating or drinking anything.

"Elie, eat something."

Elie scrunched his face at the food tray. "I'll try. Maybe just the Jell-O and some tea to wash it down."

"Elie, you've got to eat more than that."

Elie looked disgusted. The smell of the fish was making him nauseous. "No, I will be all right with the Jell-O and tea."

"The hell you are. Listen, Elie, eat your damn food! You ain't allowed to die right now. And I have selfish reasons."

"Really? What might those be?"

Grabbing Elie' chin and tilting his head to face him, Stanley said, "You know damned well what those reasons are. You still have a lot left to tell me and I won't let you die until you're finished with me. So there!"

"So there," Elie said and stuck out his tongue. They both giggled and then Elie protested, "Don't make me laugh, Stan! It hurts."

"Then eat your food."

"Okay, if you insist." Digging into the plate with a plastic fork, he took a mouthful of fish and shrugged. "Eh, not so bad. Shoshana does it much better."

"You're a spoiled brat," Stanley said, his eyes twinkling.

"I guess I am."

"No shit, Sherlock."

"Well, of course I am! After all, I am - ta da! - Elvis Presley."

"Ain't you ever!"

They both laughed. Then Stanley's face turned serious.

"You're never going to tell her."

Elie shook his head, "No. I don't think so."

Stanley walked to the window, looked out, but didn't really notice the view. "Is she the one you truly loved?"

"I love Shoshana very much."

"But she isn't the one you loved the most?"

"Stanley, why does it matter to you?

"I don't know." Then stopping for a moment, Stan opened his mouth but paused. "Forget that...It matters, my friend, because it gives a tremendous value to your life."

"I don't understand."

"You gave up your greatest love to find happiness in a new life.

You must think of her often and compare for yourself what might have been if you had been mature enough to handle it."

"Stanley, who are you talking about?"

Stan cocked his head to one side. "Priscilla, of course."

"What makes you believe that she was my greatest love?"

Stan looked intently at Elie closely, who edged up taller in the bed. "Stanley, why do you assume that the great love of my life was Priscilla?"

Now Stan was confused. He stammered, "Well…I just kind of assumed, you know."

"Because we were together so long? Yes, we were together from the time she was a young teenage girl. Yes, she was a tremendous part of my life and a great love. But believe it or not, she couldn't hold a candle to Shoshana."

"Huh. Who was it then? Linda Thompson?"

Elie shook his head.

"Ginger Alden?"

Elie made a face.

"Then who?" Stan started to pace around the room. "I got it. Of course - it was Ann-Margret."

Elie grinned. Stan laughed in triumph, "I knew it! I'm right, Elie, aren't I? I should have guessed that first."

"If you had guessed that first, you would still be wrong."

"What? Well, if it wasn't her, then…?"

Elie's smile turned cryptic, like the Cheshire cat's.

"Then whom?"

"Come on Stanley. You know the answer to that."

Stanley sat down with a confused expression. He scratched his head in total confusion. Elie interrupted his thoughts.

"Stanley, there is one person I would do anything for…" He said in a soft voice.

Stan drew a blank. Elie repeated, "One person I would do anything for…"

Stan, seized with a thought, jumped up from his chair. "Not your mother?"

Elie pointed a finger and said, "Bingo."

"Your mother? Gladys?" Stan was agape. "When I said that you had given up your greatest love, I meant a woman who –" Stanley waved his hand, "you had a relationship with."

"I did have a relationship with her. Just not the kind you are thinking of."

"But your mother was dead, many years before you ran away to this life."

"Yes. That is true, but without her constant reminders of my real roots, I would never have had the courage to abandon my unhappy state and live the life I have lived here in Brooklyn. Gladys was my one true love. All other women are a distant second."

"Even Shoshana?"

"Yes, even her."

Stan closed his eyes. "I don't understand. You and Shoshana have been together for years."

"Yes, she has been the woman in my life longer than everyone else. And she is as different from Gladys as I am from you. But it worked. It worked well. And I have loved her more than any other romantic partner in my life. But I have never loved anyone more than my mother."

"Doesn't that strike you as strange, Elie?"

"Sometimes. Sometimes, it seems odd. But no one ever loved me like my mother did. No one sacrificed her everything like Mama."

"Elie, don't you realize that if you had given your wife the same kind of unfettered love that stuck in your head for your mother, she would have loved you the way you were loved by Gladys?"

Elie looked stunned and closed his eyes. A tear dropped onto his cheek.

"Is it too late for me and Shoshana?"

Stan shrugged. "Who knows? But you'll never know unless you start your chemo."

CHAPTER SIXTY-SIX

Shoshana sat in the hospital cafeteria, sipping on her coffee. She was exhausted. She had been with Elie for hours and hours. Her friend Breindy Frankel was watching the kids. It was a relief that Stanley was visiting. It freed her up to recharge a little before going home. She reached into her pocketbook and pulled out a candy bar. Opening it, she shoved a piece into her mouth. She swallowed and followed up with a sip of her coffee. The candy went down hard and she reached for her belly and rubbed it until the pain subsided.

Finishing the snack and downing the rest of her coffee quickly, she walked towards the elevator bank. She thought she would say a quick good night to Elie, go home, collect her kids and collapse. The elevator doors opened, and she wove her way around nurses and patients on the way to Elie's room. Stan was sitting in the chair next to Elie, and they were chatting when she came in. Elie saw her come in and interrupted his conversation with Stan.

"Shoshie, I want you to know that I've decided to start the chemo."

"Oh, thank G-d!" she said, as she began to tear up. "Thank G-d! Stanley, what did you say to him to change his mind?"

Stan flashed a quick look at Elie and then turned to Shoshana and said, "You got me! We talked. He changed his mind. Did I get that right, Elie?"

Elie nodded.

Shoshana remained on topic. "Well, however you did it…thank you! I couldn't get him to agree. I'm glad you were able to do it, Stanley."

"No problem! Glad I could help."

"Elie, are you sure about this?"

"Yes."

"I mean you were pretty adamant about not doing this."

Stan interrupted the conversation. "Shoshana, leave it alone! He said he would do it. Let's not overanalyze this. He agreed. Period. Don't try to dissect it. Okay?"

She raised both brows but inclined her head. She looked at him, then at Elie. Speaking very slowly, "Okay. I'll leave it alone."

"Good."

Shoshana nodded.

Then she walked over to her husband's bed and bent to kiss him. "I will see you tomorrow. Try to sleep well."

Elie kissed her back. "If they will let me sleep and quit sticking me in the middle of the night."

"I'll talk to the nurse."

"Thank you, honey."

Stanley stirred in his chair, agitated. Elie and Shoshana looked at him with curiosity and he blurted out to Elie, "When are you going to tell her? Does she have to find out after you're dead?"

Pointing to Elie, then to himself, Stan said, "I don't want that responsibility, Elie. I don't! After all we have talked about tonight, don't you think it's time she knew?"

"Knew what?" Shoshana asked, alarmed. She studied her husband. "What's going on, Elie?"

Elie shifted uneasily in his bed. Stan stood up and yelled at him. "Damn it! Elie, tell her who you were before you came to New York. Tell her now! Tell her, or I will.

"Tell me what's going on, Elie!" Shoshana spat out. "What are you guys talking about?"

Elie fell silent. He was too terrified to speak. Shoshana turned on Stan and poked his chest. "What's going on here? What is it that I need to know? Why are you yelling at my husband?"

He ignored her to appeal to Elie's conscience one more time. "Tell her right now!"

Elie closed his eyes. His mouth started to move, but no words came out. Stan yelled, "Tell her, damn it!"

Elie couldn't get himself together. He was breathing heavily, sweat beading on his face. Stan eyed him in disgust. "Don't you think she has a right to know that you …."

Shoshona interrupted, "That he … what?"

Stanley let out a breath. He spoke softly to minimize the shock.

"Elie, in light of all the possibilities that could happen, she needs to know that before you came to New York, you were a very famous person."

Shoshana tensed up visibly.

"Shoshana, your husband is …"

Her expression lightened, and she interrupted him finishing his sentence, "actually Elvis Presley!"

There was total silence for a heartbeat.

"Yes, I know. I've always known!"

Elie looked stricken. "For how long?

"Since before we were married. Father told me."

Elie said under his breath, "You knew and you were still willing to marry me?"

With one glance, she looked at him as if he was asking a stupid question."

"I married you, didn't I?"

Stanley rubbed his forehead and took a seat. He didn't know whether to stay or leave.

"But why?" Elie stammered tenderly.

Shoshana dragged the other chair over to Elie's bedside. "Because I loved you. Why do you think? You were trying so hard to turn your life around and I saw that. I love you, Elie." Her eyes misted and then suddenly she laughed at herself.

Elie kept looking at her. "Why didn't you tell me you knew? "Why didn't you tell me yourself? You've had thirty-five years to do so. One might have thought that a secret like that was a very big deal, no?"

Elie shook his head silently. "Your father told me never tell a soul."

Shoshana looked at him ridiculously. "I think it was all right to tell me."

"Probably so."

Stan, seeing that this might be the right moment, rose from his chair and eased to the door. Shoshana stopped him.

"Where are you going?"

"I just thought this might be an appropriate time to leave you two alone. I would say you have a lot of things to discuss."

"Stanley, sit back down. Do you think I don't know what you have been talking about these past few months?"

Elie and Stan exchanged glances.

"Well, I don't know…"

"I am a lawyer." she said, arms crossed. "It may seem that I am only an ordinary, overwhelmed housewife, but I am still a lawyer. I even renew my license in case I ever need it."

"Oh, uh…He responded sheepishly as he slipped back into his chair, waiting for her to explain.

"You two would sit on the porch and talk. My little private space, my office is right behind that window. And I hate to break the news guys. I heard every word."

Stan turned red in the face. "I'm sorry, Shoshana."

"For what?"

Stan started to say something, then stopped and looked away.

"You're sorry for what, Stanley?"

Stan threw up his arms and shrugged. "You know, like everything.

It was wrong!"

"What was wrong?" Elie butted in.

Shoshana said, "Stay out of this, Elie."

"But he was trying to help me."

She looked at her husband. "Maybe." She looked towards Stan. "You are a big name in the newspapers here. I sometimes read your stories myself."

Stanley's lips curved up. Shoshana continued, "If it were up to me, I don't know if I would have chosen you to tell this story. I mean really a sportswriter to chronicle my husband's life. But shrugged, and her smile was slight." "I always worried that someone would figure it out. I was sure that when it happened…" she turned to Elie, "our lives would have gone to holy hell in a moment."

Turning to Stan, she added, "You could have broken this story at any time and I wouldn't have blamed you if you had. It must be taking a lot out of you to keep this secret. I am only thankful you didn't. There is something very special in you. It has to be killing you to sit on the biggest story of your life."

Stan sat there mesmerized.

"So, tell it well, Stanley," she said. "You and I are still in the dark about much, and time is not our friend here. You need to speak to me, as well. There is a lot I can fill in."

With effort, Stan slowed his breathing. "Thank you, Shoshana."

She dipped her head. Turning to her husband, she said, "And as for you - chemo! Starting tomorrow. Yes?"

Elie looked at her and felt such love and admiration for her. "Yes." "Good. And whatever deal you guys cooked up about this, you will run it by me. You hear me, guys. Run it by me because it involves the children and me. Elie, we will talk more about this tomorrow. Get some sleep." She got up and kissed him.

"Come on, Stanley. Let him get some rest," she said as she motioned him out the door and followed him out of the hospital.

CHAPTER SIXTY-SEVEN

Shoshana sat at her parents' kitchen table. She was wearing a robe and slippers and sipping coffee. A plate of cookies was on the table, covered with plastic wrap. Tempting treats to look at. Pondering whether to take one, her finger lit lightly onto the plastic. Lifting up the edge of the plate, she brought it to her nose, and sniffed at the cookies. Looking down at her waist, she put them back and pushed them away beyond her easy reach. She moved the chair next to her and pulled it alongside, so she could rest her feet on it. Thumbing through a bridal magazine for what seemed like the hundredth time, she looked at the clock above the refrigerator and saw that it was after one in the morning. She lifted her brow and took another sip.

She got up to put the cup in the sink, but it slipped from her grasp and fell, shattering onto the floor. Muttering to herself, she grabbed the broom and dustpan, and was in the middle of cleaning up when her father appeared in the door.

"Is everything all right?"

Grunting, he bent down to hold the dustpan for her,

"It's okay," she said. "I just dropped my coffee cup. I am cleaning it up."

"You didn't cut yourself; heaven forbid?"

"No, no. All good!"

Rabbi Aaron relaxed. In less than a week, his daughter would be getting married. At long last, the child he worried so much about would take the big step of marrying.

He stood there beaming at the kitchen entrance in his robe and slippers, with his skullcap precariously perched on his head. His glasses were skewed down on the right. She didn't know how he could see from them.

"Papa." She removed his glasses and straightened the metal rims. Clearly, he had been reading when he fell asleep with the glasses still on. They must have bent when his head touched the pillow. She laughed and placed them back on his nose.

"Thank you, my dear. What are you doing up so late?"

She shrugged.

"Are you worried about the wedding?"

She returned to her chair and drummed her fingers on the table.

"I wouldn't say worried." Her father pursed his lips, nodding.

"Not worried. Then, what?"

"Concerned."

"About what? Has Elie done anything to make you have doubts?"

She sighed and looked away. Getting up from the table, she said, "Papa, would you like some tea?"

He looked at her. She was troubled about something. He normally wouldn't drink tea at this hour, but she might need to vent. He was there to listen. "Yes, a tea would be nice. Some chamomile, please, so I can sleep."

She rustled around in the cupboard and pulled out a box of tea. She set the water to boil and wiped the sink with a towel. When the pot whistled, she poured a cup, dunked a teabag in the steaming water, and placed it in front of her father. He sat at the table opposite her.

"None for you?"

"I just had coffee, Papa. I've had enough for tonight."

"So be it. Shoshana, may I have a plate? I would like a cookie. Your mother outdid herself it would seem."

"I baked them, Papa."

"Well then, you outdid yourself. So, what troubles you Shoshanela?"

"I am not really sure, but to answer your question, Elie has done nothing wrong. He is a good man."

"Are you concerned that he is much older than you?"

"No. In many ways, he is not."

"Not what?"

"Older."

"I am afraid, I do not understand."

"Elie may be older than me in years, but he is so naïve about things.

Often, I feel that I am more worldly than he is."

The rabbi stifled a smile as he drank his tea. He lowered his cup and his gaze rested on his daughter. Such a smart girl. No, a woman. He remembered her as a baby. The first baby of his new life. The baby who defied the odds just by being born. His memories extended to Europe. She was the symbol for him of how he beat the Nazis.

And now she was getting married to a man she loved, but she really knew nothing about him. Yet he was sure Elie loved her with all his heart. On paper, none of this should work. But on paper, the rabbi should be dead along with the family he had lost. And just as he had defied the odds and beaten the Nazis, Elie had defied his own odds and driven back his demons.

Rabbi Aaron had been determined that Shoshana should never know about those demons. As it became increasingly clear that Shoshana and Elie were getting close, he held his breath. He was trying to balance the needs of Shoshana against those of Elie.

He had spoken to Elie about the challenges ahead of him. He had elicited a pledge from Elie not to divulge his past as Elvis Presley to her. He wanted his daughter to have a normal life, free from the doubts and distractions that knowing Elie's past would bring upon the couple.

But he knew better. He exhaled heavily.

Shoshana looked at him with a question in her eyes.

"Papa, what's wrong. why the sigh?"

He smiled softly at his wonderful daughter. Such a joy! Self-reliant, strong, determined. And she had such a sweet spot for Elie. Her kind face warmed whenever she looked at him.

Elie was so much younger than her in that emotional way of men. As her father, he thought how Shoshana would be so good for Elie. She was more grounded than the other women from his past.

"I sigh because I hope for much for you and Elie."

"So why sigh? It's a good thing to hope we have a life together with all that entails."

"I know it really is a good thing." He pushed his teacup to the side and leaned into the table, speaking in a hushed tone.

"Shoshana, there is something you need to understand about Elie, but you must promise to never tell him you know. In fact, you can tell no one else, ever, even your Mother."

"Papa, what are you talking about? You're scaring me."

"There is nothing to be frightened about and if you truly love him, you will understand why you have to always protect this secret."

"What is this secret? And I am to keep it even from Elie?"

"Yes. He must never know that you know! And what's more I made him promise to never tell you."

"So, both of us will know this secret, but we can never talk to each other about it?"

"I'm afraid so."

She started to say something but stopped herself. She studied her father carefully. She had not seen him so serious in a long time. He would not ask this unless there was a good reason. She took a calming deep breath. "Okay, Papa."

"Well you see, my dear Shoshana, it goes like this…"

CHAPTER SIXTY-EIGHT

"You like being alone, don't you?" Shoshana stood by his side of the bed. Elie stirred and rolled over to see her in the darkness of their bedroom.

"Huh?"

"You heard me! You enjoy being alone."

Elie reached for his glasses on the nightstand and put them on to see her better.

"I don't think so."

"Sure, you do!"

"No, I don't."

She snorted and left the room.

Elie had been home for six weeks. The chemotherapy he was going through knocked him out, and he felt awful. He didn't want Shoshana and the kids to see him suffering, so mainly he stayed in the basement, stretched out on the old couch there. He would come up for meals if he could, but otherwise he would stay put in the basement during the day.

When he came into the kitchen, she was waiting for him. She handed him the guitar that had been collecting dust in the basement for years.

"Play this for me. You are Elvis Presley and I, your wife, have never heard you play. In fact, I have never heard you sing anything other than Jewish music. Show me what the big deal was. Let me hear!"

A smile swept across his face. He cradled the guitar in his arms and smiled. Expertly, he reached up to tune the guitar by ear. In a few deft motions it was ready and he strummed the steel strings lightly. The sound was like a cool breeze to him. It had been years since he last picked it up. Elie's smile lingered as he put the guitar back on the table.

Her face fell. In confusion she asked. "You don't want to play it?"

Elie rested his palm on the face of the guitar. "Oh yes. Yes, I do! It's been… a while. How can I explain it?"

She sat beside him. Reaching for the guitar, she took it from his grasp and placed it on her lap. She strummed the strings and smiled. She picked at them with her fingers. "When I was a young girl, I always wanted a man who could play the guitar. Who knew I always had a guy like that? I knew you were Elvis Presley, but I never knew what that meant until now. I have started listening to your music. I went out and bought a bunch of your albums."

He raised his brows. She answered the unspoken question. "Yes, even your gospel and Christmas albums. I've also seen all your movies."

"When we don't have a television or a VCR?"

"I borrowed a TV from one of our friends. It had a VCR built into it. It was not large, maybe thirteen inches, but it was large enough for me to see you act. I saw them while you were in the hospital. Some of them were rather silly. I understand why you hated making them. But most of them were funny and cute. I liked them. I wish we had shared them years ago."

His lips curved up, but there was a tinge of sadness in his eyes. "Me too. It would have been fun."

"Yes, it would have been." She handed him the guitar again. "Play for me now."

He nodded as he strummed the strings and then sang for her.

Tears ran down her face. Speaking to the guitar as if it were human, she said, "Say hello to your old friend, Elie. You see, it's been crying out for you. Sing for me, Elie, as you sang for your Mama. I love you that much, too."

CHAPTER SIXTY-NINE

Stanley kicked at the narrow strip of dirt alongside the gravestone. His toe loosened up a round stone, which he picked up, placing it atop the marker. Leaning against the headstone was one of the folding lawn chairs he had brought from Elie's front porch. He had asked to borrow it for the day while visiting the grave, tucked away in Queens. He looked at the marker with the evergreen bushes in front. Musical notes marked the smooth gray surface, and, centered between them in Hebrew letters were Elie's Hebrew name and his date of death. Hidden behind an outgrowth of the evergreens, if you looked very carefully, was a second row of smaller letters spelled out in English: "Elvis Aaron Presley." An engraved heart circled his name. It was the only sign that this was Elvis Presley's final resting place.

Stanley opened the chair in front of the grave and sat down. He reached into the pocket of his windbreaker and pulled out a slim flask. Opening it up and taking a sip, he said "L'Chaim," and pointed the flask at the grave, as if to offer Elie a drink. He took another sip, repeated the toast and screwed the cover back on. He put the flask on the grass in front of him.

"Well, buddy. How the heck are you?" In the absence of a response, he continued to talk. "Buddy, that was a great way to end a show." Then, inexplicably, Stanley started to cry.

It was only a few months since they had buried Elie. It seemed surreal to Stanley. Elie had become a great friend in the short time they had known each other. The loss felt particularly profound. He had returned to the grave when Shoshana had erected the marker, but since that time, he had resisted, half out of being so busy and half out of an uncomfortable feeling that he would not be able to tolerate seeing the grave.

It had been over a year since Elie had passed on, and Stanley had summoned the nerve to visit. It was a sunny, warm spring day in April, and he ventured out to St. Albans in Queens to the Old Cemetery, where Elie was buried. The grave was on a small rise next to a tiny pathway. He parked in the lot near the cemetery office and walked the short distance to the grave, carrying the lawn chair. From the pathway, you could clearly see the gravestone, as no others were blocking the view.

As he sat, Stanley thought back to the last few months he had spent with Elie. While undergoing the chemotherapy, Elie had initially holed up in his basement and refused to come out except for a few visits with Stan. The visits were short, and Elie looked worse every time Stan saw him. He might have been right about how difficult the chemo would be.

Then one Sunday morning on a warm autumn day, Stanley heard the strumming of a guitar and soft singing on the porch. He stepped out of his front vestibule and saw Elie playing and singing. Shoshana sat next to him in the other lawn chair and beamed as he sang. As he finished a song, she would reach out to touch his shoulder or hold his hand. Recharged, he would sing some more for his wife. They were like two teenagers and he was showing off to her. Stanley watched them, a smile playing across his lips.

Shoshana waved, and Elie called out, "Stanley, how you doing?"

Stan said to them. "Now, you two behave yourselves!" and they all laughed.

Shoshana spoke to Stan as she patted her husband's knee. "He looks pretty good today, doesn't he?" Elie leaned over and kissed her on the temple.

Stan nodded and chuckled to himself as he stepped back into his house. He heard them continuing for quite a while.

Over the following months, this scene would repeat itself several times. Sometimes, Shoshana would sit with him. Other times it was the kids or grandkids. But each time Stanley witnessed it, he saw that Elie was getting stronger.

Sometimes, Elie would sit alone on the porch and play by himself, as if he were working out some sort of musical puzzle in his head. His tears would flow copiously and he would have to take a break to pull himself together.

The chemo went on for several months. It sapped Elie's energy for a week or so after each round, but soon he was back out on the porch, even on a cold day, playing his guitar and singing softly. When it got too cold, he would play inside. Sometimes, Stanley heard him playing the piano from the other side of the dividing wall between their houses.

Throughout this time, in spurts of energy, Elie filled in the gaps of his story while Stan scribbled rapidly in his notebook. Stan also sat with Shoshana and got her side of the story.

They had lived a surprisingly good life. Money was often tight, but they managed to raise a family, and Elie felt safe with her. By Elvis Presley standards, their life seemed very dull. But by Elie Pressler standards, their life was full, rewarding and happy.

As spring warmed the air, Elie returned to playing on the porch. One day, Stanley and Elie were sitting out when Stan asked, "Elie, now that I see you playing the guitar so often and singing your old songs…do you ever wonder, I mean just for a second, what it would be like to go back out on stage?" Then Stan trailed off, not quite knowing how to finish the sentence.

Elie finished his question, "And play for an audience one more time?" He peered over his glasses at Stan. "Is that what you're asking?"

Stan's eyes twinkled as he looked at Elie, "Well, sort of." He paused. "Something like that." He laughed at the thought.

Elie laughed as well. "All the time, my friend!"

The two of them looked at each other in silence for a moment. Stan said, "Really! I thought you had this all figured out?"

"I did, but it was always a passing thought. I never took it seriously and of course, now...the closest I have gotten to that is when I sang as a cantor in synagogue. I would say to myself, 'if they only knew who was singing for them right now, they would go wild.' I would smile to myself and it would give me the lift to go on. But I never was going to betray myself or my family or my mentors."

Stan sat transfixed. Elie had never let the dream die inside of himself. He had transformed it and controlled it. And because he was able to do that, he had built himself a life to be proud of.

"Elie, if the chance ever came up, would you do it?"

"What's the chance of that happening? You're kidding around."

"But Elie, really, what if, say, that opportunity really did happen...?"

"Miraculously."

Stan leaned over on his chair. He punched himself lightly on the noggin. "Yeah, miraculously, would you do it?"

"Hypothetically, sure!"

"What if it wasn't hypothetical? What if it was real? No hypothetical nonsense, the real deal."

Squinting at Stan, Elie was a bit confused. "How would I even consider something like that? First of all, listen to this conversation. We are two old men talking about a fantasy. Secondly, I chose not to do that many years ago."

"But Elie, that was when you were younger and healthy. And you would have had to take up where you had left off. Now, you are old, and you know..."

"Sick!"

"Yes. This time, it could be a one-shot deal."

"Are you talking about me doing an open mike or a real concert?"

"The full Monty, a regular concert. Then you could disappear again into obscurity."

Elie frowned, "Stan, are you talking about me revealing myself?"

"That I am, my man."

"That's crazy! They would argue that I was some old Elvis impersonator."

"Could be! But not if the venue was so big that there would be no denying that it was you."

"Right! Never happen!"

"But if it could?" Stanley lifted his brows and looked at Elie. Elie leaned back and closed his eyes, stroking his beard.

"Ah, isn't craziness fun?" Elie murmured.

Stan got up and opened the screen door to Elie's house. "I'm going to chat with Shoshana."

CHAPTER SEVENTY

Everyone likes to hold onto an important secret. The trick is finding the right people who know how to and are willing to wait for the big reveal without giving it away.

Stanley had rubbed shoulders with movers and shakers for decades. He knew how to do this sort of thing. Just as Vernon knew how to make Elvis disappear, Stanley knew how to make him reappear.

CHAPTER SEVENTY-ONE

Madison Square Garden had always been a great venue for a music concert. The acoustics sucked, but the energy was hyperdrive alive. That night, the Grammys proved it. Great performances dominated the evening from all the genres of music.

To end the show, an assembly of great bands and musicians crowded onto the stage to produce one of the greatest group efforts of music seen on a stage. It didn't matter that they were rockers or country, rappers or jazz guys, these artists blew the house away. As they bowed, suddenly the lights went dark and the crowd heard an announcement.

"Ladies and gentlemen, we are not done yet. We have a special guest coming to the stage."

A dim spotlight pointed to stage left. A tall, very thin man with a walker, wearing a white shirt with suspenders and simple black trousers shuffled slowly across the stage, guided by a young woman holding his right arm. They were followed by a single spotlight. Otherwise, the stadium was black. This man wore a black velvet skullcap and white fringes hanging from his waist. He had a long white beard and wore silver-rimmed glasses. A stool had been placed center stage. As they approached the stool, she let go. He stopped, folded up the walker, and gave it to a stagehand. Then he climbed up on the stool and was handed a guitar.

There was confusion in the crowd and murmuring in the crowd as this was all happening. Nobody recognized this "special guest." People whispered to each other, swapping guesses to figure out who was onstage.

Smiling at the crowd, the man plucked at some strings to see if they were in tune. Satisfied, he started to sing, ever so softly.

"Love me tender,
Love me sweet,
Never let me go.
You have made my life complete,
And I love you so."

He didn't look at the audience. Rather, he peered intently at the frets on the guitar neck as he played out the notes. The audience didn't know what to think or whom they were seeing, but they knew his music and his voice were magical. Some of them felt an inkling of recognition. There were some whispers, some jostling. The man continued.

"Love me tender,
Love me true,
All my dreams fulfilled.
For my darlin' I love you,
And I always will."

Curiosity was turning to excitement. People in the audience were not sure what they were experiencing, but they knew it was a treasure. For some of the older people in the audience, the voice they heard told them that they were witnessing something amazing. They recognized the voice and they recognized that it was the real thing.

"Love me tender,
Love me long,
Take me to your heart.
For it's there that I belong,
And we'll never part.

Someone in the audience yelled out, "Hey man, who are you?"
The man just smiled and sang,

"Love me tender,
Love me dear,
Tell me you are mine.
I'll be yours through all the years,
Till the end of time."

"Someone else yelled out, "Are you a Jewish Elvis impersonator?"
The singer laughed and pointed to the audience. Now some of
the musicians still on the stage moved forward to listen intently, as
they started to realize that this "guest" was somebody very special.

"When at last my dreams come true
Darling this I know
Happiness will follow you
Everywhere you go."

Then suddenly, with great energy, he jumped off the stool,
started swinging his hips and strumming the guitar really hard:

"Well, it's one for the money,
Two for the show,
Three to get ready,
Now go, cat, go.

But don't you step on my blue suede shoes.
You can do anything but lay off of my blue suede shoes."

With the broadest smile, he started dancing around the stage. For a man who came onto the stage with a walker, he strutted the stage with an energy that surprised everyone onstage and in the audience. The crowd went wild, even though they still didn't know who he was. Elie looked offstage to where Shoshana and Stanley were standing. Shoshana was clapping and dancing with tears streaming down her cheeks. Stanley caught Elie's eye and gave him a thumbs-up.

"Well, you can knock me down,
Step in my face,
Slander my name
All over the place.

Do anything that you want to do, but uh-uh,
Honey, lay off of my shoes
Don't you step on my blue suede shoes.
You can do anything but lay off of my blue suede shoes.

You can burn my house,
Steal my car,
Drink my liquor
From an old fruit jar.
Do anything that you want to do, but uh-uh,
Honey, lay off of my shoes
Don't you step on my blue suede shoes.
You can do anything but lay off of my blue suede shoes."

"Well, it's one for the money,
Two for the show,
Three to get ready,
Now go, cat, go.

But don't you step on my blue suede shoes.
You can do anything but lay off of my blue suede shoes.

He bowed deeply and spoke for the first time to the crowd. "Thank you, thank you very much," he said in that Southern drawl that was unmistakably Elvis. He launched right into his next song, still on his feet, stalking both ends of the stage. He waved to the back of the stage to all the musicians there, beckoning them forward to join him on the front of the stage. They were not sure exactly who he was, but he was singing up a storm and they wanted to be a part of it.

> *"You ain't nothin' but a hound dog*
> *Cryin' all the time*
> *You ain't nothin' but a hound dog*
> *Cryin' all the time*
> *Well, you ain't never caught a rabbit.*
> *And you ain't no friend of mine*
>
> *Well they said you was high-classed*
> *Well, that was just a lie*
> *Yeah they said you was high-classed*
> *Well, that was just a lie*
> *Well, you ain't never caught a rabbit*
> *And you ain't no friend of mine"*

A voice yelled out from the audience, "Hey, you're Elvis Presley!" That was acknowledged with a nod as he strode around the stage. One of the musicians came up and started playing with him, and the whole Madison Square Garden was going wild.

> *"You ain't nothin' but a hound dog*
> *Cryin' all the time*
> *You ain't nothin' but a hound dog*
> *Cryin' all the time*
> *Well, you ain't never caught a rabbit*
> *And you ain't no friend of mine*

Well they said you was high-classed
Well, that was just a lie
Yeah they said you was high-classed
Well, that was just a lie
Well, you ain't never caught a rabbit
And you ain't no friend of mine

His energy seemed relentless. His voice was strong and true.

Well they said you was high-classed
Well, that was just a lie
Ya know they said you was high-classed
Well, that was just a lie
Well, you ain't never caught a rabbit
And you ain't no friend of mine

You ain't nothin' but a hound dog
Cryin' all the time
You ain't nothin' but a hound dog
Cryin' all the time
Well, you ain't never caught a rabbit
You ain't no friend of mine"

He bowed again, high-fived the musicians on the stage, and returned to the stool. The crowd fell silent as he tuned the guitar again.

Adjusting the microphone, he spoke to the audience with the ease of a performer who had been doing this all his life.

"Thank you all. Thank you so much. My name is Elie Pressler, but you probably remember me by my old name…Elvis Presley." Gasps swept through the audience went silent, and then it went wild. Reporters ran toward the front of the stage. The lights dimmed once more, and a spotlight illuminated the performer's stool. Elie looked longingly at the neck of the guitar, closed his eyes and sang.

"And now the end is near
And so I face the final curtain
My friend, I'll say it clear
I'll state my case of which I'm certain

I've lived a life that's full
I've traveled each and every highway
And more, much more than this
I did it my way

Regrets, I've had a few
But then again, too few to mention
I did what I had to do
And saw it through without exception

I planned each charted course
Each careful step along the byway
Oh, and more, much more than this
I did it my way
Yes, there were times, I'm sure you knew
When I bit off more than I could chew
But through it all when there was doubt
I ate it up and spit it out
I faced it all and I stood tall
And did it my way

I've loved, I've laughed and cried
I've had my fill, my share of losing
And now as tears subside
I find it all so amusing
To think I did all that
And may I say, not in a shy way
Oh, no, no not me
I did it my way

For what is a man, what has he got
If not himself, then he has not
To say the words he truly feels
And not the words of one who kneels
The record shows I took the blows
And did it my way
The record shows I took the blows
And did it my way!"

Elie removed his glasses. He was crying and reached into his pocket for a tissue to wipe his eyes. He leaned into the microphone. "Thank you very much. G-d bless you all." Then he stood up as the crowd jumped to their feet and gave him an extended standing ovation. The musicians on stage shook his hand and hugged him. He bowed to the audience one last time, and the arena went dark.

When the lights came on, Elie was gone from the stage, and the stunned audience heard the announcement: "Ladies and gentlemen, Elvis has left the building."

CHAPTER SEVENTY-TWO

They jumped into the back of a white construction van like kids who were free and happily partying with abandon. They laughed and high-fived each other as the van sped out from under Madison Square Garden. Sitting on the floor of the van, they held onto the shelving in the van, and steadied themselves as the truck raced up Eighth Avenue, hoping to avoid the press. By Seventy-Second Street, it appeared that no one was chasing them, so they turned right and sped across Manhattan to the FDR Drive, barreling south. They eventually ended up in the Battery Tunnel and worked their way to Ocean Parkway and to their home. They piled out of the van in front of the house. Stanley hugged Elie tightly, patting him heartily on the back. Stanley winked at Shoshana, and she gave him a big hug. This surprised her as much as it surprised Stanley. They said their good nights and went into their respective homes.

At Madison Square Garden, it was pandemonium. The press, caught flat footed, was thunderstruck. They did not know where the possibly-still-alive Elvis was heading, and they didn't know his vehicle. There were crowds milling around, with the press interviewing major artists about the story that had everyone buzzing and which turned the night on its head. It was very late, so the major networks' coverage was limited, but the internet lit up. Details were so scant that the story simmered in rumors and half-truths. By the time the press figured out who Elie really was and where he lived, it was the early morning. News vans could not find where to park in front of Elie's house, and the police had to force them onto Avenue P to keep the travel lane open.

None of this was going to help them. The night before, as Elie and Shoshana had walked in the door, they grabbed suitcases and the children and drove upstate to an Orange County hotel, where they had a reservation for two rooms. They checked in around two in the morning and soon the children were asleep in one bedroom, and Elie and Shoshana climbed into bed in the other room.

In the morning, Shoshana awoke as the sunlight streamed into their room. She got out of bed and put on a robe. Coming over to Elie's side of the bed, she brushed her fingertips across his shoulder to wake him. Usually, he would move his shoulder, and then would roll over to speak with her. This time she got no response. She shook him harder and still there was no movement. She rolled him over to her. Lifting his eyelids, she saw that he had passed on in his sleep. She kissed his head, pulled the covers up around his neck and adjusted his yarmulke. Then she picked up her phone and called Stanley.

CHAPTER SEVENTY-THREE

Stanley woke up the morning after the concert to a hullabaloo in front of his door. He could not honestly tell them where Elie had gone. When asked what he knew about his neighbor, he smiled and shook his head closing the door. His cell phone was ringing off the hook. He put it in silent mode and took a shower. He dressed for work and walked toward the subway with a line of reporters following him. But he knew that if anyone told this story, it was going to be under his byline. When he got to the office, people crowded around him, but he marched past them into the editor-in-chief's office. This story was his and his alone.

When he was done with the editor, he stepped over to his desk. He had left his cellphone on a pile of papers. It was ringing, and there were many calls from Shoshana. He called her back, and she broke the news.

They buried him that afternoon. The majority of the mourners at the graveside did not yet know they were burying Elvis Presley. The news of Elie's performance had exploded all over the news, just as the news of his first faked death had shaken the world years earlier.

Now Elie was really gone, and a handful of men and women laid him to rest. Stanley stood off to the side. Tears rolled down his face as the family and friends threw shovelfuls of dirt into the grave. Shoshana waved him over to pick up a shovel. He shook his head no, but she came over and whispered into his ear. He trudged to the pile of dirt, placed the shovel into the pile, and threw the soil into the grave. When the dirt thudded onto the casket, he felt a sharper pang of grief. Planting the shovel back in the dirt for another person to use, he to where he had been standing. Shoshana was still there.

"Stanley, you didn't kill him. He wanted it and we all agreed to it. We thought it would never happen. We dreamed of the impossible, and you helped it come true."

Stan glanced away and back to her. "I know. It was an incredible long shot."

"That's right; It was. You know how you dream about something you never think will happen? Like winning the lottery. We got lucky. We won the lottery! You're a lucky man, Stanley. You helped him make his final dream come true. He was able to come full circle and maintain himself as the man he really wanted to be - and was. I hope someday you get to understand that." She turned and walked back to the grave.

Soon the grave was filled, and the mourners recited the Kaddish. Stanley let his tears flow to the ground. After the mourners had dispersed, Stan stood in front of the grave and stared at the mound of earth and the temporary marker provided by the funeral society. It read "Elijah Pressler." He touched the marker gently and went to his car.

CHAPTER SEVENTY-FOUR

"My Conversations with the King" was a tremendous literary success. It sold millions of volumes, was made into audiobooks, and eventually was sold as a movie.

Stanley embarked on a book tour that lasted several months throughout the United States, Europe, and the Far East. After hundreds of signings and radio and television interviews, he at last came home in the middle of the night and stood on his stoop. He looked left toward the Pressler stoop as if half expecting Elie to be sitting there with his guitar.

He lifted a hand to knock on their door but thought better of it. Surely, Shoshana and the kids were fast asleep. He returned to his own front door.

He reached into his pocket for his keys and let himself in. He placed his bags in the vestibule and entered the kitchen. He filled the coffeemaker with water and coffee, letting it brew. Stan reviewed the piles of mail that Shoshana had neatly placed on his table while he was away.

After skimming through the envelopes, he relaxed. The interviews were not over yet. He still had several scheduled in New York, but the tour was over and he hoped for a relatively normal existence from now on. The Elvis story was so compelling. A faked death, an extended life spent under the radar, and an amazing reveal followed by a quick death. What a story!

Stanley had written many biographies before. This biography got under his skin,

The question interviewers had asked the most frequently was where Elie had been buried. Stan never revealed the location. If it was ever identified, it would be soon overrun by Elvis fans who would have turned it into a makeshift memorial. Or worse, it might have been vandalized by fans seeking a crass bit of memorabilia from his grave.

Elie could rest in peace. The proceeds from the book and tours had left Shoshana and the kids financially secure for life. Stanley had also secured his future with the proceeds, so if he wanted to, he could have retired to someplace warm and never worked again. But he wasn't ready for that.

Over the following months, Stanley returned to the paper and to reporting sports. But a restlessness stayed with him all of the time. One morning, he walked into Elie's old synagogue and asked to speak to the rabbi. The next morning, he returned and brought his old phylacteries with him. He put on his prayer shawl and his phylacteries and sat down to pray.

And that's how it was every day afterward.

END